RED HEELS

The LBD Project, Book 2

Kim Black

Published by Steepledog Productions
PO Box 50814
Amarillo, TX 79159
www.kimblackink.com

Printed in the United States of America

Cover design by Samuel and Sean Black

DEDICATION

To Brandi, Donna, and Suzana, my sisters in the Lone Star Women of Letters. You are brilliant lights in my universe.

ACKNOWLEDGMENTS

My heart swells with gratitude to you, my readers. Your time is precious to me, and I pray that my words bring joy to your quiet hours. You truly make my dreams come true. Thanks to my ARC and Beta readers, for asking all the right questions and pushing me forward. Thank you to my cover designers and artists, Sam and Sean. You guys are phenomenal. To James Quiggle, thank you for your incredible knowledge of seemingly everything. Your keen eyes and editing skills put the perfect polish on my work!

CHAPTER ONE

For most women, a cliffside lunch date with a handsome man in Marseilles, France, overlooking the turquoise blue waters of the Mediterranean Sea, would be a dream. For covert agent, Evan Tyler, it was Tuesday.

Her date, French Economic Minister Gerard Boulette, looked as overcast as the sky. Evan thought that, like the sky, Gerard appeared so dark and burdened, if someone so much as sneezed hard, the storm would ensue. His suspicious gaze darted around the outdoor café, bouncing from patron to patron, never landing on her.

The café had only a few other patrons. Brave souls ready to snatch the umbrellas from the backs of their chairs or flee indoors when the clouds let loose. They were hunched over their lunch plates and coffee as the clouds dropped lower. The storm was close. Evan felt it in her bones.

This afternoon was the first time she'd met Boulette face to face, though Evan had seen him on television and, more recently, in a video recovered from her ongoing mission.

Gerard had been recorded in some impressively flexible but compromising positions with blonde model, Xandra Yakovsky, who now sat in a detention cell in DC.

Poor sap. Last week this guy had everything going for him. A wife, two kids, a job any man would envy, and a vague, month-old memory of a secret night with a fashion model in Paris. Evan had infiltrated and stopped the extortion ring, but not soon enough for Gerard.

Evan tried to maintain eye-contact, but Gerard refused to cooperate. He fidgeted with his coffee cup. His lip twitched as a bead of sweat formed on either side of his nose. "I can't do this. I'm beyond help." His voice trembled. The couple at the table nearest them glanced up at him and whispered. Evan guessed that they recognized him.

Evan shook her head. "You got caught doing something you shouldn't, but you're not beyond help. I have important friends. We can get you out of this situation if you just talk to us."

"Good girl," Agent Kirk whispered through Evan's ear-canal receiver. "Just bring him to us, and we can clean this up before dinner."

Evan reached out for Boulette's hand. "Anton Hrevic is no longer a threat. Neither is Xandra. If you'll just trust me—" Before she could finish, Boulette jumped from his chair and sprinted for the parking lot.

"He's running," Evan said to Kirk. "I'm in pursuit." She chased him out of the café and toward his Mercedes, wishing she was wearing her running gear instead of three-inch red pumps and a pencil skirt. She reached his car just as the engine turned over, and dove into the passenger seat before he had the chance to protest.

"Don't you understand? I am in chains. My wife's family holds more sway with the government than the Prime Minister himself. Micheline has seen the video. She took my children and left." Boulette shook his head and sped out of the parking lot and down the narrow street.

Kirk's voice rattled in Evan's ear again. "You caught him. I can see from your signal that you're moving. Where is he taking you? Hedge and I are getting the gear together, and Ramos went for the car. Find out where you're going, and we'll meet you."

Evan kept her voice calm. "Gerard, where are we going? I really can help." She knew his life would never be the same, but she also knew that she could help minimize the damage.

Gerard had shared only a little of his tragedy with Evan. He had confessed what he remembered to his wife. She had stormed out with the children, becoming an easy target for whoever was behind the scheme. Micheline and the children were taken, and a ransom was demanded. But the kidnapper didn't want money. Money would be easy. They wanted Gerard's influence. They wanted his power.

Evan just wanted to connect the dots, find the scum, and save Gerard's family. *Easy as pie.*

Gerard kept his eyes focused straight ahead and said nothing. His hands held tight and turned the wheel as though it was an extension of his arms. He took corners much faster than Evan thought possible, especially given the man's state of mind. Evan was reminded of how her daddy talked about the famous Formula One racers and their cars. *Maybe it's a French thing.* Within another minute, they pulled inside an empty warehouse somewhere between the city and the Port of Marseilles-Fos.

Gerard parked inside, hopped out without a word, and began pacing as if Evan was not there. She got out of the car and looked around for a clue to their location. "Guys," she said to the rest of her team. "We're in a warehouse. Not sure where. Just ping the shoes again and get here fast."

The warehouse was dark. No overhead lights, just the meager gray sunlight filtering in from the high windows on either side of the structure. Dark building. Dark clouds. Dark man.

"Gerard, please let me help." Evan approached him and saw that he had something in his hand. A pistol. Her heart raced, and her brain went to work. Her Springfield was strapped to her thigh under her skinny knee-length gray linen skirt. *Why didn't I wear the dress? Retrieving my sidearm from this skirt will only set him off. Just talk him down.*

Evan took a slow step toward the broken man. Yesterday he wielded world power. Today he soaked himself in a cold sweat of shame and despair. "I want to help you."

Gerard moaned. "She took my children."

Evan dipped her chin and advanced another three inches. "And I can help you get them back." She kept her voice calm and quiet, but her thoughts cried out for Hedge. She needed him right now. *This was not the plan. Alone in a warehouse with a desperate man. Gerard's finger was on the trigger, and his hand was shaking. Not the plan at all.*

"The man said that he would hurt them. He said that if I didn't do what he wanted, he would hurt my family. He wants me to change my stance on European trade with the Middle East. He says that if I don't, he will change it for me." Gerard's words ran into each other like a derailed train piling up on the tracks.

Evan knew she had to play for more time. "We don't even know what he can do. Let me look into this man. Perhaps I can negotiate."

"Stop!" Gerard blurted out.

Evan froze in place. She could hear him breathing. His body flinched as he groaned. Evan watched as he seemed to age before her eyes. His face turned ashen and the creases in his forehead deepened. He looked much older than forty.

Just a few days ago, Evan's team leader, Hedge Parker, had told her how much he needed her. His words, his embrace, it made her feel safe. That feeling was miles away now. *You need me? I need you. Right here. Right now.*

Gerard's eyes darted to the overhead door to his left. Evan turned to look, too. She thought she heard an engine humming outside. A crackle in her ear meant that Kirk was within one hundred meters of her location. His voice murmured, "We're almost to the warehouse, Tyler. You okay?"

"Who is here?" Gerard asked.

Evan nodded. "They're my friends, and they just want to help you."

Gerard's anxiety distorted his face like a disease. His lips twisted as he struggled to make them work. "How did they know we were here? Nobody knows. If they can find me, then he can find me."

"No, Gerard," she said, consciously willing her shoulders to relax. "You're safe with me."

Gerard Boulette's body changed. He squared his shoulders and relaxed his face. He took a deep breath and stood at attention.

"That's right, Gerard. Everything is going to be all right."

He nodded back to her. "You are my friend?" he asked.

"I am."

A side door opened with a loud clatter. Evan maintained eye-contact with her man, and a smile fell over his lips. "It is good to have a friend at the end."

"NOOO!" Hedge yelled from the open door.

And in that split second, the clouds tore open, and the storm began.

Gerard Boulette raised his right arm as if to salute and pushed the muzzle of his revolver to his head and fired.

Evan lunged for him but was helpless to do anything. Her lean, muscular arms reached out to where Gerard's body lay in a heap. It seemed to happen in slow motion, but too quickly for Evan to stop.

Blood and gray matter spattered the floor. Gray matter. *But not gray. Bright pink. The only color in the whole gray place.* Evan released a heavy breath as thunder rolled around her. The rain pounded on the warehouse, drowning out any other sound.

The storm had just begun.

CHAPTER TWO

Hedge Parker ran to Evan's side. Teo Ramos cleared the area in a quick sweep with his Glock.

"What just happened?" Kirk's voice thundered in Evan's ear.

Hedge held a tight grip on Evan's shoulder and tapped his own earwig. "Boulette's down, Kirk. Come in and take Tyler back to the truck."

"Yes, sir," Agent Kirk answered.

Hedge addressed Evan with a furrowed brow. "I thought you had Boulette under control." His voice was official. All business.

"Sir, I thought so, too. He was calm on the phone. He just wanted to meet. He started acting nervous at the café, then raced here." Evan squeezed her eyes closed for several seconds, trying to erase the last fifteen minutes of her life. "I thought we could talk, but he lost it. I don't understand. How does suicide solve anything? Why?"

"And where is your sidearm?" Hedge asked.

"Still in the holster on my thigh," Evan said. "I believe that if I had drawn my weapon, things would have ended this same way. Perhaps just more quickly."

"Or you might have had the chance to wound him and to prevent him from harming himself." Hedge almost barked. This was not what she expected of him.

Ramos joined their exchange after examining the body. "Sir, we're not trained to wound. You know that. When Agent Tyler draws her weapon, it's for keeps."

Hedge nodded. "I know." His face lost its ferocity. Evan couldn't decide if he was angry or maybe just recovering from the shock in his own way. "Are you hurt?" he asked.

"No, sir," she answered. She appreciated his concern. She wanted to take him into her arms, but that wasn't possible in this situation. Too much work to do.

Rowan Kirk stood in the doorway, barely clear of the rain, his tall, lean figure silhouetted in the frame. "Is she hurt?" he asked.

Hedge nudged Evan toward her old friend. "Let him process you while Ramos and I clean this place up. We won't be long."

Evan nodded to her commanding officer and staggered the ten yards to Kirk's side. She pulled herself out of the shock one shaking step at a time.

"You have some blood on you," Kirk said, pointing to the darkening droplets on her skirt. "I've got some stuff in my kit that will take it right out." He put his arm around her shoulder and led her through the cold rain.

"Of course, you do." She wanted to throw up. The man she was sent to help killed himself standing six feet in front of her. His blood was drying on her clothes. His wife and children were hidden somewhere in France, thinking horrible things about him, because he'd been drugged, seduced, and videotaped.

Only two weeks ago she'd joined a covert team of agents to test the LBD field suit, a high-tech weaponized cocktail dress designed with state-of-the-art surveillance gear, body armor, and defensive technology. She'd not only used it to take down a ring of blackmailing super-models, but she had fought and defeated Xandra, who had stolen the dress and tried to use it against her. Evan had even made herself bait to stop Jarrett Brawn, her own teammate, who was working as Xandra's hitman.

Anton Hrevic, the man she first thought was behind the blackmail ring, was ice cold in the Paris morgue right now. The woman pulling Hrevic's strings, Xandra Yakovsky, was in the custody of InDIGO, the International Discretionary Intelligence Gathering Organization, for whom Evan worked. Now they were on the trail of someone else. Either Xandra had a contingency plan that could operate independently, or there was another tier to this pyramid.

"Kirk, I wish we were done so I could call my daddy. I just want to hear his voice." As they reached their black SUV, Evan looked up at her friend and partner. Tears flooded her eyes, and she pushed them away with the back of her hand. Crying was the last thing she wanted to do. It wasn't professional.

Kirk grimaced and arranged a stray shock of Evan's red hair into place behind her ear. "I know, kid. You've had a rough week."

"Gerard has a family. His wife, Micheline. His children." Evan heard her voice and was angry at herself. She sounded like a child. Kirk gazed at her like a father worried for his daughter.

"They all have families. Whoever this rat is, he uses that to make his plan work. He's pushing their buttons." Kirk held her hand to steady her as she climbed into the SUV. "Are you in?"

Evan let her head rock back against the headrest. "I'm in." At least Kirk wouldn't care if she cried. Only now, she couldn't tell the tears from the rain.

Kirk walked around to the back hatch and retrieved a black nylon bag of field supplies. He slid into the seat next to her. "Let me get the blood out before it stains for good."

Evan watched as Kirk worked his magic with a small bottle of clear liquid and a swab. He dabbed at the drops on her skirt until they disappeared. When he finished, he dropped the swab into a small clear tube and sealed the top. He pulled a black sharpie from his pocket and labeled the cylinder with the name Gerard Boulette, as well as the date and his own initials.

"Protocols," he said, as he dropped the evidence and the bottle of cleaning solution back into the black bag. "Gotta love 'em."

Evan stared at her hands for several seconds while Kirk tapped away at his notebook computer. She jumped when Kirk said, "Yes, sir. We're ready to go."

Hedge and Ramos exited the warehouse and joined them in the vehicle, waiting for the Marseilles officials to arrive on the scene.

"Did he say anything about who it was—who was trying to manipulate him?" Hedge asked. He didn't turn to face her. Instead, he stared at the steering wheel. His grip tightened on each side.

Evan stared at the side of his head. She watched the muscles in his jaw tighten and relax as he waited for her reply.

"Sir, just that it was a man. Not that *that* means anything. He said only that the man wanted him to change his stance on European trade with the Middle East, and that if Gerard didn't, that he would change it for him."

Teo Ramos shrugged and turned to face Evan and Kirk. "So, what does that mean? Is this all about oil?"

"We always follow the money," Kirk said, not raising his gaze from his computer screen. "Remember, all of the flash drives we found in Hrevic's vault were labeled with the names of cities in Europe. They were all port cities. Marseilles and Barcelona are the major oil hubs on this side of the Mediterranean."

Another flash of lightning lit up the sky, and when all that was left was the thunder, everything seemed darker than before.

Teo raised his eyebrows. "You think this guy has the cajones to blow up a platform?"

Hedge noticed the string of black sedans approaching and opened his door. "I gave the list of cities to Agent McKinnon-Grey along with the list of subjects indicated on the flash drives. I'm sure Eleanor has her top analysts working on every conceivable angle. I'd bet every platform and every tanker going in or out of Marseilles and Barcelona are getting a thorough inspection."

"Are you all right, Tyler?" Hedge asked as the sedans parked along the side of the warehouse.

"I'm good to go, Sir." Direct, professional, as it should be; she was shaking off the shock of Boulette's suicide.

"Glad to hear it." He turned to Kirk. "Notify McKinnon-Grey about this incident and tell her that we are heading back to our hotel to await her instructions. I'm going to brief these officers on how to proceed."

Hedge hopped out and met the French team at the door into the warehouse. Teo twisted in his seat to lay his hand over Evan's. "There was nothing you could have done to stop him. He had run out of options."

Evan put a smile on her lips, making it fit; time to let it go and move on. She slipped her hand from beneath Teo's and smoothed her hair back from her face. His concern was sweet, but she didn't want to send the wrong signal.

Thunder boomed again. Close this time.

She watched as Hedge returned to the SUV, looking over his shoulder toward the sea. He had his hand on the door when his phone rang. "Hello?" A look of stunned disbelief fell over his face like a grotesque Halloween mask. He opened the vehicle door but paused before getting inside. It was as if he was oblivious to the rain.

"Yes, ma'am," he said. He put his phone away as he slipped behind the steering wheel. "That was McKinnon-Grey. There was just an explosion in the Marseilles shipyard. They're sending us to Barcelona. It's not just blackmail anymore. We're hunting a terrorist."

CHAPTER THREE

The thunderstorm had let up, but the clouds still hung low over the ancient city. Every channel on television reported the explosion at the shipyard, though the cause was still under investigation. Most reporters' speculation ranged from terrorist attack to faulty wiring to a vehicle accident. That was the game. Keep them guessing, making wild accusations, and see what plays best for the powers that be.

By the time the team was back at the small generic hotel in downtown Marseilles, the TV in the lobby was reporting exactly what Evan expected.

In other news, French Economic Minister Gerard Boulette has died unexpectedly of a heart attack. Boulette was forty-two years old. The Deputy Minister will assume Boulette's duties until an official appointment is made. Boulette's wife, Micheline, and their children have yet to make a statement.

Evan shook her head. Heart attack. It was broken, that was true. Whoever this man was—if it was a man at all—he knew how to play it. She kept silent until they were secure in their room. "Any news on Boulette's family?" she asked as Teo bolted the door.

Hedge nodded. "Just got another quick report from Agent McKinnon-Grey. The family was released, unharmed. About ten minutes after we left the warehouse." He frowned at his phone. "He, whoever *he* is, must have ears in important places."

Evan dropped into the small tan club chair by the desk where Kirk was robotically setting up his notebook. "And the Deputy Minister? What is his stance on French trade with the Middle East?"

Teo sat on the arm of Evan's chair. "Yeah, we should check on that." He patted Evan's shoulder. "You handled a bad situation like a champ. We let you down."

Evan shook her head, looking up into his deep brown eyes. "You got there as fast as you could."

Hedge's phone buzzed in his hand, and he disappeared into the bedroom without a word.

Evan glanced at Kirk and whispered, "Is Hedge mad at me?"

Kirk stopped typing and shook his head a fraction of an inch. "I don't think he's upset with you. I think he had high hopes of finding out who is pulling strings."

"And Boulette's suicide cut that line of inquiry?"

"Something like that." Kirk resumed his computer work as Hedge returned to the room.

Evan straightened herself in the chair at Hedge's serious demeanor, and the men followed suit.

Hedge cleared his throat and made eye-contact with each of his team members in turn, finally settling on Evan. "Eleanor wants us in Barcelona this evening. Our documents will be here in half an hour. Get the gear together. It's time to go."

Teo stood and nodded quickly to Evan. "See? It's cool. Don't worry about it."

Hedge lowered his brow and squared his shoulders. "Agent Tyler, may I speak to you in private for a moment?"

"Yessir," she answered as she stood. She shot a fast glance toward Teo and shrugged as she followed Hedge back into the bedroom.

She hoped they could get this official crankiness out of the way.

"Agent Tyler," Hedge said, crossing his arms.

Maybe not. "Yessir?" Evan tried a softer stance while keeping her voice crisp.

"About this afternoon." He stopped.

She waited for him to continue, but after several seconds ticked silently away, she decided to take a chance. "I apologize that I misread Boulette's state of mind. By the time I saw that he had a revolver in his hand, it was too late to draw my sidearm. I should have been more prepared."

She dropped her gaze to her shoes and waited for him to assure her that she'd done all she could. That it wasn't her fault that Boulette went off the rails. She waited for him to pull her into his arms and tell her that everything was fine and that he needed her as much as ever. She waited.

Hedge kept his arms crossed and his jaw level with the floor. "Next time you're in a situation like that, you'll be ready."

Gut punch. "Next time? Gerard Boulette doesn't get a next time," Evan blurted out. "I have his blood on my hands."

Hedge didn't defend her. He didn't move a muscle. "Yes, and the blood of everyone else who dies at the hands of this guy until we catch him."

Evan choked on her own breath. His words hit her squarely in the face and stung as hard and as surely as the back of his hand would have.

"I should have had my weapon in my hand. Is that what you want me to say? The man was terrified. But sure, maybe if I waved a pistol in his face that would have calmed him right down." Evan pushed out a heavy sigh. "I don't get you, Hedge. You want everything to be by the book, and then you tell me you need me. I thought maybe you meant more than just another body on the team."

"I did."

She didn't slow down. "I can be whatever you want, you know. That's part of the job. I just thought that you wanted something more. That's what I get for thinking."

Hedge let his arms fall to his side. "I did."

"What?"

"I did want more. I do want more." His words came slow. He shrugged. "I want more. And I thought we could be more." He paused and raised his hands to rest carefully on his hips. "But not yet. I don't know how this can work. I just know how it can't work. I've been down that path before, and my partner suffered for it."

Evan held her breath. She had hoped. She had wanted. She thought she had found whatever it was. But it seemed as elusive as the man they hunted.

She nodded. Back to official. She could do official.

Hedge shook his head. "You're a good agent. Your instincts are right on. You know as well as I do that you did all you could. Boulette couldn't see any other way out. He couldn't change his stance for no reason, and he couldn't let his family suffer for his pride."

Evan's brain clicked back to the job. "His family was released, unharmed. The man we're chasing doesn't have a hitman anymore. We took Brawn from him. He needed Boulette out of the way. He set up the scandal. He would have made it look like a suicide anyway. But Brawn wasn't available."

Hedge jumped in. "So, he forced Boulette's hand. Pushed him to suicide and kept his own hands clean. It's not about Boulette's position on trade. It was about having his man in position."

"Right. But this is just speculation until we have evidence." Evan nodded and reached out for Hedge's hand without thinking. "Kirk can find whatever we need."

Hedge squeezed her hand but then pulled back, frowning. "Kirk will dig. While he's doing that, we must run down every possibility. Until we have this wrapped up, we have to stay focused. We can talk about our situation later."

Evan nodded. She hated the idea. But if she stayed busy enough, maybe it wouldn't be awful. "I can keep everything professional for now, but please don't give me a dressing-down just because you're in a foul mood."

"I'm not in a foul mood. I am your superior officer, and you are not a damsel in distress who just needs a hug and a puppy. You can't turn those perfect lips of yours into a pout and work your magic on me." He paused for a second and knit his brow. "And I said we'll talk about this later." Hedge crossed his arms over his chest again. Heat seemed to radiate from his skin, and not in a good way.

Evan turned away from him and picked up her suitcase to pack. "Yessir."

Hedge sighed, and Evan heard a slight groan attached. She

turned around fast enough to see a grimace start to form beneath his eyes. Pain. He was still hurting from the knife wound in his hip. He shook his head and left the room.

Evan yanked the dresser drawer open and grabbed her clothes, tossing them into the red suitcase with a scowl securely fixed to her face. *I don't pout.* She tossed another handful into the bag. A loop from her bikini caught on her finger. *Thirty-six hours in Marseilles and not a single trip to the beach.* She scooped up the last of her things and dropped them in the pile.

A soft knock sounded on the door. Evan quickly shook off her anger and took a deep breath. "Come in."

Kirk poked his head into the room, keeping his eyes directed to the ceiling.

"I'm dressed, Red," she said, almost laughing at his attempt to protect her modesty.

Kirk stepped into the room and smiled. "Boss says five minutes."

Evan laughed. Kirk always seemed to know how to sense her frustration and diffuse it. "Better not let him hear you call him Boss. He's not in the mood."

Kirk nodded. "I'm careful." He opened the armoire door and pulled out the black garment bag. "Can I help you pack our baby?"

"Knock yourself out." Evan dropped down to her knees and bent low to check for anything that might have rolled under the bed. Finding nothing, she pulled herself up to sit on the bedside. "Hey, Red, can I ask you something?"

Kirk slipped the black bag over the weaponized dress and slowly pulled the zipper to the top, fastening it securely with a titanium padlock. "Sure, Evan. What's on your mind?"

Evan moved to the dressing table and began to fill her cosmetic bag, carefully putting everything into place. She glanced into the mirror to see Kirk sitting on the bed, watching her reflection. She wanted to ask the right question. She searched for the right words. This was always easier with targets and assets than with friends.

Kirk's short silver hair reflected the traces of sunlight that filtered through the window, now that the storm had lifted. His hazel eyes must have seen her struggle and softened. "What is it, kid?"

Evan took a deep breath. "How are you?" she asked. As soon as the words were out, she realized they were too generic.

Kirk laughed as though he expected much worse. "I'm fine, Evan. How are you?"

"Kirk, I'm serious." Her Texan drawl became more pronounced around him—he gave her the space to feel comfortable.

He laced his fingers together and rested his hands on his lap. "What are you asking?"

"You were shot in the shoulder last week. Twice." She turned to face him for emphasis.

He dipped his chin. "Yes, and you were beaten and strangled, and Hedge was stabbed in the backside." Kirk sounded as though he was reciting a grocery list.

"Are you still in a lot of pain?" she asked.

Kirk cocked his head to the right and grimaced. "Well, 'a lot' is a relative term. If I raise my right arm—or my left arm—over my head, it hurts like a sword stabbing up through my chest to the back of my neck. That hurts *a lot*." He nodded. "If I keep my arms down, I don't really have any pain. I get a little sore if I sit too long at the computer. But an aspirin takes care of that."

Evan sighed and tucked her make-up bag and hairbrush into her red suitcase. "So, you're mostly off your prescription?"

"I still have a few antibiotics left to take, but my painkillers are done." He leaned forward in a more serious attitude. "Are you still in a lot of pain?" He placed his hand over hers as she zipped her bag closed.

She shook her head and patted his hand. "Not me. I think Hedge is still hurting pretty badly, though."

Kirk released a heavy sigh. "Evan, you have to remember that I was shot in a place without muscles. I know I look like a male model," he joked, "but I don't have any muscles at all. This," he said, sweeping a gesture over his slim frame, "is one-hundred percent brain."

Evan laughed and gently reached out for his shoulder. Before she actually made contact, he doubled over.

"Ouch! That hurts!" he wailed.

She instinctively pulled her hand back but laughed when she realized he was teasing.

"Seriously, though." Kirk stood and took her hand again. "Hedge puts weight on his injury every time he stands, walks, or runs."

Evan nodded. The two of them scanned the room for anything left behind. Nothing. The room was clear. Evan wheeled her case to the door and took the black garment bag from Kirk.

He moved a tress of her glossy red hair behind her ear. As a former fashion model, she was accustomed to having her hair, make-up, and clothing arranged and straightened for a job. Since becoming a covert agent for InDIGO, Evan's appearance had become even more important. Evan behind closed doors, Kirk made sure she looked just right. He made sure everything was right. "I'll keep a close eye on Hedge. Don't worry about him."

"Thanks, Red."

Kirk pointed to her earlobe. "Your stitches are almost completely healed."

Evan rolled her eyes and turned her head to show her other ear. A bio-bandage had been spackled over where Xandra had ripped Evan's earlobe in two by yanking her earring out. "Wrong side, Einstein."

"Yeah, okay. Forgive me for thinking both of your ears look sexy."

Evan smiled. As they turned off the bedroom light and started into the sitting room, a knock at the main door silenced everyone.

Hedge opened the door and greeted a courier. He took a small parcel and closed the door again. "Time to go," he announced. "Our Lear jet awaits."

CHAPTER FOUR

The small charter jet bumped as the wheels retracted into the belly of the plane. Within seconds the team was over the edge of the shipping port of Marseilles, veering south toward the Mediterranean, headed to Barcelona.

A pillar of black smoke billowed up from an unnatural crater of twisted metal that once had been neatly arranged shipping containers. Scorched and broken concrete showed the extent of the impact. Emergency vehicles pumped water over the still-glowing wreckage. The whole team leaned toward the small cabin windows to study the devastation.

"We're in the air," Hedge said into his phone, without looking away. "The damage looks substantial from up here."

Evan sat back in her seat and kept her eyes tightly closed for a few seconds. The plane leveled off, creating that lighter-than-air sensation in her tummy for a split second. Woozy. Too much for one day, and she knew it wasn't over. She turned to look at Hedge as he listened to Eleanor McKinnon-Grey detailing the next step of their assignment. She couldn't make out Eleanor's instructions, but that didn't matter. Hedge would lay it all out soon enough.

Teo unlatched his lap belt and shifted in his seat to face Evan. His dark brown eyes looked wide with excitement. "This is getting into my territory," he said.

Evan raised her eyebrows. "My dress is water-proof, fire-retardant, and impact-resistant, but I doubt it would offer much protection from an explosion like that."

"You weren't hurt when that car bomb went off in Paris. It must have helped a little, right?" he asked.

"A large Russian man standing between me and the bomb was what blocked the shrapnel. Poor Sergei." Evan did feel sorry for

Sergei Bershkov. He had been just one more victim of Xandra's greed for power. She looked around the cabin. She had Hedge and Kirk, and of course Teo, on her team. A little worse for wear, but still uncorrupted. Teo smiled as their eyes met. She wondered what he was thinking.

"Yes, ma'am," Hedge said, clicking off his connection with Eleanor and slipping his phone into his shirt pocket. He regarded Evan with a subtle flip of his wrist. "Whether it's explosion-proof or not, you need to get the dress on. As soon as we land in Barcelona, we're on our way to the shipping yard."

Kirk tapped on his computer. "Are there more?"

Hedge nodded. "The team in Rome confirmed your theory, Kirk. They found shipping documents for containers in seven more ports in the western Mediterranean sent by Alan Smithee Enterprises."

Kirk guffawed.

"Why is that funny?" Teo asked.

"Alan Smithee is the name that movie directors use in their film credits if the movie is a stinker and they didn't want anyone to know who directed it," Kirk explained. "Our terrorist thinks he has a sense of humor."

"That's awful," Evan said. She removed her seatbelt and stood to retrieve her garment bag from the overhead compartment. A pocket of turbulence bumped her off her feet and into Teo's lap.

"Whoa! Sorry," she said, finding herself only inches from her partner's face. She inhaled a trace of his aftershave, still clinging to his jaw after a long day. She felt the warmth of his body beneath hers for the first time. Taut muscles. Big smile. *Oh dear.*

"Nice of you to drop in." Teo helped her back to standing, and Hedge pulled the bag down for her.

"When you're dressed I'll give you the details," Hedge said. He gave the bag to her and held her arm to keep her steady as she walked back to the small cabin at the tail.

She closed the door and stared into the tiny mirror on the wall. "What was that?" she whispered to herself. "Are we back in the eighth grade now?"

She slipped off her gray skirt and white blouse and began the process of gearing up in her little black dress. First, she put on the corset of body armor and then re-secured her thigh holster. Once everything was in the right place, she slipped into the black strapless sheath and adjusted the ruching on the sides, lengthening the hem to just below her knees.

She stepped out of the red pumps and carefully pulled the black heels from the lower pocket of the garment bag. She dropped the red shoes into the pockets and zipped the bag closed. She stepped into the black ones and gave herself another second for balance. She rolled her street clothes into a tight cylinder for compact packing. Tucking them under her arm, and draping the garment bag over her shoulder, she took a deep breath and steadied herself. *Focus on the job.*

She felt the downward tip of the plane's nose and knew that their descent had begun.

She made her way back down the aisle as if it were a catwalk in any fashion show. Her modeling days showed yet again. The men on her team, though specifically instructed by Hedge not to notice her graceful curves or long, lean limbs, couldn't seem to help themselves, especially when she wore the dress.

Hedge was no exception. His gaze seemed glued to every step. He put the garment back into the overhead bin and held her hand as she took her seat.

Teo's mouth fell open.

Kirk pressed his lips into a thin, tight line. He looked as though he was trying to remind himself that he was old enough to be her father.

Hedge shot a hot glance at Teo and began his briefing. "You two," he said, waving a finger between Teo and Evan, "are going to the docks posing as a couple looking for their container."

Evan raised her eyebrows. "A cocktail dress won't seem too conspicuous?"

Hedge shook his head. "Teo is surprising his beautiful girlfriend with a Lamborghini." He turned to Ramos. "You're going to change into a suit and tie as soon as we land. You'll take some cash with you and bribe the shipping master to let you in. Tell him that you're going to propose. That always works."

"I have always wanted to propose to a woman with a Lamborghini." Teo laughed.

"Once you're in, you have to find the container with the bomb and dismantle it. Simple enough," Hedge said.

"Do we know which container we're looking for?" Evan asked.

Hedge shook his head. "We don't even know if it's there yet. Kirk is doing a search of all the manifests of all the vessels that have off-loaded containers within the last week from Alan Smithee Enterprises. As soon as he has it, he'll give you the coordinates."

Ramos inhaled, filling his muscular chest to capacity. He released his breath slowly and squared his jaw. "What type of explosive are we dealing with?"

"As of yet, unknown. When and if one of the other teams has specifics, they'll relay that information to us. We don't know if any of the other containers contain bombs at all. The one in Marseilles was supposed to be loaded with office furniture, destined for a vineyard in the Loire Valley." Hedge shrugged at Ramos. "Can you handle it anyway?"

"No problem. Once I see it, it won't take me long to know how to disarm it." Teo patted Evan's hand. "This is going to be one unforgettable first date."

"If we get blown up, I won't marry you," she said.

Hedge focused on Evan. "You are there to be eyes and ears for the rest of us. You will use the dress to relay information between Ramos and Kirk and me. If Teo needs an extra pair of hands, you help him, but one word and you walk away—or run if the situation calls for it."

"I'm not leaving him there."

Teo fixed his face in his most stern expression. "If I say run, you'd better run. Don't wait for me, don't look back, just don't. I'm serious, Evan."

"I'm not okay with that, Sir," she protested.

"Don't care," Hedge responded. "If Ramos tells you to clear

the scene, you do it. He's not just protecting your pretty face. Remember, that dress you have on is a major investment for InDIGO. It's part of our assignment to use and protect that weapon."

Evan nodded, humbled. "Yessir."

Kirk raised his right index finger. Evan knew it was his way of letting the others know he had something important to say at the next break in conversation.

"Yes?" Hedge said, turning to Kirk.

Kirk turned his notebook so that the monitor faced the team. "There is a container shipped from Smithee Enterprises located somewhere in this area of the shipyard." The screen showed a satellite shot of the Barcelona port with rows and rows of brightly colored freight containers. Kirk motioned to a small area at the edge of the port.

"That doesn't look like an explosion there would do too much damage. The one in Marseilles was right in the middle of the lot." Ramos sighed. "An impact in this area could send most of the blast out into the water. Maybe it's not a bomb."

Kirk shook his head. "Odds are pretty good that it is some form of explosive device."

Hedge furrowed his brow. The sounds of the jet engine grew louder, and his voice seemed to strain above the hisses and whines. "Has one of the other teams reported back?"

Kirk tapped away at his keys and a red digital square formed over an area of the shipyard. The picture on the monitor suddenly panned out to a broader view. "No, but see this," he said. He pointed to a large man-made structure jutting out in front of the shipyard.

"What is that?" Evan asked.

"It's a platform," Hedge said. The expression on his face indicated a realization of the terrible possibilities.

Kirk leaned forward in his seat. "Not just any platform. Barcelona Harbor is the home of the largest—the main oil platform in the Mediterranean Sea. If there is an explosion in the shipyard, even a small one, it could set off a chain of blasts that could detonate the whole platform into a massive eruption. Something like that would affect world oil supply, and rates, for months, possibly years to come."

Hedge swallowed hard. "And if either of you is out there, you have no place to run."

Teo sat up straight in his seat, addressing Hedge. "Sir, I'd like to request that you allow me to go out there alone. I can wear an ear receiver. I'd rather keep Evan out of harm's way."

Evan shook her head. "My job is not to stay out of harm's way. I understand that we want to protect the dress, and I will do my best. But Teo will have a much better chance at finding his target with me at his side."

Teo held up his hands. "No. With all due respect, I'd prefer that you weren't at my side for this. What if I can't disarm it?"

Evan crossed her arms in front of her. "I thought that you were good at disarming bombs. Are you saying now that you can't do it?"

"I can disarm any bomb you put in front of me."

Hedge held his hands up to stop their exchange. "Hold up!" he commanded. "Agent Ramos, your request is denied. Unfortunately, Evan is correct. You need her out there."

Before Ramos could say a word, Hedge turned to Evan. "But you must be willing to walk away from Ramos at my word. I don't like it any more than you do, but if you refuse, I won't let you go."

Evan didn't even want to think about a situation that called for her leaving a partner behind. A few years before in Italy, she'd been told to leave Kirk behind when they'd been forced to jump from a yacht and swim to shore, and she had refused. She had saved her friend's life. She had received a mild reprimand but never regretted her decision. She blinked away the thoughts of these types of complications. "Yes, sir."

Teo opened his mouth to speak but stopped short.

A ding sounded in the plane, and the overhead seatbelt light blinked on. Everyone straightened themselves in their seats and latched the safety straps. Kirk swiped his hand over the computer monitor to push the image onto his hand-held device. Once the program loaded, he closed his notebook and put it away in its bag.

Kirk glanced over his shoulder at the other team members. "Don't worry. I still have contact with my resources. As soon as we know anything for sure, I'll tell you." He turned back to face forward and cupped his hands around his mouth. He whispered, "Evan, receiver check. Can you hear this?"

Evan smiled when she heard the soft hum of Kirk's voice coming through clearly in from the audio receiver implanted in her ear canal. "Loud and clear."

Teo turned to face her. "What was that?"

Evan patted Teo's arm gently. "I was just letting Kirk know that I can hear him."

"Right, yeah," he said. He let his hand cover her fingers that still rested on his arm.

Evan tilted her head back against the seat's headrest. Teo's hand was warm over chilled fingers. *Evan, girl, you need to settle yourself. You haven't even given Hedge a chance. He's still hurting. You haven't had a quiet moment to get into the swing of whatever that relationship will be, and now you're making eyes at Teo? Get a grip.* But her hand had a grip. On Teo's solid biceps.

The plane bumped as the hatch under the fuselage opened, jostling Evan back to her senses. A mechanical squeal signaled that the landing gear was engaging and locking into position. Everyone peered out their windows to the brightly colored spires of the ancient city sprawling out beneath them.

"Buckle up tight, boys and girls," Hedge said. "This is where the fun begins."

Evan turned her head to see the land below. "Look at the size of that port," she said. The shipyard looked like it stretched out for miles. The point where the oil platform resided was obvious. Dozens of massive tankers radiated out from its sides.

Teo shook his head. "It looks like a momma dog with a litter of pups gathering for dinner."

"It sure does," Evan agreed. "That's our target, right down

there."

Teo nodded. "We can't let any kind of explosion happen anywhere near those tankers. If one goes up, they all do."

"The price of oil will quadruple overnight," Hedge said. "Our job just got a whole lot tougher."

The jet tilted to the right as the pilot aligned the plane with the landing strip. Kirk tucked his chin to his chest and squeezed his eyes closed. His fingers gripped the armrests until his knuckles turned white.

Hedge shook his head. "Kirk, you know that flying is still the safest way to travel, right?"

"I'm aware that the facts support that theory," Kirk said.

Evan smiled. "If you still had your computer in your lap, you'd be fine, wouldn't you?"

Kirk nodded stiffly.

"Since your eyes are closed, just imagine that it is, Red."

Her voice seemed to comfort him. He opened his eyes and glanced back at Evan. He looked down at her feet and back up with a sharp glance. "You're wearing the black shoes. Why?"

Evan shrugged. "I assumed the red heels were mostly for when I couldn't wear this dress."

Kirk shook his head. "No. Well, yes, you should wear them if you can't wear the dress, but you should also wear them when you have the dress on, too."

"Oh," she started. She wondered what difference the shoes would make.

"The shoes can help me track you in three different ways. One, the red dye is a special formulation that can be picked up with a special filter, so that I can easily spot you in a crowd of people. Second, there is a GPS tracker in each heel. That's what I used to find you earlier. And third, they contain a tiny radar tracker chip."

"What?" Evan asked. "You can't track something this small with radar."

Kirk grinned and nodded. "Yes, you can." He turned his head to face her.

Evan noticed that her idea was working. Kirk's nerves seemed to disappear.

"It's a technology developed to help researchers track endangered baby horned lizards in Texas and Oklahoma."

"Baby horny toads?" Evan asked, excitedly. "I love horny toads."

"Yes, well, the babies are too small for traditional tracking tags that emit signals. There's no place for a power source." Kirk used his hands to talk now, and his voice rose in excitement. "But the little microchip will ping if you sweep with radar."

Evan nodded. She glanced over at Hedge who smiled at her calming manner with Kirk. The plane touched down on the runway.

Everyone leaned forward as the brakes engaged and the plane slowed to a casual taxi up to the private airport.

Hedge waited for the jet to slow to a crawl before he jumped from his seat to deplane. "Grab your gear, folks, we're here."

Evan, Teo, and Kirk all stood and reached for their luggage. Evan switched back into the red heels.

"How do I look?" she asked.

Kirk gave her a smile. Hedge nodded in approval.

Teo wiggled his brow. "You wanna get married, sweetheart?" he teased.

"I'm waiting for a man with a Lamborghini." Evan turned her head to shoot an air kiss to Teo over her shoulder.

"Baby, today is your lucky day."

CHAPTER FIVE

Evan twisted her hair around her fingers and smiled with a blush as Ramos handed a roll of cash to the guard at the shipping yard gate. The uniformed man offered instructions to the appropriate area of the port and wished him luck.

"My mother never spoke Spanish as fast as that guy," Teo said as he took Evan's hand and looped it over his arm. He walked her back to their rental car and maneuvered through the gates. The guard gave him a wink and a salute.

Evan waved.

"You speak Spanish, right?" he asked.

"O'course I do; I'm from Texas. But back home Spanish is real different than anywhere else in the world. It's as much Tex-Mex as the food." She gestured to the row of containers on their right. "You don't suppose they have fajitas over here, do ya?"

"I doubt it," Teo answered. He parked at the end of the drive. "I think we walk from here."

"Okay," Evan said. She hopped out of the sedan and took Ramos' arm again.

He pulled his bag from the back seat. "Do you think we keep up the cover out here, too?"

"Never drop your cover," she said. "I'm walking, breathing proof that you never know where a camera might be hidden."

"Good point." He moved the bag's strap up on his shoulder and snugged her waist with his arm. "Let's find this bad boy."

Kirk's voice hummed in Evan's ear. "You guys are heading in the right direction. Do you have the key?"

Evan smiled at Ramos. "We have the key you gave us. How certain are you that it will unlock something?"

Kirk laughed. "I can just about guarantee it will unlock something—but I'm not sure exactly what that something might be."

Ramos gestured with his chin. "Lots of the freight boxes with locks. As far as the eye can see."

Evan scanned the ends of the containers around them. Most did have padlocks hanging from their bolt hasps. "I thought they had to be inspected—the contents, I mean."

Kirk answered. "They are supposed to be. But lots of these places take the word of the shippers that the contents have been inspected. It's like a note from home. Not every country has the budget for a TSA."

"And our terror suspect knows this. He puts a padlock on the outside, writes up an efficient looking manifest, gives it an official fake signature, and voila!"

"Yeah, that's about it," Kirk said.

Evan relayed the information. "Why don't you wear an earwig?" she asked Teo.

"I do when I must. But when I'm on bomb-squad duty, it's best for me to focus on only what's in front of me."

"Got it." Evan looked up and down the aisles of containers to be sure that Kirk could get whatever readings he needed from the dress.

"How do we know which one?" Ramos asked.

Evan shrugged, waiting for Kirk to answer.

"Ask him," Teo said.

"I can hear you both just fine," Kirk said. "I'm doing a scan on the area for electronic heat signatures."

Evan raised her eyebrows. "If it's giving off heat, wouldn't that mean it's about to blow?"

"Not necessarily. Just active," Kirk explained. "Evan, can you two walk about twenty yards or so to your left?"

"He wants us to head up here a-ways," she said. "How's this, Red?"

They walked down a row of double-stacked containers marked with a dozen different languages and numbers on the ends. None of these had padlocks.

"Closer?" Evan asked.

"A little further," Kirk instructed. "I think I have something. Maybe another thirty feet."

Ramos and Evan went on. The sunlight was slipping away behind the mountain range in the west. Dock lights were fluttering on all around them.

Evan shivered in the cool evening breeze blowing in from the sea. Teo seemed to notice, and he moved his arm up across her bare shoulders. She smiled. "Thanks, Teo."

"Don't want you catching pneumonia out here on the job," he said, matching her grin.

Evan imagined his warm arms around her. She wandered through that idea for a moment and then scolded herself for it. *Stop it with those thoughts, already.*

"Stop where you are," Kirk said sharply.

Kirk's voice startled her, and she wondered if he could read her mind. She shook it off and halted, squeezing Ramos' arm to stop him, too. They looked around. Right in front of them was a stack of two containers, both with padlocks.

"Which one?" Ramos asked.

"Hmm." Kirk said. "I have a minor heat signature coming from about nine feet off the ground in front of you."

"Roger that," Evan said as she pointed to the container on top.

Ramos dropped the bag and sighed. "Of course, it's the one that involves climbing."

Evan laughed. "I suppose I'll be giving you a boost," she said. "Do we have any idea what he's dealing with? What kind of gear should he use, Kirk?" she asked.

Kirk scoffed. "The dress doesn't have x-ray vision—not yet. You'll have to climb up and let me see what we're dealing with."

Evan handed Ramos the bag. "He says for you to climb up, and then pull me up with you so he can see. You'll have to take everything with you."

Ramos slid the strap back over his shoulders. Evan knelt and held her laced fingers out, offering Ramos a foothold.

"I thought I was supposed to be the one getting down on one knee."

"Things change." She flashed a broad smile.

Ramos shook his head and reached up. He took the door rails in his grips and placed his foot in Evan's hands. She easily boosted him to the level of the upper car as he pulled his muscular frame into position. He took the key from his slacks pocket and tried it in the lock.

"No go with the key," he said. "Do we pick it?"

Evan shrugged. "Help me up. I'm good at picking locks."

Ramos hooked his bag strap to one of the lever handles and positioned his toes more securely on the two-and-a-half-inch lip of the lower box on which he stood. He squatted down, gripping the vertical strapping bar with his right hand and reaching for Evan's hand with his left.

"I hope this doesn't mess up my new shoes," she said as she scaled the end of the container to Teo's side.

Once up, she shifted her back to Teo, almost spooning with him. "Hang on around my waist, if you don't mind."

"It's a dirty job," he teased.

Evan pulled a tool that looked something like a cross between tweezers and scissors from her neckline. She lowered herself slightly, until the padlock was at eye-level, and began manipulating the lock. A few seconds more and the lock clicked.

The sudden drop of the body of the lock from the shackle surprised Evan. She jumped and lost the last of what precarious footing she had. She yelped as she fell, and Ramos reached out and caught her arm.

Evan dangled from her wrist within the tight grip of Teo's strong hand. "Are you alright?" he asked.

"I think so," she answered, trying to catch her breath. With her other hand, she steadied herself on the lower freight car, intending to climb back up, but the metal under her fingers was warm to the touch. "Aww, crap," she whispered.

"What's wrong? Did you break a nail or something?" Teo kidded.

Evan scowled. "Let me down easy, and then throw me the key."

Evan dropped to the paving and caught the brass key from the air. She shook her head as she slid it into the padlock on the lower car and it opened easily.

"Did it work?" he asked.

"Yeah," she said with a nod. "Lock that one back up and get back down here."

Teo climbed down to her side as she removed the padlock from the horizontal hasp.

"Don't just start pulling things open," Teo warned. "We don't know where the bomb could be."

"Tell me what's going on," Kirk insisted, raising his voice slightly to recapture Evan's attention.

Evan nodded to Teo and then gestured to her ear. "We found the freight car, and we opened the lock."

"I can see that much on the monitor. I'm reading the heat signature from above you, though." Kirk's voice sounded nervous. "Oh, no. Evan, you guys have trouble."

"The box itself is hot," Evan explained. "What should we do?"

"Poner las manos en el aire! Put your hands in the air," yelled a voice from behind them.

Evan and Ramos stopped in place, letting their hands slowly rise to eye-level.

"No vengas aqui a proponerle matrimonio," the port security officer said. "¿Que haces aqui?" he asked. "What are you doing here?"

From the corner of her eye, Evan could see two efficient-looking guards holding pistols on them.

Teo turned a slow circle to face the man. "No, I didn't come to propose. Soy un official federal. Ambos somos," he said, gesturing to Evan, too.

"Evan, the temperature is rising. You two need to get that thing shut down," Kirk said with a defined urgency.

"Uh-hunh," she hummed. She turned to face the armed guards. "Tenemos que ver lo que hay en este envase," she pieced together through her nerves. "We just need to see what's inside."

The guards wanted none of it. "Vienen con nosotros. Come

with us," the taller of the two men said.

Teo took a step toward the men, and Evan unbolted the vertical locking bars on the box.

"We can't wait, Teo," she said. "Kirk says it's getting hotter."

"Alto! Alto!" the first guard yelled.

"Don't open it!" Ramos hollered, too.

Evan stepped back and let the door swing open. Teo cringed.

Kirk scolded her, too. "Tyler, the bomb could have been rigged to the door!"

Evan ignored all the fuss as her gaze fixed on a shoebox-sized mechanism strapped to the ceiling of the box. Wires and a timer glowed in the blackness of the container. On the floor below sat a few dozen unmarked barrels.

Evan took another step away as her life began flashing through her mind like the vacation slideshows her family would watch after a long trip. Her breath became short and choppy.

Ramos saw the device about the same time as the guards. Everyone froze.

"This is bad," he said.

"This is worse than bad," Kirk whispered. "We have to assume that those barrels are filled with something combustible and probably worse."

The port guards realized what they were looking at right away. "¿Quien hizo esto?" the shorter one asked.

"What difference does it make who shipped it?" Teo said, half-laughing. "I can stop it." He gestured to himself. "Puedo deternerio."

The taller guard grabbed Evan's arm and pulled her away from the freight box. "Avanzamos. Move away."

"Let go of me," she said. "No me toques, por favor."

Teo motioned to Evan while pleading with the guard. "I need her. La necesito."

Evan took a step into the container while Teo opened his bag of tools. The shorter officer held up a flashlight into the darkness.

"Dios nos ayude," he said, forming a cross over his chest with his fingers.

Evan smiled. "Estamos aqui para ayudarle. No te preocupes." She tried to make her voice sound calm.

"Hotter, Evan," Kirk insisted. "I need to get a better look if I'm going to be of any help to Ramos."

Evan stood as close to the device as possible. "What can I do?"

Teo carefully climbed on top of two barrels and handed her the flashlight. "Hold this for me and tell the guards to stay back. Thanks."

Evan took the torch and nodded to the guards. "Tell anyone else out here to stay away. It's too dangerous. Es demasiado peligroso."

The men nodded and headed back to the end of the dock.

Evan made sure that the tools in the bag were all within her reach. "What can you tell us, Kirk?" she asked.

"I'm having to switch between infrared and night vision. This thing is getting warm. Can you read the timer, Ramos?" he asked through Evan.

"Can you tell what the timer says?" she asked.

"Looks like zero-four-thirty," he answered.

"Hedge wants to know if that's enough time?" Kirk asked.

"Do you have enough time with that?" she asked.

Teo glanced down and forced a smile. A bead of sweat gathered in his thin mustache. "I'm good."

"I have faith," she said.

Kirk hummed, "How complex is the configuration?"

Evan took a breath. "Kirk wants to know how complex is the configuration?"

Ramos nodded to himself. "Looks pretty basic. Lots of wires, but they're all the standard colors. This is pretty textbook."

Evan wiped a bead of moisture from her forehead.

He pushed his wire cutters into the multi-colored web. "This one here," Ramos said, as he nipped.

The timer stopped.

Teo let his shoulders sink as he exhaled. "One minute thirty left on the clock. We're good."

Evan sighed. "Red, send in the authorities to empty this car. We have disarmed the device."

"Roger that," Kirk answered.

A light blipped on the device.

"Hold," Ramos said. He focused on the bomb again. "The timer is back on, running fast-forward. Evan, get your butt out of here."

"Not leaving you," she responded.

"Evan, get out, now," Kirk shouted. "That's direct from Hedge."

"No, sir!"

She took a deep breath. Teo scrambled with his wire-cutters, trying to decide where to snip.

"I have an idea," she said as the timer approached the ten-second mark. She pinched the notch at her neckline.

The dress instantly sent out a sonic-electromagnetic pulse.

Evan hiccupped.

The flashlight went dark. Teo's watch stopped.

"Did it work?" Evan asked.

Teo's voice shook. "I guess it did. I saw the digital display readout four seconds. But there's no display at all now."

"Didn't mean to surprise you, but I didn't have much time for a warning," she explained. "I figured if anything could stop the blast it would be the SEMP."

"Don't apologize, Tyler. You saved our lives. I like that kind of surprise better than having my head blown off, any day of the week." Teo reached out for her hand. "Can you help me down?"

Evan caught hold of his hand and helped steady him on his landing.

"Are you guys okay?" Kirk asked. "Or are you dead?"

Evan laughed. "We're not dead. We stopped it." She followed Teo outside the freight car. "Hey, Red, how come I can still hear you? I thought the pulse would knock out everything."

"It did for a second," he said. "But your shoes got everything up and running again. They have a surge shield in the heel, along with a few extra capacitors. The shoes will automatically synch up and recharge if the dress or your ear receiver loses power."

"Nifty," she replied. "Is there any chance that the bomb we just disarmed will have anything like that? I don't want it coming back on again."

"Hmm," Kirk began. "How close were you when you flipped your switch?"

"About three feet below it."

"There's almost zero chance it had a surge shield, so I would guess you fried the circuit completely." Kirk tapped away. "I'm instructing the port authorities that your scene is all clear. Hedge has a team on the way now. Once they arrive, do you think you and Ramos can extract the device? We need to be able to tell other port teams what they're dealing with."

She looked at Teo. "Kirk wants to know if we can extract it."

"Yeah, we can do that."

Evan watched as Teo rolled his shoulders forward and back to loosen the stressed muscles. She gently patted his arm. "It's okay now. We got it."

Teo smiled and snugged her shoulders in a hug. He faced out to the black water where the lights of the city glistened on the surface.

"It's beautiful like this, isn't it?" he said with a quiet calm.

"It is," Evan answered. "Now it's time to get that bomb out of there."

Teo nodded, turning back into the container. He leaned over his open tool bag and sighed. Evan noticed a shiver run down his back.

"Are you all right?" she asked.

He didn't answer.

She put her hand on his shoulder. When he looked up, she put her hands on either side of his face. The stubble of his five o'clock shadow felt rough on her palms. She gazed into his dark brown eyes until his smile matched hers.

"You're going to be all right. We both are." She patted his cheek. "Tell me what you need."

Teo nodded and straightened his back. He handed her an

old-fashioned battery-operated flashlight and gestured to the menace on the ceiling of the box with his cutters. "You want to give me another boost?"

CHAPTER SIX

"When you are told to get out," Hedge started.

Evan waved her finger in his face. "With all due respect, sir, you're treating me like a little girl. If I had run the bomb would have detonated."

Teo sat on the small modern couch in the hotel suite. "I don't even want to think about what would have happened, Parker. Agent Tyler saved lives by staying."

Kirk looked up from his computer. "Not to mention saving the world from skyrocketing oil prices. Eleanor says two more teams have located bombs. That makes nine so far, with two more ports being searched as we speak."

Teo shook his head and began unbuttoning his shirt cuffs and collar. "I don't care what the rest of the world is paying for gasoline if I'm dead, you know."

Hedge wanted to continue his scolding but knew it was futile. "I understand what happened." He faced Evan and shrugged. "You saved lives. More than you know. I just have to remind you of the protocols."

"I get that there are protocols in place for all of our protection. I do get it. But when I saw the timer counting down, I knew what had to be done." Evan paused for a moment as she heard those words out loud. "I knew what had to be done," she repeated. This time the words had a quiver in them.

Teo nodded and stood by her side. "And you did it, Tyler. Thank you, you know, for saving my life."

Evan couldn't think to smile. The adrenaline she'd been riding on for the last half hour had come to an end. Her elbows weakened. Her knees wobbled.

Teo hugged her as if as much to keep her upright as for affection. "Come sit here beside me," he said.

"Ramos," Hedge directed as the other two sat. "What kind of bomb-maker are we looking for? How technologically advanced was this piece?"

"It was sophisticated enough. It was clean. At first glance, it looked like a pretty good mess of wires and tape, but that was mostly for show. When the timer really got going—after we thought we had it taken care of—well, it was pretty artfully done." Teo nodded. As he got more excited, his hands became involved. "The thing about bombers is that they are consistent. They find their preferred type, and they usually stick with it. Maybe they slick it up as they go, but that's about it."

Evan watched him talk. She allowed her shoulders to loosen. Her breath became more stable. "Hedge, Ramos was perfect out there. Calm and collected."

Hedge Parker nodded. "I know. You both did your job, but your job isn't over. We seem to have the ports secured now—or nearly so—but we still don't know who is doing all of this or why."

Evan chewed on her lip. "Can we search intelligence files for a bomb-making signature?"

Kirk waved a finger in the air. "I'm doing that now. The parts are all pretty generic thus far. Whoever he is, he knows how to fly under the radar. He purchased the timing mechanism from an electronics distributor in Germany and the main housing from a wholesale steel manufacturer in France. The wires were ordered online from a home-improvement outlet in Michigan."

Evan laughed. "What about the actual explosives? You can't order those from any Home Depot."

"You would be surprised what you can cook up in your sink," Kirk said.

"No, I wouldn't," Teo said. "I've got some cousins that make all kinds of cocktails. But that's a little different, I guess."

Hedge held his right hand to his side again and then balanced the motion with his left. "Eleanor wants us to track down any leads we can while we're here in Barcelona. Kirk found a few contacts that might help us find this guy." He looked at his watch. "It's after midnight, local time. Let's all try to get some rest tonight. Tomorrow will be challenging enough."

Kirk shot a glance to Evan. "I'm bunking with you tonight. I want to talk to you about the dress if that's okay."

Evan nodded. "Can I go take it off now?"

"Sure," Kirk said. "Go ahead." He pointed to the door behind him.

Evan raised an eyebrow to Hedge. "Are you done with me?" She didn't like stringing those words together. It was an innocent question, but the implications might be bigger than she wanted to admit.

"I'll see you in the morning," he said.

Basic answer. *It's fine.* But she wanted him to say *no. No, I need to speak with you privately.* She paused a few more seconds to give him the chance to change his answer. He didn't. He was already in another conversation with Kirk.

She stood to leave the room, and Teo followed her to the bedroom door. Evan sighed as he opened the door for her.

"What can I say?" Ramos whispered. "I owe you my life."

Evan patted the side of his face. "Yeah, and you owe me a proposal with a Lamborghini."

"I want you to hold me to that," he said with sly smile.

Evan patted his cheek and let her thumb brush over his bottom lip as she walked into the bedroom, and he closed the door, leaving her alone. *Alone.*

Her red travel bag sat in the middle of the bed next to the window. The garment bag for the dress hung on a hook on the closet door. The lamp between the two beds was an apple green ceramic elephant with a white linen drum shade perched above. Everything in the room was green or gray-toned. The prints over the beds were modern interpretations of oversized palm leaves. The room was pretty but hardly cozy.

She pulled her clothes out of the bag and tossed her yoga pants and tee onto the chair at her side. The rest of the clothes went into the small dresser on the opposite wall.

In less than a minute, she was comfortable, hanging her dress into the bag for charging. A tap at the door caught her attention.

"Come in," she responded.

Kirk grinned as he sidestepped into the room. Evan realized that this was one of his new habits since spending more time in the field. He looked as though he was ready to dodge a bullet or slip behind a shrub for cover.

"What do we know?" she asked as he planted himself on the foot of his bed.

Kirk grimaced. "Lots of stuff, but nothing we really need to know."

"Is Hedge really angry?"

"Not angrier than me," he said. "We're both just worried about you."

Evan rolled her eyes. "You know, I made it. You should be proud. Both of you should. It's because of the dress that Teo and I are still alive. You and Hedge did that—and Eleanor."

"Hmm, Eleanor," Kirk muttered. "Hedge is getting an earful from her right now. She's second-guessing her decision to let us continue this mission."

"How can she do that?" Evan exclaimed. "Does she think the bombs wouldn't have been set if we had gone back to DC? We found the keys to the shipping containers before we were approved for this extension."

"You know that, and I know that," Kirk said with a sigh. "And of course, Eleanor knows that, too." He began pecking away at his keyboard again. "I'm sure Max Fischer is giving her grief about the whole assignment. By his timetable, we should have been back home three days ago."

"I understand," she said. "It's just frustrating. I guess I'm feeling a little low because we haven't caught the guy." She pulled her feet up under her. "We don't even know who he might be."

Kirk raised his head to stare at her for several seconds. It was long enough to make Evan nervous. "What is it?" she asked.

"How was the dress?" Kirk's eyes lit up like a kid on Christmas morning. "You set off the SEMP all on your own. How was it?"

Evan pulled her shoulders up around her ears, crunching herself into the smallest size she could manage. Her voice sizzled with excitement. "It was pretty great."

Kirk beamed. "Did it hurt?"

Evan laughed and flopped her feet back over the side of the bed. "Nope! I was afraid that it might. You know, the first time you set off the pulse, I was out cold. The second time it went off automatically when Brawn tried to shoot me."

"I know. I was worried you would hesitate to initiate the pulse. But you did it. I'm really proud of you." Kirk reached for his notebook bag from under his bed. "I need to run a set of diagnostics on you, okay? I know you've had enough time to calm down from it all, but I need to make sure that the pulse isn't doing any physical or physiological damage."

Evan raised her eyebrows and held out her right arm. "Yes, please let's be sure about that."

Kirk pulled out the familiar wires and plugged them into his computer. He secured the other ends to Evan's wrist, temple, and throat. "Just breathe normally."

She nodded. "It did sort of feel like a hiccup. Like the kind you get when you drink a soda too fast."

Kirk nodded.

"It was like a quick squeeze around the middle," she added. "A nice little hug."

Kirk fixed his gaze on the monitor. "You seem a little upset."

Evan shook her head. "I'm not upset. Is my blood pressure up or something?"

"No, everything is fine," he said. He glanced up at her vibrant blue-green eyes. "I don't know. Maybe Gerard's suicide bothered you more than you think."

"Well, yes—it bothered me. How could it not bother me?" She clenched her fists. "I tried to talk to him. He just couldn't see a solution. He wasn't willing to give his wife a chance to understand him or forgive him. I just don't understand."

Kirk patted her balled hands. "That's what I mean by *upset*."

Evan stretched out her fingers and flexed them a few times. She hadn't realized how high-strung she'd gotten over the situation. "I just felt like I could help him. It was as if we had a connection," she tried to explain.

Kirk shifted his computer to his side and began removing the wires from Evan's pulse points. He scooted to the edge of the bed so that his knees were only an inch or so from Evan's. "I want you to listen to me because what I'm telling you is important."

Evan nodded. She knew he was serious. "I will."

"You have an amazing ability to connect with people. I've seen it up-close." He leaned closer to her and softened his voice. "You've saved the lives of several people because you have a knack for seeing the good in everyone. You remind people of what they can do. You see it, and you make others see it, too."

Evan pressed her lips together and tilted her face forward. "But?"

"You forget that the connection is a two-way street. You may be lifting these people up, but Evan, they can just as easily pull you down."

"I'm careful."

"You are. You have been." He reached out and patted her hand like a caring father with his daughter. "We are looking for a terrorist. There is a madman out there right now, and he's plotting against not just a single country, but against the world."

Evan squeezed Kirk's hand in appreciation. "I know this, Red. He's using people. He's hurting people."

Kirk lifted his chin and nodded. "And that's the point I'm making. You see people who are vulnerable—who are being pushed around by this bully. You want to help them."

"What's wrong with that?"

"Nothing." Kirk shook his head. "There is nothing wrong with that, but that's not your assignment."

"I think it *is* part of our assignment." She drew her hands back.

Kirk didn't seem to take offense to her withdrawal. He casually leaned back onto his palms. "This man, whoever he is —or woman, for that matter—sees the vulnerability of these people, too. They're the ones pushing Gerard around."

"Yeah," she said.

"We have to assume, we *must* assume, that this guy is forcing them to do his bidding."

"I'm just trying to stop them from doing it," Evan argued.

"I know that. But listen, what if Gerard Boulette's suicide was his plan? What if that is what he intended all along?"

Evan let an injured breath escape her lungs. Her brain ached from thinking about Gerard. "But the bombs?"

Kirk sat up straight again. "That's why I'm going down this path of reason. Anybody with half a brain doesn't plant a dozen bombs hundreds of miles apart to go off at random times."

"We don't know they were set to go off randomly."

Kirk gestured to his computer without picking it up. "No, but if you want them to all detonate, you have them all go within minutes of each other. We had hours between Marseilles and the one here. And none of the others were counting down when they were discovered. I think he intended for them to be found."

"What good does that do him?" Evan asked. She pushed her fingers through her red hair, picking it up from the back of her neck and letting it cascade down to her shoulders. "If the bombs don't go off, we have a much easier time tracking him down."

"That would make sense if we were actually getting any useful information with which we could track him. As of right now, we aren't." He held his palms up. "No prints, no chemical signatures, nothing. All of the paperwork for the shipping containers was under Alan Smithee Enterprises, which has a working website representing the business as a toy manufacturer."

"What?"

"I think it's a message to us."

"He's playing with us?" she asked. She searched Kirk's eyes for answers.

He shrugged. "I don't know if he knows who we are, but yeah, he's playing with us."

"And you think Gerard's suicide was part of his plan?"

Kirk nodded. "I do. He's not leaving us any other trail. The bodies of Gerard Boulette, Anton Hrevic, Robert Charles, and even Jarrett Brawn—they are our only breadcrumbs."

"We have Xandra Yakovsky in custody," Evan said. "We should talk to her. She may still be the one pulling strings."

Kirk cocked his head to the side. "Maybe she is. We don't know for sure. The problem is that she's not talking yet. Until she does, we won't know whether she's got a boss, a pawn, or a partner."

Evan took a deep breath and stood up.

"I'll let you get ready for bed, Red."

"I'm not telling you that you did anything wrong, Evan. I just want you to be careful out there." Kirk stood, too. "Your instincts are top-notch, but if you get personally involved with a target, be they victims, suspects, assets, or whatever, you're going to get hurt."

She smiled. "I understand, Red." She stood and kissed his cheek. "Thanks for caring enough to set me straight."

Kirk grimaced and shook his head. "And none of that kissing between personnel, either. You know where that leads."

"Where?" she asked. She gave him a wink as she opened the bedroom door.

He shook his head, trying to hide the faint blush settling into his cheeks. "Are you going for some warm milk to help you sleep?"

"I think I owe Hedge an apology."

CHAPTER SEVEN

Hedge sat with his legs stretched out across the small couch, dressed only in a pair of faded jeans, reading from the tablet in his hand. When he noticed Evan, He grabbed his gray tee shirt and pulled it over his well-built but still bruised chest and shoulders.

"You don't have to dress fancy for me," she said with a playful tone. She pretended not to notice his perfectly formed pectorals, biceps, triceps, and trapezius. He looked good, not just for a man approaching forty-five; he looked good for a man of any age.

He smirked. "I thought my instructions were for you to get some sleep."

"Yeah, like you haven't noticed I stopped following your instructions back in Paris," she joked.

Hedge didn't laugh. "I noticed."

Evan walked to the end of the couch and tilted her chin, silently asking permission to sit down.

Hedge sighed and dropped his feet from the sofa to the floor to make room for her.

"Maybe I came out here to tell you that I'm sorry for my insubordination out there today on the dock."

Hedge raised his left eyebrow. "Really? You're sorry for remaining in position after you were told to get out of there?"

Evan stretched her arm across the back of the sofa toward him. She let her index finger poke at the top of his shoulder. "No, sir. I'm not sorry that I stayed with Teo. But I am sorry for telling you *no* when you ordered me out."

Hedge couldn't help but laugh. "You just can't resist, can you?"

"Would you like me to apologize for making light of this serious situation?" she offered.

"Are you actually sorry for that?" he asked.

She twisted her lips to one side. "If I answer that honestly, it might make any following apology sound insincere."

Hedge slid his tablet onto the narrow coffee table in front of them. He turned to face her, and she matched his attitude.

"Did Kirk send you out here?"

Evan shook her head. "Nope. He wanted me to stay in there and watch him undress. I don't know what it is with you guys, but for some reason y'all all want me to see you topless. Are you having some sort of contest or something?"

Hedge rolled his eyes. "What do you want, Evan?" he asked.

She let her hands fall to her lap. "I am sorry. Kirk talked to me about getting too personally connected on the job. He helped me to see what it was doing."

"You're great out there. You have good instincts."

"I know. I think you and Kirk are reading from the same playbook." She sealed her lips together quickly. "Sorry for that, too."

Hedge raked his fingers through his light brown hair. "I don't have the greatest track record for keeping things professional on the job. You know how it was between Eleanor and me when she was my partner."

"I know enough," she said.

"It was bad," he began. "That's not true, exactly. It was great —in the beginning. But then judgments went cloudy. People got hurt. It's just never a good idea."

"In Paris, when we first found these keys," she said, gesturing to an invisible pile of keys on the table. "You told me that you needed me."

"The team does need you. Your country needs you." Hedge shifted in his seat. "Don't ever doubt that."

"I don't. But that's not what you said at that moment. You told me that *you* needed me. And later, when you kissed me. You said that you needed me." Evan tried to take a mental step back from the conversation. She didn't want to spill out her heart and tell him that she desperately needed him, too. Maybe she did, but she refused to do it. Especially right after being chided for getting overly involved.

"What difference does that make?" he asked. His voice was quiet and calm.

Evan wanted to scream. *What difference? What difference!?* Her thoughts were spinning. She had no idea how to respond. She took a deep breath and released it slowly. She could smell the clean herbal scent of his shampoo. She hated how much she loved that smell.

"I guess I thought Marseilles would be different," she heard herself say. Her tone was professional—exactly the opposite of how she felt inside.

"Different how exactly?" he asked. His dark blue eyes stared unswervingly into her gaze.

She blinked. It was too much. She had made excuses for him. He was in pain, he was overwhelmed by the assignment, whatever. She wasn't sure what happened in the last 48 hours, but something definitely had changed. Her emotions were on a Tilt-a-Whirl, while he seemed to be riding a Lazy River. She took a deep breath. Professional. She could keep it professional. Kirk had been right about her being upset. Maybe she did just need some rest and a little time.

Hedge sighed. "I have to get some sleep. Eleanor is doing her best to keep us up and running out here. Fischer is on the warpath. We need some results." He got to his feet slowly.

Evan guessed he was in more pain than he would want her to know. *Give him time, too.* It will work out. Evan nodded, standing up. She decided to take the light approach once again. "Yes, sir. Oh, and Hedge?"

He picked up his tablet and took a step toward his bedroom door. "Yeah?"

"If you guys *are* having a contest with the shirtless thing—don't take this the wrong way, but—"

"Go to bed."

CHAPTER EIGHT

"I know Fischer wants results," Hedge said. "We'll have them soon. We're making progress." He angled his tablet to prevent the glare from the table lamp distorting Eleanor's image as they communicated online.

"Gerard Boulette was to have made a presentation at the European Trade Summit next week. France has yet to name his replacement, but I'll keep you apprised," Eleanor said with a sigh. "How is Evan holding up?" she asked.

"She was shaken a bit by Boulette's death, but she's all right." Hedge nodded. "Ramos and Tyler operated well as a team out there this evening." Hedge glanced down to see the time. It was nearly three in the morning in Barcelona. "Everyone is just anxious to catch this guy."

Eleanor grinned. "I'm sure you're taking good care of your team."

Hedge knit his brows together, trying to decipher her meaning. "They're all asleep right now."

"You look tired, Hedge," she said. "Are you sleeping?"

He rocked his head to one side and stretched his shoulders back. "I'd be sleeping right now if I wasn't reporting to you."

"You know what I mean," she insisted. "Are you healing? Is Evan taking good care of you?"

"Elle, Evan isn't the medic on this team; Ramos is. And he's keeping both Kirk and me healthy." He knew where her fishing would lead next.

"I just thought that perhaps you might be giving each other a little comfort and support in the field." Eleanor's eyes sparkled, even across thousands of miles.

Hedge rubbed at his temples. "Elle, things aren't like that here."

She frowned. "I wouldn't blame you if they were, you know. I remember the nights we spent in the field."

He cut her off. "Kirk said that you sent him some names to look into. Is there anything I should know before we go hunting tomorrow?"

Eleanor sat back in her chair. "Xandra Yakovsky hasn't given up any more information. She absolutely refuses to talk to anyone. I've tried three times to question her, and all I get from her are giggles or growls."

Hedge shrugged. "Your strength is interrogating men, Elle, not women. Your baby-blues work like truth serum on men. Women, not so much."

Elle circled back around. "They never seemed to work all that well with you, Hedge. Maybe that's why I liked you so much. I always enjoyed a challenge."

Hedge blinked away his fatigue. "I've got to get some sleep, or I'll be worthless. Is there anything else you want to tell me—regarding the job?"

Eleanor smiled and tilted her chin. "It's always about the job, Hedge." She leaned forward again. "The three names I've sent Kirk were all gleaned from the main computer from Anton Hrevic's home in Paris. They have similar notes attached to their files as did several of the men who Xandra ordered killed at the hands of Jarrett Brawn. It is possible, maybe even likely, that they are targeted for assassination, too. With Brawn dead, Xandra may have ordered another hit man."

Hedge shook his head. "If she did that, it would have had to be from wherever you're keeping her. We had her in custody before Evan killed Brawn."

Eleanor nodded and squared her shoulders. "It's possible that she had a back-up in place. We still don't know that she's not the one calling the shots."

Hedge yawned. "We'll look through the names, and I'll get back with you tomorrow—later today—whatever."

Eleanor repeated his yawn. "Get some sleep. I have a man here working on any possible connections between all of these names. The only obvious ties they have to each other are that they all work for their government agencies or for businesses closely associated with the government."

"Yeah, I'll bet Kirk can connect some dots."

Eleanor grinned and sighed again. "I do miss being in the field at your side, Hedge."

"Tell your husband that I say *hello*," he said, hoping to make her uncomfortable. "Your little senator is a good man."

Eleanor's expression changed from coy to angry in an instant. Before she had a chance to respond, Hedge ended his call with her. He yawned again as the room went dark. He stood up to go back to his bedroom and tossed a glance over his shoulder to where a slit of moonlight fell across Evan's closed door.

"Comfort and support," he muttered.

CHAPTER NINE

"Douglas Mabry, Benito Tambar, and Michael Cooper," Kirk listed. "All three of these men were on Hrevic's computer. Xandra wouldn't give us any information about them at all, but Nastya seems to be cooperating. She gave a little information about all of them."

Evan nodded. Nastya Alenko was one of Anton Hrevic's muse-models, who had been secretly gathering information and video to be used for blackmailing and manipulating men with power. Evan had spent the last two weeks in Paris infiltrating their circle and befriending the muses to stop the scheme. Nastya was the one who always met with Cooper. "Cooper is the one we looked at before. I remember his picture—the young, good-looking type," she said. "What do we know about them?"

Kirk tapped at his keyboard, and the pictures popped up on his monitor. "Mabry is the secretary to the US ambassador to the UK. His apartment is in London, but he is currently on a sight-seeing tour of Europe with his wife and children."

The monitor showed a picture of a man with dark features, in his mid-forties, with a receding hairline and a too-perfect nose. Another photograph showed him flanked by two blonde children with straight, white teeth and freckles. The woman standing behind him was platinum blonde, in her mid-thirties, wearing an expensive silk scarf and Tiffany earrings.

Kirk continued, "Tomorrow they will be arriving in Barcelona. He is scheduled to deliver a parcel to the American Embassy in preparation for the European Trade Summit."

"That takes place next Thursday," Hedge interrupted.

"Yes," Kirk said, switching to the next photo. "Tambar is also expected to be at the Trade Summit. He works for the Spanish government in their energy department."

Tambar appeared to be in his sixties. He was bald, but with a thick black beard and mustache tinged with silver at the corners of his mouth.

"His wife lives with him here in Barcelona. She was diagnosed with cancer last year and has been in and out of the hospital since then."

"Sad," Ramos commented.

"And lastly," Kirk said, changing the picture once again. "We have Michael Cooper. He is an Irish entrepreneur—billionaire. He is single, and a world traveler. He also will be in London for the Summit, though not officially. He is meeting with some of the representatives for a private conference. He owns several oil fields throughout the world and is presenting a lecture about new drilling standards."

Evan listened to Kirk's voice, but couldn't peel her gaze from the photograph on the monitor. Cooper's piercing blue eyes stole her breath. His high, chiseled cheekbones cut sharply back into a clean-shaven jaw framing a perfect cleft-chin.

"He's just so dang pretty," Evan heard herself say out loud.

Hedge blinked. "Well, he's the one that doesn't seem to be a victim of extortion. Nastya assures us that he's an old friend of hers."

Kirk nodded. "Mabry and Tambar both have photos and videos from multiple encounters with Hrevic's party girls. Tambar especially enjoyed their company. We haven't found anything with Cooper on it at all. When he is seen at the house in Paris, he's talking to Nastya. He spends the night with her and leaves the next morning. No wild parties."

Ramos shrugged. "Maybe they are just friends. Did Nastya say anything about what Hrevic or Xandra was doing? Did she know that they were blackmailing all of these men?"

Hedge chewed on his lip. "She never indicated that she or the other girls had any knowledge of Xandra or Hrevic's operation. She knew that they were supposed to take care of the men, but she still insists that it was because they were Anton's friends."

"She kept telling us that if we wanted information about the men, we should ask Anton," Kirk added.

"She doesn't know he's dead?" Evan asked.

"Not until we told her," Kirk said. "Eleanor's interrogation team let her go this morning, along with Olga, Maria, and Tatiana. We'll keep tabs on them all, but we had no reason to keep them any longer."

Evan shook her head. "If any of them do know what's going on, maybe they'll lead us that direction." She couldn't help but stare at the photo of Cooper. "Where is Cooper right now?"

Hedge rolled his eyes. "Agent Tyler, Mr. Cooper is not our top priority right now; no matter how badly you might wish that he was."

He made a quick gesture to Kirk, who took Cooper's picture down. Evan's focus returned to Hedge.

"Today Kirk and I are going to meet with Tambar. We're going in as American businessmen interested in Spanish energy investments," Hedge explained.

"I have a power point ready," Kirk added.

Teo and Evan exchanged an amused glance.

"We'll try to get a feel for if he's being pushed around by anyone," Hedge said.

"You don't want me to go as your secretary?" Evan asked. "No offense, Red."

"None taken."

Hedge shook his head and picked up a red neck-tie from the back of the closest armchair. "We might need you to visit him later. He tends to work late a lot—usually at the bar around the corner from his office."

"So he's kind of a pig?" Evan asked. "Of course he is. Otherwise, nobody would be able to blackmail him in the first place."

"You felt sorry for Boulette," Kirk reminded her.

"Yes, but Boulette's wife wasn't dying of cancer," she answered.

Ramos tapped the coffee table with a pen. "We don't know if the blackmail has anything to do with his wife. Maybe with her cancer, she gave him permission to fool around. The extortion might be job-related. Most government positions have ethics clauses."

Hedge finished knotting the tie and snugged it up to his collar. "We'll see what we can find out about him." He motioned to Ramos and Tyler. "You two stay close here just in case we need you."

Kirk pulled on a gray sports jacket and loaded his attaché case. "Evan, I'm going to turn off your canal receiver for now, but Hedge and I will stay connected to you through the tablet. If we have anything actionable, we'll let you know right away."

"Thanks, Red."

Ramos walked the men to the door of the hotel suite. "Good luck," he said, offering his hand to them as they filed out.

When they were gone, he turned to Evan. "Let's get us some room service."

CHAPTER TEN

Kirk studied the hall outside the office of Benito Tambar. His foot tapped nervously on the marble tiles as they waited.

"May I bring you some coffee or tea?" the curvy young secretary offered. "Señor Tambar will only be a few more minutes."

"No, thank you," Kirk said without making eye-contact. He was busy assessing exits and obstacles.

"I would love some coffee," Hedge said with a broad grin. The brown-eyed woman smiled and nodded.

As soon as she had cleared the doorway, Hedge turned slightly in his seat to favor Kirk. "You have to calm down. You're tapping SOS in Morse code with your toes."

Kirk stopped instantly. "It's been a while since I've been out like this."

"Be glad I didn't make you wear a tie," Hedge joked.

The woman returned and handed Hedge a Styrofoam cup. "I didn't know if you wanted sweet or no," she shrugged. "I made it sweet."

Hedge grinned. "Gracias," he replied, and then took a sip. The sugar overpowered any coffee flavor completely. "You surely did. Thank you."

She curved her ruby red lips into a smile and returned to her desk. Hedge pretended to take another sip.

"How bad is it?" Kirk asked in a whisper.

"Plenty bad," Hedge said under his breath.

"What do you think is going on with this summit?" Kirk asked. "They have a couple of these a year. They renew a few trade agreements, adjust a few rates, and pat each other on the backs. They're always pretty routine. What's so special about this one?"

Hedge cast his gaze out the window on the opposite wall to a garden beyond. "I don't know. Our sources haven't heard anything out of the ordinary until this mess out here on the Mediterranean ports."

"Now these guys are scrambling—talking about terrorists wreaking havoc with their oil treaties," Kirk added. "Is this what Xandra had in mind all along? Does it come down to oil—like everything else on this side of the Atlantic?"

"Why not?" Hedge asked.

A light flashed on the secretary's desk phone, and she stood and directed her attention to Kirk and Hedge. "Señor Tambar will see you now."

The men followed the dark-haired beauty through a short, arched hall and into an oak-paneled sitting room. The vaulted ceiling ran from a pair of eight-foot-tall carved double doors to a cut-stone fireplace at the far end. The stucco ceiling was braced with heavy gothic timbers and punctuated with ornate wrought-iron chandeliers. The secretary gestured to a pair of matching leather chairs opposite a glass-topped desk, and they took seats.

Benito Tambar entered the double doors as if he was being hailed with a chorus of trumpets. Kirk and Hedge stood.

"I hope you did not have to wait too long," Tambar said, offering a handshake to each man.

The sheen of his beard was matched only by the reflection from his head. Kirk averted his eyes and took a seat. Hedge smiled and waited for Tambar to sit at the desk.

"Your assistant offered us coffee," Hedge said, waving his hand toward the hall.

"For that, I am truly sorry," Tambar said with a robust chuckle.

"Señor Tambar," Hedge began, "My name is Brandon Hedger, and this is my colleague, Roland Curtis. We have been discussing the possibilities of investing in Spanish resources. In California, which we call home, we have all sorts of solar and wind opportunities. There is always oil and natural gas, and of course, coal. We have a company that is even working on extracting energy through a desalination process with ocean water. We have our hands in all sorts of investments at home."

Tambar listened and nodded. He didn't seem to understand where the conversation might lead.

"I have heard that Americans like to diversify their investments," Tambar said.

"Quite right," Kirk said, nearly startling himself just by participating in the exchange.

Hedge nodded. "Yes, well, we've just about run out of American opportunities," he said. "And we've decided we need to find another country into which we can expand."

Hedge stroked his goatee as a gesture to help identify himself with Tambar, but Tambar's face suddenly appeared ashen.

"I am not sure what you want from me," he said. His eyes shifted from side to side.

Both Kirk and Hedge became concerned with the change in Tambar's appearance.

Kirk raised his hand in hopes of calming the man. "We just thought that you might point us in the right direction. With your position, we assumed you would have information that would lead us in more profitable ways."

Tambar's body language became erratic. "I cannot help you." He stood, pushing his leather desk chair to one side. He looked at the door and then back to the men.

Hedge shook his head. "We don't want you to do anything illegal or unethical. We are just asking for a name—maybe a list of names. Where would your country benefit the most from outside investors?"

Tambar backed away another step. "I have done what you asked," he stammered. "¡Dejame en paz! You must leave me alone!"

He trotted to the carved doors.

"Wait, Señor Tambar," Kirk called after him.

Tambar was on the run.

"Crap," Hedge muttered. "Let's go."

Kirk grabbed the attaché and followed as Hedge ran after Tambar.

"Me voy para el resto del dia," Tambar yelled to his secretary as he ran through an exit and into the garden.

"He's leaving for the day," Kirk translated.

"I know," Hedge said. "Get to the car. I think I can catch him."

Kirk shook his head. "He's going the opposite direction. I'll stay. Maybe we'll have the chance to cut him off." Kirk could see that Hedge was in pain as he ran. He didn't want to leave his side.

Tambar raced across the courtyard and back into the building. Kirk and Hedge almost caught up to him in the hall, but Tambar slipped into a closing elevator car.

They assessed the situation. Kirk looked back at his partner. "You take the next car up, and I'll take the stairs."

Hedge knew his friend was giving him the easier task, but with the fire in his hip, he was grateful. He ran to the next elevator.

Kirk ran to the end of the hall where a glowing glass sign indicated the stairwell. He began his ascent. At each floor, he pushed open the door enough to see if Tambar was getting off the elevator. Nothing.

At the fifth floor, he saw a door closing across the hall. His breath was failing. His shoulder ached. He had nearly forgotten about his gunshot wound, but now every move of his right arm stabbed through to his lungs.

He darted from the stairwell into the hall and across to the just-closed door. He pushed the door open with his foot and sidestepped inside. "Alto!" he yelled to a shadow silhouetted against the window on the other side of the room.

A stout woman with silver-rooted orange hair stepped into the center of the room, into the light so that Kirk could easily identify that this was not Tambar.

"Lo siento," he apologized. "Debo tener la Oficina equivocada."

"Salte," she replied.

Kirk nodded. "I'm going. Just the wrong office," he said. "Lo siento. Lo siento."

He left the woman and returned to the hallway. The elevator light across the hall lit up with a ding, and Kirk readied himself to tackle Tambar, should he come out.

The doors parted, and two elderly men strolled out. They eyed Kirk as though he were a sculpture of modern art. Kirk realized he had been standing with his hands out in a pseudo-judo position.

"Ridiculo," one of the old men spat out.

The next elevator car stopped as well. Kirk turned to face it, altering his stance to a more casual attitude. Hedge waited inside.

"You don't have him either?" he asked.

Kirk joined him. "Nope."

Hedge shrugged. "Do you want to continue pursuit?"

Kirk shook his head. "No. Let's go to the car. I'll do some hacking, and maybe I can get his car tags or something like that."

"If we don't find him soon, we can try out Plan B," Hedge said.

"What's Plan B?" Kirk asked, punching the elevator button for the lobby.

"Let the uninjured members of the team do the chasing."

"I like that plan."

CHAPTER ELEVEN

Evan sat on the couch, reviewing her cover information. She was to be Eve Taylor, professional problem-solver to the rich and powerful of the world. She practiced her Spanish and French and debated whether to use her Texas drawl or not. Her accent charmed most men, but not all. She decided that maybe she would keep the accent, but tone it down to that of a more refined Southern Belle. It could work.

Ramos brought a tray of hot tea and fruit to the coffee table. "I'm hungry," he said. He poured out a cup of tea for Evan and then one for himself. "I doubt that this will fix that problem, but it's all they have right now."

Evan smiled. "I'm good with it."

"Yeah, but I'm hungry," Ramos insisted.

Evan picked up a wedge of apple and took a large bite. Her eyebrows dipped and her eyes watered. Her pink lips puckered. "Ooh, that's a sour one."

Ramos picked up a piece and popped the whole thing into his mouth. He blinked several times as he chewed and swallowed. "Yes, ma'am. Tart."

Evan took a sip of tea and sighed. "I wonder how the kids are getting along," she teased.

"I'm sure they're fine," he said. He scooped up a handful of grapes and munched away. "They'd call if they needed anything."

Evan nodded. "I suppose."

"I wanted to talk to you," Ramos said, putting down his teacup after a long sip. "It's about yesterday."

Evan put her tablet down and pulled her foot up under her. "What's wrong?"

She had been trying to decide if Teo's comments and familiar gestures were just part of their cover, or if he was becoming fond of her. She was struggling to determine how she felt about him as well. Until yesterday, everything was easy.

Kirk was her first partner and a father-figure. He took care of her and guarded her as he taught her the basics. Hedge was her new team leader. Handsome and protecting, he brought out the best in her. He gave her confidence to do things she never imagined were possible. And then there was Teo.

Last week, Teo was a tough guy with a good sense of humor. He took care of the stuff that needed to be done. He stood in the shadows and kept the operation smooth. He was there, but quiet.

Yesterday, Teo put on a tie and took her hand in his. He teased her about proposing. He had called her baby. His big brown eyes smiled at her—maybe more. Now he wanted to talk about yesterday, and she wasn't one hundred percent certain how she felt about it. She took a deep breath.

"I think we have a problem with the bombs," he said matter-of-factly.

Her breath left her. She tried to inhale again, but the action turned into a weak laugh. She shook her head and took a sip of tea. "I'm sorry. Go ahead; I'm listening."

"Are you okay?"

"Yeah, I just breathed in wrong," she explained. She felt like an idiot. *I'm off on some eighth-grade daydream, and he's on the job.*

Ramos waited until she was steady.

"What do you mean by *problem*?" she asked him.

"I spent all night looking over the schematics of the bomb, and then as each new one was found, more schematics were sent along for me to examine."

"What's the problem? That should help us determine who the terrorist is, right?" Evan asked.

"It should," he answered. "Maybe it will, but you know how I said that bomb makers pick one style of bombs and stick with that?"

"Yes, you said that they might make improvements, but that they pretty much have one design that they prefer. Or something like that." Evan shrugged. "Have you matched our guy's style with someone in particular?"

Ramos sat next to her and pulled up photographs and diagrams on his tablet. "No, that's my problem. Look at these."

He flipped from one diagram to the next. Evan recognized one of the sketches. "That's the one we disarmed here."

"Yeah," he said. "Compare it to the others."

She looked at several of the photographs either direction through the slides. "They aren't the same."

Ramos stared her in the eye. "Not even a little bit. This one was planted under a pick-up truck in a freight car in Genoa." He switched to the next sketch. "This one was in Malta. It uses stick dynamite. This one was made with plastics like C-4."

"What does it mean?"

Ramos scrubbed his face with his palms. "I don't know. Except that every one of these devices was a bomb and was found in a freight container on a dock on the Mediterranean Sea, they have nothing in common. I haven't been able to trace, with any certainty, any of the components to a single person or even a definitive location."

"Okay, let's think about this for a minute," Evan reasoned. "What does this tell us?"

"My first inclination is that we have more than one bomb-maker."

Evan pulled both of her knees up to her chest, wrapped her arms around her legs, and rested her chin on her knees. "That would explain why they weren't all set to go off at once, I suppose."

Ramos shrugged. "Even so, an organization with resources for multiple devices all shipped under the same name?" He paused. "You would think they would be organized enough to get the timing closer."

"You said that nothing has been traceable yet?" she asked.

"Yeah."

"That's a pretty big coincidence, don't you think?" she asked. "A terrorist group is coordinated enough to keep all the components of all these bombs completely discreet, but can't time it for them all to blast at the same time?"

"Unless that is the plan," Ramos suggested.

"That's what Kirk said last night."

Ramos leaned back against the arm of the sofa and stared at Evan. "We could be dealing with a much larger organization than we thought."

"Do you think we should message Kirk and Hedge?" she asked.

"They'll be back soon," he answered. "I'm sure."

Evan rocked her head back and stared at the ceiling for several seconds. Ramos placed his tablet on the table by the snack tray and put his hand on her shoulder.

"It will be okay," he assured her. His hand was warm and strong on her arm.

She let her feet drop back to the floor. Her arms fell to her sides. She shot a light glance to Ramos, and then let her gaze wander back to the food on the tray. "I'm hungry, too," she said. "Why don't you stay here, and I'll run down to the corner for something?" she said, more in a statement than a question.

Ramos nodded. "Be back here soon, though."

Evan pulled her sneakers on. "I know you're hungry."

Teo walked her to the door and smiled. He took her arm gently in his left hand, pulling her around to face him and drawing her close. He took her face in his right hand and placed a kiss on her lips.

Evan blinked. *I'm not crazy.* "I'll be back in just a few minutes," was all that she could think to say.

CHAPTER TWELVE

"You're ridiculous," she muttered to herself as she stepped out onto the street. The morning sun shone brightly in her eyes. She took a deep breath of air to clear her thoughts.

"As soon as you make up your mind to keep things professional with Hedge, you get all wrapped up with feelings for Teo." She realized how much she enjoyed talking to herself. She had spent the last two years training herself not to do it, because of the receiver implanted in her ear canal. Now, knowing it was off, she felt free to scold her conscience out loud.

The aroma of butter and corn caught her attention, and she turned to her right. A few blocks of jogging brought her to a small market. She found several items to make a good lunch for both her and Ramos. There was bread and a seasoned fish. She found a small bottle of wine to share as well. She purchased a basket and gathered her finds together.

From the corner of her eye, she thought that she saw a man looking at her. She moved to a polished shop window to use the reflection for confirmation. She had good instincts; both Hedge and Kirk thought so. Examining the reflection, however, revealed no watchful eyes.

She was about to turn back toward the hotel when she noticed him. A tall man in a gray silk pinstriped jacket stepped from inside the shop across the street. His hair was combed neatly, and though he wore very dark sunglasses, the high cheekbones, sculpted jawline, and cleft chin left no doubt in Evan's mind who the man was. Her heart skipped a beat.

"Absolutely do not approach Mr. Cooper without backup," she whispered to herself. She forced herself to turn in the opposite direction. She walked several paces away from him, keeping a steady watch on his reflection. Michael Cooper seemed to be shopping for accessories at a boutique that sold straw hats and leather goods.

Evan stopped to watch. She wanted to see if he was alone or if he had a bodyguard or lady-friend. Nobody talked to him except a sales clerk. He didn't regard anyone else on the street. He found a hat and inquired about a leather portfolio. The clerk received the payment for the hat, but apparently had disappointing news about the leather folder.

Evan wished she was wearing the dress. *Kirk could tell me exactly what he's saying.* "Of course, a red-headed woman roaming the street in a black cocktail dress at eleven o'clock in the morning wouldn't be conspicuous at all," she murmured. She rolled her eyes.

He started in her direction. She couldn't risk allowing him to see her now. It could ruin her cover later. She stepped into the small store at which she'd been pretending to shop.

"Buenos dias," said the young shopkeeper. Her accent was definitely American.

"Good morning," Evan answered.

"I'm from Indiana." The clerk offered her hand to shake.

Evan took it and smiled. "I'm from Texas."

"Don't you love henna?" Indiana asked.

"What?" Evan responded, pretending to browse while moving into position to look out the front window without being spotted.

"You were looking at my henna ink kits. You'd look amazing with henna art."

Evan smiled. "Do you really think so?"

The brunette extended her sandaled foot for Evan to see. The top was covered with blue-black paisleys and curls. "Cool, huh?"

Evan nodded. "It's very nice." Cooper ambled in front of the shop. He stopped next to the door, looking at a brass-handled walking stick. Evan turned to her right. "How much are your henna kits?"

The clerk stepped between Evan and the front door, allowing Evan the ability to watch Cooper over her shoulder without being seen.

"I have this one for only eleven American dollars. It's a small starter kit, but it has everything you need." The store-keeper handed Evan a small green box covered with Moroccan designs.

Cooper continued down the street without looking up and into the shop.

Evan sighed with relief. "I'll take it."

CHAPTER THIRTEEN

"You won't believe who I just nearly ran into on the street," Evan announced to Ramos when she slipped back into the suite.

"I don't know. Oh wait," he said. "Was it one of the security guards from the dock?"

"No," she said. She took the basket of lunch and emptied it onto the table in front of him. "I saw Michael Cooper. He was out shopping here in Barcelona."

"Are you sure?" Ramos asked.

"I am."

"Maybe it was just somebody who looked like him," he suggested.

"No. I studied his picture," she said. "It was definitely him."

"Well, what's he doing here now?" Ramos mused. "I don't like these kinds of coincidences."

"I know. I don't either."

Ramos raised his eyebrows. "You didn't let him see you, did you?"

Evan shook her head. "Absolutely not." She handed Ramos his share of bread. "Do you think that we should contact Hedge about this?"

Ramos shook his head. "Kirk just called me a few minutes ago. He said that they would still be another hour. What do you think?"

Evan pulled out the bottle of wine. "I guess we'll have to wait an hour."

Teo picked up the green box and looked inside. "Is this henna?"

Evan laughed. "I ducked into a shop for cover, and it turns out they sold henna."

Ramos laughed. "I am an amazing henna artist. Do you want

me to paint you a tattoo?"

"How long will it last?" she asked.

Ramos took a bite of his fish. "That depends on where you let me paint it. The softer the skin, the shorter it lasts." He gestured to her feet. "If I put it on your foot or ankle, it will last for at least a week." He reached out and ran his finger down the inside of her upper arm. "Someplace like here, or on the back of your knee, and it will only be there for a few days."

Evan giggled at his touch.

"Think about it while we eat." Ramos grinned. "I'll put it wherever you want, but remember," he said. "Hedge won't like it if the tattoo shows beyond the boundaries of the dress."

Evan raised her eyebrows. She knew Teo was right. She hadn't really even wanted a henna tattoo before, but now it seemed like a necessity. "There isn't a lot of territory that the dress actually conceals."

"If you're scared, we don't have to do it," Teo said with a shrug. "I understand."

"It's not that I'm scared," she insisted.

"Oh, I didn't mean it like that," Ramos said. He sipped at his wine. "It doesn't hurt like a real tattoo. It's just stain. I know you're not afraid of a little stain."

"I know it's just stain," she said. "I just don't want Hedge to be angry."

Teo blinked. "If we put it in the right place, how exactly will he see it?"

Evan pressed her lips together tightly. "Good point."

CHAPTER FOURTEEN

Hedge and Kirk plodded up the steps of their hotel and into the lobby. The two hosts at the front desk nodded a welcome, and then exchanged a looked of concern.

"Are you all right?" the younger man asked. He took a few steps to round the end of the desk.

Hedge held up a hand to stop him. The simple motion of raising his arm caused pain to shoot through to his hip and buttocks. He groaned. "We're fine. Are there any messages?"

The older of the clerks, who was still at least a decade younger than Hedge Parker, smiled in pity. "No messages, sir."

Hedge walked stiffly to the elevator, where Kirk already leaned against the wall.

"Does your shoulder hurt?" Hedge asked Kirk.

"No," he lied, trying to hold his right arm straight. "Does your hip hurt?"

"No."

The *ding* signaled the arrival of the elevator car, and Hedge and Kirk stepped inside. Hedge closed his eyes for a moment, as the lift surged upward to the third floor. The men stood in silence, staring at the doors. When the doors slid open, they filed out into the hall, grateful that no one was around to see them.

Kirk opened the door to their suite. "Honey, I'm home," he announced.

A thump came from the bedroom on the right. Hedge and Kirk each drew their sidearm and took positions at either side of the door.

Hedge called out, "Anyone here?"

He could hear a murmur from the bedroom. Kirk carefully turned the knob and pushed the door open while stepping out of the opening.

"Hands in the air," Hedge yelled as he rushed the small room.

Evan was stretched out on her bed, lying on her stomach, holding her hands up. Her tee shirt was pulled up in the back on one side, exposing a patch of skin covered in a dark purple butterfly design. Ramos was on his knees on the floor, holding his hands over his head.

"Hold, it's just us," he said.

Hedge and Kirk relaxed their stance and lowered their weapons. "We could have blown your heads off. Why didn't you answer when we came in? Didn't you hear us?" Hedge asked.

Ramos stood up and came around the bed. "We heard you. You startled us, man. When you yelled, Evan jumped and knocked the bowl of ink onto the floor. I was trying to get it cleaned up. I didn't think you'd bust in with guns blazing."

Kirk laughed, relieved that everything was all right. "What are you guys doing with ink?"

Hedge eyed the artwork on Evan's lower back. "Yeah, what is that?"

"It's a butterfly," she answered. "At least, that's what Teo told me he was painting." She reached for the hand mirror from the nightstand. "It is a butterfly, right?"

Kirk peeked at her back and then raised his brows. "Yes, that's a butterfly."

Hedge's face flushed red. "You didn't ask if you could have a tat."

Kirk holstered his pistol and backed out of the room. Ramos picked up the ink and brush and set them on the night table.

Evan sat up on the bed and pulled her shirt down to cover her new body art. "I wasn't aware that I had to ask permission."

"Maybe nobody has mentioned this to you before, but in this line of work tattoos can be dangerous," Hedge said, pushing his words through aching lungs.

"Really? Dangerous?" Evan's tone dripped with sarcasm.

"Sir," Ramos tried to intercede. "This is on me. I talked her into it."

Evan scowled at Teo and then at Hedge. "He did not talk me

into anything."

Hedge ignored Ramos. "Tats are really only good for one thing in our jobs, and that is identifying bodies."

Ramos continued to try. "Also, I'd like to add that it's just henna ink, sir. It's not a permanent tattoo."

Evan rolled her eyes. "It doesn't matter whether it's real or not. He can't tell me what I can and can't do."

"I am your commanding officer out here, and I certainly *can* tell you what you can and cannot do." Hedge narrowed his eyes and took a step toward her. They stood toe to toe at the foot of her bed.

Ramos seemed to have given up and left the room without either of them noticing.

"If you had come back to the room ten minutes later, you would never have even seen the tat," she insisted. "We were careful to put it somewhere out of everyone's view."

"What's the point of having body art if nobody is going to see it?" Hedge growled.

"Teo saw it. He knows where it is," she said with a bite.

"And what if an asset or a target sees it?"

Evan glared. She looked as though she wanted to slap his face, but resisted. "Just because Evan Tyler doesn't have a tattoo, doesn't mean that Eve Taylor can't."

"It's a liability," he started, but the pain in his side took control. His eyes winced, and he turned his face away. He bit down on his bottom lip and held his breath.

"What's wrong now?" she asked.

Hedge shook his head. "Nothing. I'll leave you and your ink alone." He started back to the sitting room, but a sharp pain held him frozen for several seconds. He reached out to the wall for support.

Evan ran to his side and helped him down to the foot of Kirk's bed. "You're hurt. What happened this morning?"

Hedge inhaled and exhaled, trying to ease the cramp in his side. After a few seconds, he could speak again. "We tried to meet with Tambar. He took off."

"What do you mean? He wouldn't see you?" She pulled the small chair around and sat down in front of him. Her eyes studied his face. "You need some meds."

"I'm fine. I just need to rest for a while." He thought about moving into the other bedroom but didn't want to have another bolt of pain immobilize him again. He stared back into Evan's eyes. She didn't appear angry or defensive anymore. She looked concerned.

He swallowed hard. "We saw him," he said. "But something we said—I don't know what, exactly—but it spooked him, and he ran."

Evan shrugged. "And you chased him?"

"Yeah, we chased him. I took the elevator, and Kirk took the stairwell. He lost us five floors up. We never got close enough to tag him." He held his hand to his side. "My problem is that I forgot that we decided that you could catch up with him later at his nightclub."

Evan grimaced. "Your problem is that you forgot that you were still injured. Until you get all healed, you can't be running all over Spain. You'll tear out your stitches."

Hedge nodded. "I may have already."

Evan let her shoulders slump. "Lean over and let me look," she ordered.

He shook his head. "You aren't the medic on this team."

"Teo, I need you in here," she called out.

Ramos poked his head into the room. "What is it?" he asked timidly.

She pointed to Hedge with her thumb. "He needs you to look at his backside. He may have torn his stitches."

"I'll get my bag," Ramos said, ducking back out.

Hedge shook his head at Evan. He laughed to himself when he saw how quickly she jumped from defending herself to being his fierce protector. *She can be such a pain in the ....*

"Turn over," she demanded.

"I'll go into my own room," he said. Hedge started to push himself up from the bed, but the pain prevented him from fully straightening.

"Yeah, let me know how that works out for you," Evan taunted. She shifted her weight to one side and crossed her arms. "Just let me help you."

Evan pulled him across the bed as Ramos returned.

Hedge unzipped his slacks and lowered his waistband until his wound and his pride was bared. Ramos shook his head and opened his medic bag. He handed Evan a small bottle of alcohol. "Open this for me, please."

"Sure," she said. She pulled the zip strip on the lid and popped the top back.

Hedge took a deep breath as he pulled out some gauze and other necessities. "Kirk said you both did a fair piece of running?"

Hedge nodded, gritting his teeth as the cold antiseptic was swabbed over his wound. "Yeah."

"Okay," Ramos said, examining the swollen gash in Hedge's flesh. "Your stitches are still intact, but you pulled them pretty good. They can't handle any more stress for a while. I'm going to apply a fresh dressing, and then you're going to get some rest. I already told the same thing to Kirk. No running, climbing, no picking up anything heavy. Don't do it. For at least three full days, you both have to take it easy."

"That's easier said than done," Hedge responded.

"I know," Ramos said. "But lucky for you, you have a team who has your back-side." He laughed.

Evan gathered the bloodied dressing and dropped it into a plastic bag. "Tonight is all me, anyway. You and Red just sit by the monitor and wait up for the kids."

Hedge wanted to jump back into a scrap with Evan. He wasn't really angry, but he liked the way she was fighting back these days. Drawn out across the bed with his trousers down didn't seem like a great position of strength, though. He decided to wait until he was fully clothed again.

Ramos handed him a couple pain-killers. "Take two of these and call me in the morning," he said with a chuckle. He grabbed his bag and gave Evan a wink as he left the room.

"That wasn't so bad, was it?" she asked.

Hedge sighed. "I'm never a very good patient," he said. He rolled to his able side and pulled himself to his feet, with Evan's help. He noticed that her hair smelled like lavender as he let her support him while he regained his balance.

"Maybe not, but you're a good team leader," she admitted.

Evan walked Hedge into his bedroom. "Do you need me to help you change clothes?" she asked.

Hedge raised his left brow. He wondered if she was serious. She smiled and left him alone, closing the door between them.

He thought about the purple butterfly resting in the small of her back. He didn't care if it was vegetable dye or not. *What difference does that make?* Of course, he knew that it made all the difference in the world. He wondered if he was more upset because it was there, or because of who put it there. He liked Ramos, but he wasn't sure he liked how Evan had taken to calling him Teo. Too familiar.

He thought about her soft red hair as he pulled his shirt back from his shoulders. He drew a deep breath, imagining the scent of lavender. "Crap," he whispered. "I can't do this again."

The memory of Eleanor, soaked in blood, on the floor of that warehouse all those years ago floated back into his mind's eye. "Not again."

He changed into his faded blue jeans and a tee shirt and joined the rest of the men in the sitting room. Kirk wore a Hawaiian print shirt and a pair of khakis. His shirt was unbuttoned from tending his injury. Ramos stood at the small mirror by the door, buttoning the cuffs of the silver blue dress shirt he was sporting over black slacks. His shirt was unbuttoned as well.

Hedge furrowed his brow and cleared his throat to get his team's attention. He gestured to both of the men. "Let's get these barn doors closed before Evan gets out here. She doesn't need these images seared into her brain before she meets Tambar."

Kirk laughed and buttoned his shirt.

Ramos grinned at his reflection. "That's a good point. We

don't want to spoil her."

Evan walked out of the bedroom, still putting in her earrings. "Who are you spoiling? If it's me, I'm really okay with that," she teased.

Hedge took a step in her direction. He always inspected her before she left wearing the black strapless cocktail dress.

Tonight she wore the hem about two inches above her knees. Her calves slimmed perfectly into the red heels. The ruching at the side seams of the skirt formed soft pleats that followed every curve of her thighs and hips, smoothing to a narrow waist. Evan wore the translucent black silk scarf attached at her left hip, crossing over the bodice diagonally, and flowing freely from her right shoulder. Her red locks were pulled into a wavy knot at the nape of her neck, with plenty of loose tendrils to frame her ivory face. Her eyes shone a brilliant teal blue rimmed with smoky black eyeliner. Her lips glistened a classic red that matched her shoes.

The men were silent. Hedge wanted to say something, but he couldn't think of anything appropriate.

Evan straightened her shoulders and smirked. "Is my lipstick smudged?"

"No," all three men answered simultaneously.

She laughed. "Kirk, do we know if Tambar is out tonight?"

Kirk nodded but didn't say anything. His gaze was fixed on her.

She looked to Ramos. "Are you going to wear a tie or jacket?"

He shook his head. "I'm ready," he murmured.

Hedge shook himself free of the spell. He took a step in her direction. "You look good. Turn around and let me see the back."

Evan smiled coyly.

"I want to make sure that no one will be able to tell that you're carrying," he added. She nodded and turned a circle for him.

He scrubbed his thoughts clean as she faced him again. He wished he could be at her side on this mission—for dozens of reasons. He shot a glance to Ramos. "You need a jacket. How else will you hide your piece?"

Ramos tugged his upper lip into a smile. "Got it." He picked up the blazer from the back of the armchair and slid it over his shoulders.

Evan tucked her clutch purse under her left arm and crossed the room to Ramos' side. "How do we look?"

Hedge shook his head at the couple. He tilted his head to favor Evan. "You look gorgeous." He turned to Ramos. "You need your weapon."

Ramos nodded and disappeared into his room for his sidearm.

Hedge turned to face Kirk. "Are you two linked and synched?"

"Good to go, sir," Kirk answered, still watching Evan.

She tugged at her earlobe. "I got you." She sent Kirk a wink and kiss.

Ramos returned and took Evan's arm. "Ready to go, sir."

"Full magazine?" Hedge asked.

"Plus one," Ramos answered confidently.

"Take care of her," Hedge said, watching them walk into the hall.

"She'll take care of me," Ramos answered.

Hedge closed the door behind them. He took the chair opposite Kirk and propped his foot on a pillow on the coffee table.

"Kirk, I don't think I've ever felt older than I do today," he said, concentrating on the idea of not scratching at his stitches.

"Well, Hedge," Kirk said with a snicker. "It just so happens that you've never been older than today."

Hedge stretched his arms up and back, lacing his fingers together behind his neck. "Is this how it's going to be from here on out?" Hedge asked. "The old guys sit behind the computer while the young operatives have all the fun?"

Kirk tapped at his keyboard. "If we're lucky."

Hedge sighed. "I guess." He stared up at the ceiling for several seconds.

Kirk seemed to notice. He stopped typing and turned to his old friend. "She looked good, didn't she?"

Hedge let his arms relax and fall to the arms of the chair as he leaned forward. "She looked amazing."

"If Tambar is out there, he won't be able to resist her." Kirk looked back at his monitor. "And it appears he is out tonight. I just got a hit on his car in front of his nightclub."

Hedge took a deep breath. "That butterfly was great, wasn't it?" he asked.

"Ramos has real talent," Kirk agreed.

"We should focus on the job," Hedge self-corrected.

"And there is our little party," Kirk said, gesturing to the traffic camera showing Evan and Ramos walking into the bar.

"We're in," Hedge said.

CHAPTER FIFTEEN

"We're here," Evan whispered, both to Teo at her side and to Kirk in her ear. She gave Teo's arm a quick squeeze as they entered the dark, smoke-filled club.

"Tambar is already there," Kirk said. "It looked like he came in alone, about five minutes ago."

Teo nodded. They found a table in a corner to the left of the bar behind the crowded dance floor. Red and blue lights flashed around the room from the ceiling. As Evan took her seat, Teo gestured that he'd circuit the place and bring back drinks.

Kirk's voice buzzed in tones just below the thump of the bass. "There is a security camera at both the front and back doors, and one at each end of the bar—all of which are static. No audio, either. Tambar is alone at the far end of the bar from you. He keeps checking his watch."

"Probably waiting for someone." Evan scanned the room as she casually pushed a tendril of hair back from her face. Dark wood paneling enclosed the room. The floor looked like black concrete, either painted or stained with decades of wear. The club was crowded with people huddled over watered-down drinks. The atmosphere was a blanket of thick cigarette smoke that stuck in the back of Evan's throat. She half-admired the dozen or so dancers able to breathe in that smog.

Kirk's voice again. "Yeah, he's most likely got a date. You may need to be ready to make him a better offer."

Evan swallowed hard. Her mouth was dry from shallow breathing to avoid the pungent air. "My dress is going to need a heavy-duty clean cycle to get all this smoke out of it."

Kirk laughed. "I don't miss the smoke." He paused for a moment. "You've got a friend at two o'clock."

Evan looked up and slightly to her right. A tall, thin man with over-bleached hair and teeth was approaching. He half-walked and half-danced to her side.

"¿Aqui esta sola?" he asked.

"No, mi amigo esta alli," she answered, pointing to Ramos. "He's coming back now."

"You are American?" the man asked, unwilling to fade away.

"Si," she said, standing to welcome Ramos back to the table with a warm hug. "Gracias por mantener mi empresa."

"De nada," he said, deciding that Ramos could probably snap him in half at whim.

"Who's that?" Ramos asked, watching him walk-dance away.

"Just somebody who thought I looked lonely," she said with a laugh. "Kirk says that Tambar is at the bar."

"I think he's waiting for someone," Ramos said, handing Evan a drink.

She laughed. "Thanks. That's what Kirk and I decided, too."

Ramos slid into the seat across the tiny table from her. "I forget we're a threesome tonight."

Evan sipped her cocktail and frowned. "I suppose the good news is that I should be able to down five or six of these before I even get a buzz. This place must make a fortune."

Ramos grinned. "Don't get over-confident with your beverages tonight. We have to stay focused."

Evan laughed and stood up. She smoothed her dress into place and leaned over Teo's face. "I'm not much of a drinker, anyway."

She picked up her clutch and drink and made her way to the bar, squeezing into an empty seat beside Tambar. The bartender nodded at her, and she lifted an eyebrow. She stared into the mirror behind the rows of liquor bottles on the opposite wall. She waited for Tambar to make eye-contact in the reflection. She smiled at him.

He checked his watch.

She sighed, and then slipped off her barstool and walked back to the table.

"You didn't talk to him," Kirk scolded.

"Two minutes," Evan whispered.

As she reached the table again, she handed her drink to Ramos. "Get ready," she whispered.

"Wow; here he comes," Kirk said.

Evan smiled at Ramos, and said, just loud enough for Tambar to hear, "Well, call them back and tell them to have everything ready in the morning."

"Yes, ma'am," Ramos answered.

Evan turned around just in time to face Benito Tambar. "Why don't we dance?" she said, taking his hand in hers.

Tambar blinked in surprise. "Si—yes," he said. He led her to the edge of the crowd.

Evan smiled placidly as she studied his features. Tambar's bronzed cheeks rose round from his thick black beard, matching his bare scalp. His eyebrows were black and bushy as well. He acted as though he might speak, but then didn't for several seconds as they danced.

He keeps his hands to himself, at least. Evan easily kept up with Tambar. His dancing was predominantly a side-sway with an occasional bounce. Evan appreciated that he didn't go full-tilt on the dance floor. She hadn't quite gotten used to the red heels, yet.

He finally gathered the courage to talk to her. "I haven't seen you here before."

Original.

"I'm an American," she said, hoping that fact would explain everything.

"Oh," he said.

Evan had no intention of leading the conversation. They danced for another minute before he continued.

"What brings you here to Barcelona?" he asked. Evan smiled as she heard the rasp in his voice. He was already getting tired.

"What if I told you it was all the handsome men in this nightclub?"

He laughed. "I like your sense of humor."

She flashed him a sincere smile.

He glanced at his watch again.

"I'm sorry," she said. "Am I keeping you from something? Your wife, maybe?"

Tambar shook his head. "No, I'm not married."

Even with the loud music, she could hear a faint ticking sound in her ear. The dress could analyze voice patterns and detect deception. It transmitted a tick directly into her ear receiver when someone was lying.

"Good," she said. "More fun for me."

"What is your name?" he asked, taking her hands in his.

Evan drew a quick breath. His fingertips were cool, and his palms were clammy. "My name is Eve." She continued to dance.

"You don't want to know my name?" he asked. His hearty voice sounded wounded.

"What is your name?"

"My name is Benito Tambar."

Evan smiled and danced closer to him. "Benito is a good, strong name."

He grinned at her compliment. After another second he looked at his watch again.

Evan stopped dancing. "Do you have an appointment?"

Tambar stopped and took a few steps away from the dance floor. Evan followed. He glanced up at the ceiling and back to her. "I apologize. I was supposed to meet a friend here, but perhaps he got delayed."

"He?" she asked.

Tambar nodded. "A colleague, I assure you."

"You are here for business, too?" she asked, trying to sound innocent.

"Yes; business."

Evan sighed. "I suppose I'll lose you when he arrives, then?"

Tambar shook his head. "Only temporarily. Our meeting won't take long. I want to spend more time with you. That is if you can be patient with me?"

Evan tilted her head and pursed her lips into a provocative pucker. "I can be patient."

"Evan, we have trouble," Kirk whispered.

At the same time, Teo appeared over Tambar's shoulder. "Ms.

Taylor, your call to Paris is on the line," he said.

Evan quickly retrieved her business card. "I have to take this call," she explained, pressing the card into Tambar's palm. "Please call me as soon as your appointment has ended." She whispered into his ear. "I'll be waiting."

Evan grinned and left Tambar at the edge of the dance floor. Ramos took her arm and handed her his phone, which she immediately pressed to her ear. "What can you tell me?"

"Don't look back, Evan. Just keep walking," Kirk instructed.

She went straight to the back door, as Ramos directed her with his hand on her back. Once outside, Ramos pulled her into a shadow.

"What was that?" she asked both of her partners.

"We had to get you out of there," Kirk said.

"Michael Cooper just walked into the bar," Teo added.

Evan rolled her eyes and drew a deep breath. The air was fresh for the first time in half an hour, and the change caused her lungs to ache. She grimaced at Teo.

"Hey, Kirk, umm, did I mention that Michael Cooper was also in Barcelona?" she said, bracing herself for whatever wrath he could send to her ear.

"You might have forgotten that detail. How did you know this?"

Evan bit her bottom lip. "I happened to see him shopping while I was out picking up lunch for Teo and me."

Kirk's voice strained. "And did he see you?"

Evan exhaled. "I don't think so."

"But you're not one hundred percent sure?" This time it was Hedge's stern voice.

"No sir, not one hundred percent."

Teo nodded to his partner, trying to offer support.

Evan shot Teo a pained grin. "Do you want me to come back to the hotel now, or would you like me to wait out Tambar's meeting?" she asked.

Hedge growled. "Well, what do you want to do, Evan? It seems that you're the boss on this little adventure. Whatever makes you happy."

Kirk hesitated. "Umm, before we start down that road, I'd like to throw this out: it looks like Michael Cooper is Tambar's appointment."

Evan listened to Kirk carefully. He tapped at his keyboard. "I'm watching the bar's security feed, and they're talking."

"Talking like acquaintances?" she asked.

"No," Kirk answered. "They sat down at a table. They're talking business. This camera feed is terrible. I wish Evan was in there—I could read their lips."

"If I was in there, we could listen to them," she reminded him.

"True," Kirk agreed.

Teo shook his head. "It's too dangerous. Tambar was already spooked by Hedge and Kirk. Confronting Cooper here would scrap our whole plan."

Kirk laughed. "What little plan we have."

Evan's brain clicked through a dozen scenarios. When she landed on one she liked, she said, "Hedge, do you trust me?"

"Not as far as I can throw you," he answered, almost automatically.

"I'm serious, Hedge."

He didn't answer right away. Then, "What do you have in mind?"

"I'd like to go back in," she stated with determination.

"What do you see happening?" Hedge asked.

Ramos was shaking his head. "Bad idea," he whispered.

"I see myself talking to both men. Reasoning with them. If I'm going to be a fixer, maybe they'll appreciate the caliber of my other clientele." She sounded confident, anyway.

Kirk rebutted. "We don't even know why they're meeting with each other."

Evan shrugged it off. "It wouldn't be unreasonable for them to meet. Cooper is in oil. Tambar is in the energy department. They're both going to functions related to the summit next week. Maybe they're friends."

"I don't know, Evan," Kirk said. "If you lose Tambar, we won't get him back."

Evan squared her shoulders. "Agent Parker, do you trust me?"

She could hear him muttering what she assumed was a curse of some kind. "Get in there," he ordered.

CHAPTER SIXTEEN

After giving a few brief instructions to Teo, Evan strode back into the nightclub. She went to the bar and ordered another drink that she had no intention of consuming, and then turned her attention to the table where Tambar and Cooper sat in deep discussion.

She tipped her chin toward Teo, who took a seat at another table. Evan started to draw a deep breath for confidence. The acrid cloud of smoke burned almost immediately, and she cut her effort short.

Evan took three long steps toward her targets. They looked up when she stood only a few feet away. She stopped and smiled at them both.

"I'm so sorry to interrupt, Señor Tambar," she said, employing the sweetest Texas drawl in her repertoire. "Is Mr. Cooper the man you had the appointment with?"

"Yes," Tambar answered, obviously glad that she had returned.

Cooper tilted his chin and grinned at Evan. "I'm sorry, have we met?" His Irish accent broadened her smile.

Evan held out her hand and shook Cooper's warmly. "No, well —not yet. My assistant has been trying to get an appointment with you for next week in London. You seem to be a real challenge to track down."

Cooper shook her hand and smiled. "Would you like to join us?" he offered.

Evan shook her head. "Oh no, you two should finish your meeting." She took a step closer to Tambar and patted his shoulder. "Benito, I'll be waiting for you at that table over there with my assistant." She gestured to Teo. "Mr. Cooper, if you have a minute before you leave, I'd love to chat with you. I'd only take a minute of your time—that is, if Benito doesn't mind."

She let her eyelashes rise and fall in Tambar's direction.

"Of course," Tambar agreed.

Cooper nodded. His gaze fell to her legs and rose slowly back to her eyes. "It would be my pleasure."

Evan grinned again and walked casually back to Teo's side.

Kirk began twittering in her ear. "He invited you to their meeting. Why didn't you say thank you and sit down?"

She held her cocktail to her bottom lip. "It's called hard-to-get," she whispered.

"It's a risk," Kirk added. "I hope it pays off."

Ramos leaned over the table for a quiet comment. "They're both staring at you."

She smiled. "That's exactly what I want them to do." She pretended to play with her phone. "Red, I need you to make sure it looks like I did try to make an appointment with Cooper."

"Done. You're already on his agenda for next Tuesday."

Teo held his drink to mask his words. "I guess their meeting is over."

Evan looked up to see Michael Cooper heading her direction. As he reached their table, Teo stood.

Cooper held out his hand. "Can we talk on the dance floor?" he asked.

Evan took his hand and followed him into the crowd.

As he drew her into his arms, Cooper said, "I'm sorry, but you have me at a disadvantage. We haven't been properly introduced."

"Eve Taylor," she said. "It's nice to finally meet you, Mr. Cooper."

"I suppose that our meeting on Tuesday has something to do with business?" he asked.

Evan was pleased that he'd already taken the time to check out her story, and even more grateful that Kirk was efficient at hacking almost anything.

"Yes, it's strictly business."

"Pity," he whispered. "What business are you proposing we

share?"

Evan smiled. "I have a feeling that you may be in need of my services."

"I am," he agreed quickly. "What exactly are your services?"

Evan laughed. He held her right hand gently in his left, while his right hand sat firmly on her lower back.

"I have a nice little specialty firm. I take care of people with particular ... delicate ... needs. In some ways, I'm like a fairy godmother." Evan let her glossed red lips curl at the corners. "I make problems disappear."

"Really?" he asked. He stared at her lips. "What kinds of problems do you treat?"

"I deal with judgment lapses, indiscretions, misunderstandings, poor choices, and things like that. You know what I mean. These types of things so easily turn into scandals, lawsuits, and other basis for extortion." Evan shrugged. "I make them go away."

"You're a fixer," he stated.

She raised her brow. "Yes."

Cooper scoffed. "And you think I need to be fixed?"

"Mr. Cooper, I've helped hundreds of people in precarious positions. Celebrities, politicians, executives. I'm very good."

Cooper looked into her eyes. "Of that, I have no doubt. But I'm not sure why you think I'm in trouble."

Evan let him twirl her under his arm and then stepped back into his embrace. "I was actually working for another client, and your name popped up in one of the files."

"How interesting," Cooper said. "Who was the other client?"

Evan clicked her tongue. "Tch-tch-tch. You know I can't tell you that."

"And how can I be sure that you're not just making things up?"

Evan nodded. "You're an acquaintance of the fashion designer, Anton Hrevic?"

"Yes," Cooper said. "Sad about his yacht accident last week."

Evan nodded again. "Yes, well, my client was a friend of his, too. And in the last two days, he's been contacted by someone who's trying to manipulate him because of some compromising pictures that were taken by Hrevic."

"Unfortunate," he replied.

"I agree. My investigation has led me to a few others in the same situation. Your name is one I've found on Hrevic's list." Evan allowed her fingertips to curl around the back of his neck. She watched his lips twitch at the sensation.

"And you think that someone will contact me to blackmail me as well?" Cooper asked.

"If they haven't yet, I expect that they will soon."

Cooper nodded toward Tambar. "I think our friend is getting anxious. I'd better return you to him."

Evan squeezed his hand. "I'd like to help you if I can."

She followed him back to Tambar's side, and he held her hand until she was seated.

"Ms. Taylor, I appreciate your candor," he said with his polished accent. "May I have your business card? I look forward to Tuesday, but I'd like to have your contact information in case a situation arises before that." Cooper waited as Evan drew a card from her clutch.

Tambar raised his brow. "What kind of business do you have together?"

Cooper didn't wait for Evan to answer. "Ms. Taylor is going to help me with a possible difficulty I may have ahead of me." He took the card from Evan's hand and put into his breast pocket. "I'll be calling you soon."

Evan shook Cooper's hand and watched him walk away.

"Now for the hard sell," Kirk whispered.

Evan faced Tambar and smiled. "I'm sorry about that," she said, taking his hand in hers. "Let's have a little fun."

Tambar's hand was still cool to touch. He shifted his eyes to either side. "What is your business?"

Evan looked down, feigning humility. "I'm like a consultant. When people have problems keeping their personal relationships private, I help them."

"How do you help them?" Benito asked.

"I don't like when people bully others or try to take advantage. I have a client who had been in a car accident after a bad night of drinking—his father had just died from cancer. I made a few calls and the charges disappeared." She tilted her head. "I got the reporters and photographers to leave him alone."

"How do you accomplish this?" Tambar asked.

"I have many friends that owe me favors. I help them, and they help me to help others," she explained.

Tambar looked at his hands. He raised his gaze to meet hers. "And you will be helping my associate, Mr. Cooper, with a problem?"

"I can't talk about other clients. I have a strict confidentiality policy." She let her eyes soften.

"Could you possibly help me?" Tambar asked.

"Oh, my poor Benito, are you in trouble? I would be happy to help you if I can," she said.

"Unbelievable," Kirk hummed in her ear.

CHAPTER SEVENTEEN

"How exactly are you able to make my problem disappear?" Tambar asked. He stared at Evan's hands, avoiding eye contact.

She reached out for his hand and squeezed it. They sat in a quiet booth in a private room in the club. It was darker, but the air was clear. From the main room, they could hear only the thump of the bass line in the music.

"First, I need you to tell me everything about the man who is trying to control you," she explained. "If you tell me everything, without leaving off any details, I can find him. Then I will talk to him and convince him that he should mind his own business."

Tambar's face looked confused. "But there is so little that I know about him."

Evan lowered her gaze until he finally looked into her eyes. She had him. "Don't worry about that. I'm a problem solver. I take little pieces of a puzzle. On its own, it doesn't look like anything. Just an odd shape that doesn't make any sense. But you see, I have been gathering these little pieces for a long time. I have hundreds and thousands of puzzle pieces."

"And what can you do with them all?"

Evan smiled at Tambar. "When you have enough pieces, you can start to link them together. They start to form pictures. The pictures make sense."

"And how do you know," he said with a fear-saturated tone, "if your pieces fit together?"

"Sometimes they don't, but I look for hints." Evan blinked her eyes thoughtfully. "I am very good at finding links. Your information might not be enough to track this man down, but when I look at all of my clues, the whole picture often points right to the solution."

"This man is very dangerous," Tambar warned. "He might try

to hurt you. He doesn't want to bargain."

Evan nodded. "Then it's important to stop him quickly before he hurts you or someone you love."

Tambar nodded. "I work in the department of energy for the Spanish government. I helped to develop the largest oil platform in the Mediterranean Sea. Have you seen it?"

Evan nodded. "Yes, it's very impressive." Her heart pounded at the thought of being back on the shipping dock.

"I am supposed to attend the European Trade Summit next week. There I am scheduled to speak about oil and other energies that are being developed throughout Europe, and how they will affect commerce throughout the region."

"You are to present a forecast for what the future holds?" she asked.

"Yes. It is my prediction, but I have a great deal of research to substantiate my outlook." Tambar sighed. "Spain has had a few problems of course, but compared to many other places in Europe, we are thriving. Energy options have never been better."

"But this man wants you to present a negative forecast?" she surmised.

"Yes. He instructed me to tell the other representatives that Spain is not equipped with the technology required to handle Europe's needs. He wants me to say that our resources are on the verge of depletion. It's not true, but that's what I must tell the others."

Evan watched his lips tremble. His dark brown eyes grew glassy and reddened in the corners. "What is it he's threatening to do?"

Tambar let his chin drop to his chest. "He says that he will. ..."

Evan waited patiently as he swallowed away tears.

"Earlier I told you that I wasn't married. I lied. You are a beautiful woman. But I am married. My wife is ill. She is dying." Tambar pulled his hand from Evan's and held his head in his hands. "She has cancer."

Evan blinked back any tears she felt surfacing. *Professional.* "What is he threatening to do to you?" she asked.

"He says that he has pictures of me. He sent one to me in an envelope. I don't know how he got these photographs." Tambar clutched at the edges of his beard. "How could I have been so stupido?"

"The pictures are real, and they are of you?" she asked. She waited for a nod. "And where were the pictures taken?"

Tambar sighed. "I was at a party in Paris a few months ago. There was a girl. She was lovely, and I was stupid. I had too much to drink. I made a mistake."

Evan nodded. "And did he say he will show the pictures to your wife?"

Tambar shook his head. "No, she doesn't care about things like that now." He choked on his sentence. "The man says that he will hand them over to the newspapers and television. I will lose my position. I will lose my house, and I will no longer be able to pay for the special care I provide for my wife. It is experimental and very expensive."

Evan exhaled. It was difficult to hear this man agonize, but she had much more to ask him.

"What can you tell me about him specifically? How did he contact you? Do you know what he looks like?" she asked. "I need to know everything you can tell me."

"I never saw him," Tambar began, forcing himself to regain a sense of calm. "I received a parcel. It had a few pictures. It told me exactly what to do and say. It had a number to call." He paused. "I have the number here." From his jacket pocket, Tambar drew a cardholder. He plucked one out and passed it to Evan.

She took the card and examined the phone number that was hand-written on the back. She was careful to hold the card where the dress could scan it, and Kirk could analyze it.

"I called it once. I told him that I couldn't possibly do what he asked. He told me that if I didn't, he would cause my country a great deal of trouble. The next day my secretary was in an automobile accident." Tambar shrugged. "He called me back and warned me that the next car accident he caused would require a body bag. Of course, I was scared, but I told him that I still couldn't do it."

"What did he say to that?"

"He threatened to destroy my beloved platform at the dock. He told me that this was a game for him." Tambar scrubbed his bald head with his fingertips. "He told me that he wouldn't give me another warning."

Evan leaned closer to Tambar. "So you thought about doing what he asked?"

"I don't have a choice. I called the number again, but a message said that the phone was no longer in service. If I don't do as he says, people will die." Tambar wiped the sweat from his forehead. "It's just one false report."

Evan pressed her lips into a thoughtful line. "I'll do my best to find him before your presentation."

Tambar nodded. "I would be indebted to you. I am ashamed for letting myself get into this situation. My poor judgment has put my whole nation at risk."

Evan stood up, prompting Tambar to rise to his feet. She took his arm and led him back to the main bar room. "Let's fix that, Benito. You go home to your wife. Keep my card in your pocket and call me if he contacts you again. You can call me at any hour —day or night."

"Gracias, Señorita," Tambar said, hugging her gratefully. "I will call if I think of anything else. Will I hear from you again?"

"Yes, Benito. I will call you as soon as I have him handled," she kissed his cheek. "Now you stay out of trouble until after the summit. Don't pick up any more women. Just be a good boy. Do you understand?"

"Si," he agreed. He shook her hand. "You are an angel to me."

As Tambar walked away, Teo appeared at her side. "You are one slick talker," he said. "You think we could sneak in one quick dance before we go back?"

Evan laughed.

"No dancing for either of you," Kirk said. "Get back here right away."

"Yessir," Evan answered. "We're on our way back now."

CHAPTER EIGHTEEN

"I can't believe you had him begging you for help," Teo said as they returned to the hotel room. "I knew you were good, but I didn't know you could work miracles."

Kirk sat in the middle of the couch with his feet propped up on the coffee table. "I did." He patted the seat cushion to his right, as an invitation.

Evan started to sit down, but Hedge took her hand to stop her.

"I'll admit it. I didn't want to make contact with Cooper unless we had to. He doesn't seem to be in the same position as the others. But," he paused, flashing a satisfied grin to Evan, twirling her under his arm. "You made it work."

He lowered her onto the sofa next to Kirk.

"I'm sorry that I didn't mention seeing Cooper earlier today. When the whole thing about the henna started, he was the last thing on my mind." Evan slipped the red shoes off her feet and snuggled her toes into the arch of Kirk's socked feet.

"He didn't act like he saw you earlier," Kirk said.

"No. I was pretty careful to move to cover as soon as I noticed him." She pulled the bobby pins from her bun and brushed her fingers through her long, loose curls. "I don't know whether he'll call for any help from us," she said.

"From you," Teo corrected.

"From me," she said with a smile. "But I still think he may be getting threatened. I don't like that he was meeting with Tambar. It's too much of a coincidence. I don't believe in coincidences."

"They're in the same business," Hedge said. He sat in the armchair, positioning himself carefully to avoid any stress on his stitches. "I'm not sure their meeting is such a coincidence."

Kirk shook his head. "I did some checking. Tambar had

Cooper on his agenda for a meeting this afternoon. When we scared him out of his office, Tambar probably rescheduled."

Teo shrugged. "They both frequented Hrevic's parties. They're both in the energy business. It makes sense that they're both being blackmailed."

Hedge inhaled and exhaled with a calm façade. "We will look into his affairs, too. I had hoped we'd find this terrorist before it got this far. Digging into the lives of politicians is fairly easy. There's always someone who wants to stab them in the back." His gaze seemed to settle, by default, upon Evan's legs stretched out in front of him. "The private lives of billionaires are harder to crack. Anybody close enough to know anything doesn't want to fall from grace and lose whatever cash flow they might have."

Evan nodded. "So, what did you need us back here for?" she asked. "Teo and I were going to do a little dancing." She laughed and winked at Teo.

"In Paris, we made a mistake of not knowing each other well enough," Hedge admitted. "We didn't recognize the evil among us. But I don't think we should overcorrect by becoming too familiar. We have to focus on the job at hand." He brought his gaze back up to her eyes just as she looked his direction.

Teo smirked. "You ordered us back to prevent us from?"

"I requested your return so that we could strategize as a team." Hedge crossed his arms over his chest.

Kirk tried to diffuse the tension in the room. "My poker buddies have been talking again."

Evan laughed. "Are these the same poker buddies who told you about the shipwreck off the coast of New Zealand a few years ago?" Kirk had spent hours telling her stories about his friends' strange intuitions.

"Yeah, it's the same group of guys." Kirk tapped away at his computer.

"What happened in New Zealand?" Teo asked.

Kirk straightened his shoulders. Evan smiled at how seriously he approached story-telling.

"Six years ago there was a small cruise ship that went down

in a bad storm about a hundred miles northeast of New Zealand. The passengers and crew all escaped safely in lifeboats. Everyone was accounted for." Kirk retracted his feet from the table, arranging them precisely at shoulders' width on the floor in front of him. "About a week after the wreck, I get a call from my buddies. They don't exactly know what I do, but they know that I have friends in high places."

Hedge loosened his crossed arms and leaned forward. "What did they call you about?"

Kirk grinned. "They told me that my government friends should look into the wreck. They said that if I did, I would find some very interesting things still onboard in the wreckage."

Evan had heard this story before but still listened with the interest of a curious child. "Tell them what you did."

Kirk nodded to her. "I made a call to another agency friend who was in the area already and then flew out undercover as a filmmaker. We put a team together and chartered a boat and went out to the site. On the first dive, my friend brought up the bodies of two of the world's most wanted terrorists. By the fifth dive, they had secured and recovered a dirty bomb that was set to go off as soon as the ship reached Sydney Harbor."

Ramos raised his eyebrows. "That was you?" he asked. "Who are your poker buddies?"

Hedge laughed. "I doubt Kirk is allowed to give us any names."

"No," he said. "But I can tell you that they are rarely wrong. When they give me a lead, I listen."

Evan stretched her arm across the back of the sofa, turning her body to face Kirk. "So what are your friends telling you today?"

"They said that they heard about the bomb at Marseilles, though the port authority there is spinning it as a small explosion from an accidental fire," he explained. "They know about the one you two disarmed yesterday, as well as the others all over the Mediterranean."

"How can they already know about this? Are any of them inside?" Ramos asked.

"No, but these guys know how to connect dots." Kirk nodded. "They say that it's all tied to the Summit in London."

Hedge shrugged. "We already know that."

Kirk curled the corners of his mouth. "Yeah, we do. But how could they?"

Evan chewed on her lip. "There's a leak. Either on our side or the other. But why would a terrorist want to give away his plan to sabotage the Summit?"

"We can't assume it's the terrorist," Teo said. "Brawn was on our team and was working against us the whole time."

Hedge winced at the name. He rubbed at his injured hip. "It could easily be one of the blackmail victims. Maybe he's letting something slip in hopes that there will be more security at the conference. He might be hoping to preempt an attack against the representatives."

Kirk drew a slow, even breath. "I don't know who's putting the information out there, but my friends aren't the only ones hearing rumors. They said that the price of oil is on the rise, along with gold, silver, and other precious metals."

Teo tilted his head and squinted his eyes. "I get the price of oil going up. If just one platform blows, the supply is interrupted, and ports everywhere get shut down. That's what we're busting our butts to prevent. But why gold? What's with that?"

Evan regarded Hedge. He started to lean forward and prop his elbows on his knees, but the strain on his stitches seemed to halt the action and returned him to his former attitude. "If oil skyrockets, the United States has a big problem. We've shut down a great deal of our domestic production. Whether we like it or not, most everything we produce and ship in the US relies on cheap oil."

Teo scoffed. "Gas hasn't been cheap for a long time."

"No, but at the moment, our market can bear the cost. It's tight, but we're managing. Even with our economy, the US dollar is still the standard currency for world trade." Hedge shook his head.

Evan picked up where he left off. "But in recent months there's been a lot of talk pushing for the world to convert to the gold standard."

Teo held up a finger as if he were a child in school. "What would that mean?"

Kirk responded. "It's complicated, but I'll try to make it simple. No government could print more paper money than they have in gold reserves to back it. And technically you can, but only by a percentage. Say, if you want to print a hundred-dollar bill, you must have eighty dollars in gold to back it. Or silver, or platinum, or oil, or another precious commodity."

"Why is that a bad thing?" Teo asked. "That sounds fair and reasonable."

"Theoretically it's a very good thing," Evan explained. "The problem comes when you factor in the human element. When the countries with all the resources decide to gang up on the countries without, they can collapse entire economies, turning great governments into third-world entities in months, maybe even weeks."

"You're talking about the United States?" Teo asked. His expression carried a look of devastation.

"Imagine all the money you have in the bank—in your wallet —becoming nearly worthless overnight," Hedge said. "You still have five thousand dollars in savings, but now that's not enough to buy a week's worth of groceries."

"That can't happen," Teo protested.

Hedge nodded. "Tell that to the people of all the countries who have been taken over by their enemies. Iran, Iraq, Afghanistan, Kuwait, and nearly every country in Europe and Africa at one time or another. War is hell."

"But we're not at war," Ramos said again.

"Aren't we?" Kirk asked. "The bombs may have been set in Europe, but the United States would be just as devastated."

Evan pulled her feet from the table and wrapped her arms around her shoulders like she was heading off a chill. "The US has been the stabilizing nation all around the world for a hundred years. If we can't even take care of our own, we won't have any way to help our allies. Think of all of the countries that would be non-existent in another decade."

Kirk put his warm hand on her bare shoulder. "We're not just rescuing a few men from blackmail. We're not just stopping a mad bomber from attacking a Summit. Our mission," he paused, "is to save the world."

The others released a meager, anxious laugh that tapered into silence. Everyone jumped when Evan's phone rang from inside her clutch purse. She quickly reached for the phone as Hedge grimaced with pain at the sudden jerk.

"Hello," Evan answered. She didn't recognize the phone number.

"Is this Eve Taylor?" Michael Cooper's voice asked.

"Yes, Mr. Cooper," she said, raising her eyebrows. The men all straightened their shoulders as she rose to her feet. "What can I do for you?" Evan gestured to her phone and to Kirk's computer as she left the living room and closed the door to her bedroom. She wanted them to tap into the conversation and didn't want Cooper to hear any echoes from the transmission.

She settled onto her bed as he continued.

"You said that I should call you if I thought I might have a problem," he said. His voice sounded soft but worried.

"Yes, Mr. Cooper. I think there might be someone out there who wants to damage your reputation."

"These days it's hard to hurt a reputation. I'm concerned about my business."

Evan laughed at his comment but promptly regained her business attitude. "Has someone contacted you—asked you to do something? Have they threatened you?"

Cooper paused. Evan could hear him breathing. "Mr. Cooper?"

"I'm here," he said. His Irish accent was sharp and short. "I'd rather not speak over the telephone."

Evan wondered what kind of threats he might have received. "I can meet you tomorrow morning," she suggested. "You pick the place, and I'll be there."

Cooper's voice seemed unstable. "I'd like to meet you at the

Cathedral. But I cannot wait until tomorrow. Can you meet me tonight?"

Evan could hear the urgency in his voice. "Certainly, Mr. Cooper. I'll be there in half an hour. Where will you be?"

"I'll be at the main entrance. There are plenty of security cameras there. We should be safe," he said.

"I'll be there. Are you all right?" she asked.

"I'll feel better when you're here," he answered. "Ms. Taylor?"

"Yes, Mr. Cooper, what is it?"

His voice had a definite tremor. "Would you mind coming without your assistant? If anyone is following me, meeting a beautiful woman at a romantic location won't seem strange. Meeting a couple late at night looks like business."

"I understand," Evan agreed. "I'll come alone."

"Thank you, Ms. Taylor." He disconnected without saying good-bye.

Evan immediately returned to the others.

"Get your shoes back on and get over there," Hedge ordered.

Evan raised her brow, surprised at his eagerness.

Kirk handed her the shoes from the floor in front of him. "Go. I'm already tracking down all the leads that Tambar gave us. Your Mr. Cooper is waiting for you as we speak." He gestured to his monitor, which was tapped into the feed of cameras trained on the doors of the Catedral La Seu.

Hedge and Teo both pulled on their black leather jackets. "We will be watching from a distance." Hedge grabbed his bag of gear. "Kirk, keep us all in the loop."

"Roger that," Kirk chirped.

Hedge and Teo followed Evan out the hotel room and watched her hail a cab. Hedge opened the taxi door for her as it pulled to the curb. "No pressure," he said, helping her into the back seat. "Just the future of the entire civilized world."

CHAPTER NINETEEN

"She's just looking for a little human touch," Ramos said, his expression showing stress.

"I understand that. It's easy to feel isolated when you're thousands of miles from your family and friends. Especially when you can't tell them where you are or what you're doing." Hedge pulled to the curb two blocks from where Evan's cab dropped her in front of the Cathedral. "We all knew this when we signed up. She knew it would be like this."

"So what's wrong with us becoming friends?"

"Nothing is wrong with friendship," Hedge answered. "You two just looked like more than friends sprawled out across the bed, her shirt up, your hands on her back."

"So, friends don't touch each other?" Ramos asked.

Hedge huffed. "It blurs the lines." He turned to face Ramos. "We are all called to sacrifice ourselves for the greater good. Sometimes, God forbid, we are called to sacrifice each other."

Teo diverted his gaze to his hands.

"That!" Hedge said.

Ramos looked back up. "What?"

"That face you just made. You're not willing to sacrifice Evan."

Ramos shook his head. "I don't think you would, either. And I know Kirk wouldn't."

Kirk's voice rose over the remote speaker. "No, I wouldn't. If anything happens to her, I'll blame the two of you. Forever."

Hedge shook his head. "We do our best to protect Evan and the dress. But the dress itself puts her on the front line. She is the most vulnerable member of our team. I don't want her to be in a position of danger, but that's where she is every time she walks out the door."

Ramos pointed to Cooper as he approached Evan. "I don't like

this guy."
　"Neither do I."

CHAPTER TWENTY

"Eve," Cooper said, taking Evan's hand as she got out of the taxi. "Thank you for coming so quickly."

"I hope that I can help you," she said.

He led her to a well-lit area in front of the Gothic cathedral. The peaked arches that covered the façade glowed gold in high contrast to the black sky. The quarried stone walls remained stoic even after centuries of wear and weather.

"This is my favorite place in Barcelona," he whispered, stepping closer. "It inspires me that something man-made can endure for generations beyond the lives of its builders."

Evan took a minute to appreciate the breath-taking architecture. It was the first time since arriving in Spain that she'd really looked around herself for pleasure. "It is lovely." After only a second, she began to feel guilty for letting her mind wander from the job. She took a breath to speak, but Cooper cut her short.

"I come here whenever I'm in the city. It lifts my spirit."

"Do you come to Barcelona often?" she asked.

"About twice a month," he explained. "I have an interest in an oil company here in Spain."

"You do?" She tried to sound surprised. "What's the name of your company here?" She hoped to glean plenty of information for Kirk to investigate.

Cooper laughed. "It's not my company. It belongs to a friend. I'm just an investor."

Evan nodded. "I see. Yet you visit twice a month?"

Cooper smiled. He slipped his hand around to rest on her back. "When your business makes as much money as mine, you look for expenses to deduct from your tax debt." He motioned to the building beside them. "And isn't this a beautiful excuse to visit?"

Evan nodded. "Mr. Cooper," she started.

Cooper placed his right index finger over her lips. He moved closer to her face and whispered. "Please call me Michael. We should appear to be on a date."

Evan nodded again. "Michael," she said softly. She felt warm standing so close to him. She moved her hands to his arms, just below his shoulders. His body felt like a chiseled sculpture beneath his tailored silk shirt. "What would you like me to do for you?"

Cooper covered her mouth with his, pulling her into a full-bodied embrace. His left hand cupped the back of her head; his fingers weaved through her soft curls.

Evan's first instinct was to resist, but she gave that up right away and melted into his kiss.

After several seconds, their lips parted, and Evan gasped for breath. "I didn't expect that," she said.

"Well, that's a shame," Michael whispered. "I should think a woman as beautiful as yourself would be used to long, hard kisses."

Evan's fingers throbbed with heat. She struggled to clear her thoughts. "I'm not in the habit of kissing men I've only just met."

He smiled, keeping his lips just inches from hers. "But I feel like I've known you for ages." He kissed her again.

"Michael," she said as she pulled gently away. "I need you to tell me who is threatening you. What did they say to you? What do they want you to do?"

Cooper looked around them. "Can we go somewhere more private? I'd feel more comfortable."

"Where?" she asked. "Do you see someone that you recognize?" She didn't want to scan the area around them. She'd allow Kirk to take care of that.

"We could go back to my flat," Cooper suggested. "It's nearby."

Evan smiled and shook her head. "It's not that I don't trust you, Michael, but in my business, I take precautions."

Cooper grinned. "Very good. Where would you prefer at this

time of night?"

Evan glanced down at her watch, giving Kirk more time to feed her a location. "I know a little place not far from here."

"There's a little bar around the corner. I have eyes all over it," Kirk assured her. "It's called Els Quatre Gats."

"Have you been to Els Quatre Gats?" she suggested.

"It's one of my favorites. It was one of Picasso's favorites as well," Cooper added.

"Can we walk?"

Cooper nodded. "Good idea. If someone is following, it will be easier to tell, yeah?"

"Exactly," Evan replied.

They made the short walk to the bar and found a table in a corner. The walls were washed in three tones of yellow and reached up to the high, flat ceilings framed with green painted beams. Original paintings of every variety of size and style hung all over the walls.

"Are you an art lover?" Evan asked. "I mean, obviously you are. What I mean to ask is if you have a favorite style."

Cooper smiled. "I like all kinds. I have a great collection of paintings, but my favorite things are tiny, detailed pieces. I love paintings that fit in your pocket but have all the details of a huge mural."

Evan listened carefully, getting swept up by the passion in his voice.

He took her hand across the small round table. "Can I tell you a secret?"

She nodded, leaning closer. "What is it?"

"While I'm in London next week, I'm going to buy a Faberge egg. Are you familiar with Faberge?" he asked.

Evan appeared hurt. "Of course. They're magnificent pieces, crusted in jewels. Each one opens up to reveal a tiny surprise trinket." Evan listened as Kirk fed her more information.

"You do know," he stated. His voice sounded pleased.

Evan nodded as Kirk's whisper faded. "Are you going to the auction at Sotheby's?" Evan was grateful for Kirk's quick research.

"I am. Have you seen the entire catalog?" he asked.

Evan wove her fingers between Cooper's, stalling for a few more seconds. "The full catalog won't be printed until tomorrow," she said with a playful smugness. "But I have scanned the website a few times. I especially like the Matisse. How much do you think it will draw?"

Cooper smiled, satisfied. "I have no idea about that one. With Matisse, the final bid is dependent upon who is present."

Evan tilted her head. "And what is your limit for the Faberge? If you don't mind my asking?"

Cooper grinned at her question, apparently amused. "I don't mind, Eve. But I don't have a limit. I will buy it, no matter what the bid goes to."

Evan forgot that she was speaking with a billionaire. His piercing blue eyes disarmed her. His hands were warm to her touch. She thought about how soft his lips felt against hers.

Their drinks arrived, and Evan picked hers up right away. Cooper scooped up his and held it at eye level.

"To art," he toasted.

"To art."

They both sipped at their drinks.

Evan placed her cocktail on the small paper napkin. "Now can we talk about what happened this evening?"

Cooper looked at her as if she spoke backward. "What do you mean?"

"You called me for help," she began. "I assume that someone contacted you."

"I knew that you would," he said with a smirk.

"I would what?" she asked,

"Assume."

Evan blinked at Cooper in disbelief. "What are you saying?"

"Crap," Kirk whispered. "He threw you a line, and you bought it."

"Was all of this a pickup?" Evan rolled her eyes. "I thought you were in some sort of trouble."

Cooper took her hand again. "In my defense, I usually don't have to resort to these tactics. Most women don't even wait for me to ask them out."

Evan drew her hand out from under his. "I'm not most women," she protested.

"That's obvious," he said. "I've never known anyone else who works more than me. Maybe that's why I'm so attracted to you."

Evan was frustrated that Cooper had wasted her evening, but flattered by his words. She couldn't help but be charmed by his scheme.

"You know, my assistant is probably scouring your background as we speak. I thought that someone had threatened you." Evan looked back at her watch. It was after one o'clock. "I should be getting back."

"Please come back to my flat tonight," he asked. "I don't have anyone here. We could have a nice time." His fingers made small circles on the back of her hand.

"I can't," she said.

"All right then," he said with a nod. "But stay and finish your drink with me."

"You should come back in," Kirk said.

"I'll stay for a little while," Evan stated. "We can talk, but I'm not going home with you tonight."

Cooper appeared content. "Fair enough," rolled off his tongue in a chirp. He picked up his drink for another sip.

Evan decided to fish. She was good at that. "I don't mean to pry into your personal life, but I've done a little research into Anton Hrevic's organization. When you visited Hrevic's home, it looked like you always spent time with the same woman."

Cooper nodded. "Yes, my friend, Nastya Alenko was one of his models. I visit her whenever I'm in Paris."

Evan pretended to seem relieved. "She's an old friend?"

Cooper laughed. "You won't come back to my flat, yet you act jealous of another woman whom you've never met."

Evan shrugged. "I didn't say that I would never come back to your place. I just won't tonight." She pursed her lips and sipped her drink. "How long have you known Miss Alenko?"

Cooper clicked his tongue. "I was in school with Nastya's older brother. He was my best friend. We were roommates in college."

"How nice," she replied.

"Her brother, Costa, was in a tragic accident nearly a year after we graduated. Nastya and I were both devastated. We took comfort in each other."

Evan softened her eyes. "I'm so sorry for you both."

"Nastya is a beautiful woman. For a long time, I thought I would ask her to marry me." Cooper sighed.

"Why didn't you?" she wondered aloud. She imagined how different Nastya's life might have been if she'd married Michael Cooper.

Cooper leaned back in his chair. "I just couldn't. She was like a sister to me. Well, not so much like a sister. I suppose that would seem twisted. But being together was how we healed. It was how we honored and remembered Costa. To marry her would be as though we were in constant mourning."

"Being connected by tragedy is difficult to overcome," Evan said.

"It affects a person," he said, staring at the door.

Evan watched as his attention wandered around the room.

"Have you spoken to your friend, Nastya, since Hrevic died?" she asked.

Cooper shook his head. "I tried to call her as soon as I heard, but I was told that she was traveling. I suppose she went back to stay with her aunt for a while. That's good for her."

"But you miss her?" Evan tried to sound sympathetic.

"I do," Cooper admitted. "I'm feeling lonely. When we met earlier, I liked your ways. You're professional but quite personal. I like you. I want to spend more time with you. When you gave me your card, you presented me the perfect excuse to call you."

Evan finished her last sip. "You should keep my card," she suggested. "Call me if you need me—in a professional sense. And maybe I'll see you in London."

Cooper pulled a small handful of cash from his wallet and

tossed it onto the table as Evan rose to her feet. He followed her to the door. "You will. Remember, you have an appointment with me on Tuesday, and I'll expect you to be there."

Evan nodded. "That's right." She looked both directions down the street for a taxi.

"Let me drive you to your hotel," he offered.

"Don't you dare," Kirk whispered.

"I don't think that would be a good idea," she said.

Michael Cooper pulled her body to his and kissed her again. Evan's arms circled his neck, and she held his head in her hands. They released each other with a hot sigh.

"I suppose you don't trust me to take you home?"

Evan laughed. "I don't think I trust myself to get out of the car, even if you did."

"I don't want you to regret a single minute we spend together," Cooper said. "I'll let you get some rest."

A cab pulled up to the curb as soon as she turned her back on Cooper, and she got inside. "Well," Kirk hummed in her ear. "That was not what we expected."

Evan directed the taxi back to the hotel.

"Not at all," she whispered. Her head was spinning. "Not at all."

CHAPTER TWENTY-ONE

"Basically, he called you up, and scammed you for a date," Hedge said, as he paced the small stretch of sitting room in the hotel suite.

"I can't help that," Evan answered, shrugging off any guilt. "We all fell for his line. Not just me, remember?" She held her red heels in her hand.

"I don't like the guy," Teo stated. "I told Hedge earlier that I didn't like him, and I like him even less now."

Evan rolled her eyes. "I'm tired, y'all. Can we argue about this in the morning?"

"Yes, just get some sleep. We have to focus on Tambar tomorrow." Hedge waved his hand toward her room. "He's a big enough problem all on his own."

Kirk was sitting in the armchair with his notebook in his lap. "Umm, hold up."

Everyone stopped in place and turned to see what Kirk had to add to the conversation.

He looked up to see everyone staring in his direction. "I—we have a problem. Tambar's tracker hasn't moved in over thirty minutes."

Hedge moved to where he could see the monitor himself. "Where is he?"

"At his home," Kirk answered, gesturing to the satellite image on the screen.

Evan sighed. "That's good, isn't it?" she asked.

Teo and Evan joined Hedge looking over Kirk's shoulder. At first, Evan didn't see a problem, but as she focused on the image, she realized what Kirk was saying.

"The tracker signal is coming from his garage." Her voice shook as she spoke. Images of Boulette's lifeless face flashed through her mind.

Kirk nodded. "Yeah. And not moving around his garage. It's a static signal."

Hedge squeezed Teo's shoulder. "Saddle up, cowboy. We're heading back out." He pointed to Kirk and Evan. "You two stay here. Kirk, we'll let you know what we find. Evan, you get some sleep."

Evan scoffed. "Right." There was no way she would sleep until she knew Tambar's status. Her stomach churned.

Hedge and Ramos left quickly. Evan was frozen in place, staring at the monitor. Kirk shook his head.

"No, you need to go on to bed," he instructed.

"How?" she asked. "This is a serious problem. Tambar is panicked. I saw it in his eyes."

"I know, Evan. I'm the one who chased him around his office building."

"He's going to be another Boulette."

"You don't know that."

Evan dropped her shoes. "Okay, so let's say he's still alive. He's just been sitting in his garage—in his car—for half an hour doing what? Thinking?"

Kirk shifted his computer to the table, and took her hand in his, pulling her to the sofa. She sat down, propping her elbows on her knees and letting her face sink into the palms of her hands.

Kirk patted her shoulder. "He may be doing just that."

Evan snorted. "Even if he is alive, we don't know that his blackmailer terrorist isn't there with him. Hedge and Teo could be walking into a trap."

"Those two can take care of themselves," Kirk assured her. "You should have heard them talking about your Mr. Cooper earlier. When he kissed you, I thought they were going to come unglued."

Evan almost laughed. She looked up. "What did they say?"

Kirk shook his head. "That information is need-to-know."

She held up her palms. "I need to know."

He shook his head. "Not from me, you don't. If you want to

know, you'll have to ask them."

Evan sighed. "All of you are crazy."

Kirk nudged her knee. "Go change for bed, at least. Get comfortable. I have some stuff to show you. I was going to wait until tomorrow, but if you're not going to bed, we have time now."

Evan went into the bedroom and undressed. She plugged the dress into the garment bag and draped the scarf over the horizontal bar on the custom hanger. She zipped the bag up and turned on the charger and the sonic cleaner. She hoped the smell of cigarette smoke would come out.

She tugged on her lounge pants and sleep tee and pulled her hair into a cloth-covered band. A few minutes later she had her face washed, and teeth brushed. She could finally breathe.

Evan sank into the couch cushions and then noticed her shoes still lying where she had dropped them earlier. "Aw, shoot. I forgot to grab those."

Kirk picked them up and joined her on the sofa. "I need them in here anyway."

"What do we know about Tambar?" she asked.

"Nothing yet," Kirk answered. "No answer at his gate. They're headed in."

Evan pulled her feet up underneath her. A chill shot through her body. "Is it cold in here to you?"

Kirk shook his head. "It's still eighty-nine degrees outside. The thermostat says it's seventy-eight in here. It's not cold."

She scrubbed at her eyes. "What's wrong with me, Red?"

"Nothing's wrong with you," he said, patting her hand. "You have a lot going on in your mind tonight."

"So what did you want to show me?" Evan took a deep, cleansing breath and pasted on a smile.

Kirk pulled a small flannel pouch from his shirt pocket and dropped the contents out onto his hand. A small black button glistened from the center of his palm.

"What is that?"

He grinned. "My latest and greatest," Kirk said. "It goes right here." He held up her right shoe and, while depressing both the inside arch of the shoe and the top of the inner curve of the sole at the heel, he twisted the heel out and opened.

"I didn't realize the heels did that," Evan said, her brows raised.

"This little compartment is empty for now, so there was no need to get into it. But this little fella is just the right size to ride in here." Kirk flipped the heel back into place. "Don't worry. The heel won't slide out of position without pressing both spots at the same time. You won't be walking along and suddenly lose your footing."

"That's good," she said with a nervous laugh. "What does this 'little fella' do?"

Kirk sat up straight to explain. "It's called a sonic agitator." He waited for her reaction.

"That's a terrific name, I suppose."

Kirk nodded.

Evan twisted her lips to one side. "What does it do again?"

Kirk smiled broadly. "You can't hear it at all, can you?"

Evan shook her head. "I don't hear anything."

He leaned back and clapped his hands together. "It's driving me absolutely nuts."

"What is?"

"The agitator," he replied. "You know what a mosquito is? I mean the noise maker, not the insect."

Evan nodded. "It's the little electronic transmitter that produces a high-frequency noise that only younger people can hear."

"Yeah, and women can hear it better than men," Kirk explained. "My agitator is the mosquito's evil twin. It emits an ultra-low frequency sound. Older men are the most susceptible."

Evan winced. "And how would this be useful to me?"

Kirk turned to face her straight on. His hands held the shoe like a prize. "Now this is just my theory. It hasn't been scientifically proven, but my experiments have shown promise." He placed the red pump gently into her hands. "There is a great deal of evidence to show that low-frequency sound waves tap directly into the limbic part of the brain—that's the oldest, least-evolved or adapted section. Some call it the caveman's brain."

"I thought this was the part of the brain all men used," Evan teased.

"Watch it," he said amiably. "If you stimulate this area for more than a few minutes, a man will become irritable, maybe even aggressive."

"I don't need that," she protested. "I have enough of that as it is."

Kirk nodded. "Yes, but that's different because most of the time a person knows exactly why they are irritated. They identify the problem and go after it. Men especially are problem-solvers."

"I suppose that's true often enough."

"But when you don't know what's bothering you, you become confused. A confused, aggressive man tends to make mistakes. They fall back on their instincts, which are giving them crossed signals." He waited for her response.

"You think that a man who is making these kinds of mistakes is more easily manipulated?"

"Yes!" he declared, rising from the sofa, his left fist raised. "Especially if the woman manipulating him is the same person offering relief."

"How do I turn this off and on?" she asked, examining the shoe for switches.

"Right now I have it on through my notebook. Tomorrow we'll sync it with the dress, and to activate or deactivate it, you'll raise your toe and tap your heel three times fast." Kirk laughed. "I thought about pulling a Wizard of Oz and making you click your ruby slippers together, but then I thought better."

"Kirk?" came Hedge's voice over the computer speaker. "We're in Tambar's garage. He's down."

Evan sank back into the couch, clutching the shoe to her chest. Tears blurred her vision. Her ears felt hot. "No," she imagined herself saying.

Kirk took position at the computer. "Is C-O-D apparent?" he asked.

Hedge's voice sounded stressed. "Yeah, we found him sitting in his car with the motor running. His wife is next to him. She's in her nightgown."

Evan leaned toward the computer mic. "Was it murder or suicide?"

Hedge swore under his breath. "Tyler, why are you still up?"

"Murder or suicide?" she asked again.

"It appears to be suicide. Nothing is out of place; doors were locked from the inside."

Evan nodded, slipping into numbness. "Who's left? As soon as we identify his next target, he kills them. He's not leaving any evidence." Her voice turned raspy.

"Kirk, Ramos is calling for a team now. Take care of her. We'll be back in half an hour," Hedge barked.

Kirk closed the notebook computer and turned to face her. He took the shoe from her and dropped it onto the couch, and drew her into his arms. "It's going to be okay," he said in his most comforting voice.

"You don't have to be my father out here," she said. "I'm not a child. You and Hedge both treat me like a child."

Kirk took a step back, still holding her shoulders. "I don't think of you as a child, and neither does Hedge."

Evan sighed. She felt safe with Kirk. She let her head rest on his uninjured shoulder. "It's just that sometimes I feel like you're both protecting me," she whispered.

His hands circled her back and climbed to the nape of her neck. He pulled the hair band from her hair and watched the red curls fall loose. "Trust me," he murmured in her ear. "I'm not feeling the least bit paternal at the moment."

His soft breath on her neck sent a warm flush over her body. She tilted her head back to look into his hazel eyes. The green flecks in his irises seemed brighter than she'd ever noticed before. "Oh," she said. She planned to say more, but her lips quickly became occupied with Kirk's.

Another full minute of kissing passed before Kirk and Evan pulled away from each other.

"My goodness gracious," was all that Evan could manage. She blinked several times, trying to piece together what just happened.

"I need to disconnect the shoe thingy," Kirk said. He flipped open his computer and tapped out a few keystrokes. Evan watched as his expression changed almost immediately. "Oh, thank heavens," he said under his breath. He turned to face her, reddened with a weird cocktail of lust and embarrassment.

She picked up the pair of heels and stared back at him. "I'm going to bed," she whispered.

Kirk watched as Evan closed the door between them. "I'm not."

CHAPTER TWENTY-TWO

Evan awoke to the bright spring sunrise streaming through the window. She blinked and rubbed her eyes as the memories of last night flooded her brain. Tambar was dead, Cooper was a puzzle, and Kirk. She didn't want to think about Kirk.

She lay still and let her eyes focus, listening for Kirk's breathing in the bed next to hers. Nothing. Maybe he was still in a deep sleep.

She rolled over in her bed, careful to appear as though she was still dozing. She let a slit of light through her eyelids as she scanned Kirk's bed. It was there, just a few feet from her, unused. The blanket hadn't been touched since she settled to sleep last night. An almost sad sigh of relief escaped her lips.

Evan got out of bed and pulled on her running suit. She brushed her hair out and looked for her hair band to tie it up. It took a minute before she remembered that the band was probably still on the floor of the sitting room, where Kirk had dropped it.

Nothing left to do but face the boys. One more deep breath and she opened her door. Kirk slept on the couch with his computer still opened on the table in front of him. Teo munched his way through a bowl of granola, and Hedge was tying his sneakers.

Evan saw her hair band on the corner of the coffee table and picked it up without a sound. She pulled her hair up into a ponytail and slipped her Springfield .45 into the built-in pocket in the back of her boy-shorts. She put on her track jacket and pulled the zipper up about six inches to keep it in place, concealing her pistol.

Hedge tossed her a small bottle of water. "Do you mind company?" he asked. "We need to talk."

"You're not allowed to run," she said. She patted her own

backside to mimic Hedge's injury. "You'll pull your stitches."

"I'm supposed to walk," he replied. He stood up and pushed his pistol into the small of his back.

"I was going to run."

"Well, now you're just going to walk."

"Yessir."

Teo saluted as they started out the door.

Hedge paused in the doorway. "Get Kirk up, too," he said. "I want you both showered and ready for instructions when we get back."

"Sir," Teo answered.

Evan followed Hedge down to the lobby and out to the street. He gestured to the north, and they both began a brisk walk.

"What are we talking about?" Evan asked after they made it to the end of the narrow city block without a word.

"I suppose we should talk about what happened last night."

Evan hoped that he referred to what happened with Tambar and Cooper. At least both of those men fell into the category of business.

"Where should we start?" she asked. She tried to keep her voice as casual as possible. Hedge didn't respond.

She took a deep breath. "I suppose I should apologize for not telling you about seeing Cooper while I was out in the market."

"That's a start," Hedge spat out.

"I intended to, you know," she added. "I shouldn't have lost my temper when you challenged me about the henna. You were right about that, too. I wasn't thinking about any consequences when we started playing with it."

Hedge nodded.

Evan kept walking, waiting for more cues, which Hedge didn't offer.

"I've been acting like an arrogant, spoiled child, thinking that I can do whatever I want. I should be more careful about listening to you." She continued to walk, and Hedge kept quiet.

"Maybe if I had listened to you, and not gone back to Tambar, he'd still be alive." She watched Hedge's face for any reaction but saw nothing.

"And I should have realized that Cooper wasn't in any trouble, that he was only drawing me out to him."

Evan walked on beside her silent partner. She wanted some reaction. She felt like she was being forced into some strange confessional, and that she wouldn't be absolved until she had spilled her very last secret.

"I suppose I've been feeling sorry for myself, too. I let Boulette's death get to me. Instead of thinking about the job, I've spent far too much time thinking about my personal feelings. I guess that's why I let my guard down with Teo and with Kirk."

"Kirk too?" Hedge exclaimed. He turned to face her and slowed to nearly a stop.

Evan's eyes rolled back, and she let her shoulders drop with a shamed huff. "That's what this is about?" she asked. "I should have known." She started to walk away without him.

"Is that why he slept on the couch?" Hedge asked.

"I don't know," she said, throwing it over her shoulder. She stopped and let Hedge catch up. "I didn't mean for anything to happen. Not with any of you. Not Teo—and least of all Kirk." She sucked her bottom lip into her mouth and shook her head. "I don't have anything against Kirk at all; I love him. It happened because of this thing he put in my shoe."

Hedge raised his eyebrows. "I don't think I want to know." He started to laugh.

Evan punched his arm. "Don't be horrible," she said. "He put this sound generator into the heel of my shoe, and it makes men have this sort of caveman reaction. And nothing bad happened, anyway. He just kissed me."

Hedge laughed harder at her nervous reaction. They resumed their pace and crossed the street to a small green park area. "I don't think you need a device that makes men act like that. Your hair is more than enough."

Evan shot him a coy grin.

"And that right there," Hedge added.

Evan shook her head. "Well, just forget about that last part. I still apologize for the rest."

Hedge scoffed. "As my granddad used to say, that's horse hockey!"

"What?"

"You didn't mean any of that. All those apologies were for my sake. Not because you regret anything. The last part was the only honest admission in the whole conversation." He gestured to a park bench in the corner of the small garden they found on their walk. "Can we rest for a minute?"

Evan nodded and crossed the small stretch of grass to the bench. "What are we going to do?"

Hedge shrugged. "Well, the thing is, you have this knack for being impulsive." He stroked his goatee and then scratched under his chin. "My problem is that you're usually right."

Evan leaned forward and tugged at her sock. "I wasn't right last night."

Hedge yawned and tilted his head to the side until a muffled pop sounded from the back of his neck. "Why don't you tell me what you would have done differently yesterday."

Evan sat up and faced him. "Well, maybe I should have been more direct with Tambar right from the beginning."

"Kirk and I tried that. It didn't work, and he ran. Your approach using Cooper was brilliant."

"If I had brought Tambar to a safe location, he might still be alive."

"I doubt he would have stayed. He would have insisted on being with his wife. Same outcome." Hedge shook his head. "Your instincts were spot-on. Sometimes we just can't change things."

Evan rose to her feet again. She stepped onto a raised curb with her toes and let her heels lower to stretch her hamstrings. "So I'll ask again; what are we going to do?"

Hedge stood and reached out for her hand, pitching his thumb in the direction of their hotel. "Let's head back. I want to watch for whomever they replace Tambar with. Maybe if we get a name, we can do some research and see if this whole thing was engineered by our terrorist."

"Hedge, after I first contacted Boulette, our guy did or said something that made Gerard kill himself. The same happened with Tambar." Evan tried not to think of the idea that now haunted the shadows of her mind. "Have I put Michael Cooper into danger just because I talked to him?"

Hedge twisted his upper lip into a snarl. Evan always liked when he did that. To her, it was the one goofy thing he did without realizing it. "He said that nobody had contacted him. If he is an old friend of Nastya's, he's probably not in any trouble. We'll watch him once he gets to London, but I don't think you cursed him with the kiss of death."

Evan rolled her eyes. "I'm trying to be serious."

"I know. I have to hope you aren't literally handing out kisses of death, or our whole team is in trouble, apparently," Hedge teased.

"At least you know you're safe," Evan said, tacking on her coy smile.

Hedge took her arm to stop her. He nodded to another bench. Evan wondered if he was still hurting.

They sat down again. "Are you okay?"

Hedge's expression became serious. "You need to understand the reason I'm trying to keep our situation professional."

"I'm listening." Evan wasn't sure she was ready for this conversation, but she wanted it all the same.

Hedge exhaled, furrowing his brow. "Evan, you're perfect."

A laugh escaped her. "Don't be ridiculous." She almost got back to her feet.

"I'm not. You need to hear me out." He shifted so that he was staring just over her shoulder, not making eye contact. Then he locked his gaze with hers just as he began again. "You have this magnetism. Every man you meet will do anything for you."

"Not every man."

"I'm not finished. You are too beautiful for your own good. And that's what makes you perfect for this job. I don't know what you looked like as a child, but I suspect you were the tallest girl in your class." He raised his brows to form the question.

"Since the fourth grade." She nodded. She tried to glance around the park, but Hedge's eyes kept her still. "In high school, I was taller than all my teachers, even the men."

"And you blossomed, looks-wise, when you were about fourteen?"

Evan took a deep breath. "About then. But I wasn't popular."

"No, you wouldn't be. Boys were terrified of you. Too pretty. And girls were rivals." Hedge finally looked away for a second.

"Rivals?"

He shrugged. "You probably had no idea at the time."

Evan shook her head. "And now you're a therapist? A mind-reader?" The bright morning sun was nearly blinding. Evan squinted.

Hedge laughed. "Ten sisters, remember?"

This was too much. *Perfect? That's his problem with me?*

Hedge continued. "The thing about perfect people is that they aren't, you know, perfect. They are usually extremely manipulative, among other things."

"I'm not manipulative."

Hedge scoffed at her denial. "Oh yes, you are. You cry on cue. You can even blush intentionally."

"When I need to." She crossed her arms and pursed her lips.

"Exactly. To get what you want. And that makes you an effective agent." He lowered his voice. "You get almost anything you want just by asking. And when you do get a *no*, that's when you turn on. You're doing it right now."

Evan straightened her spine and chuffed. *What was he talking about?*

"You flash those eyes and that thing you do with your lashes. You lick your lips or, heaven-forbid, you bite them." Hedge took a deep breath as if he was steeling himself. "And don't get me started on how you move your body."

"How I move my body?" Heat flushed up from her stomach and pumped through every cell.

"Yes, that perfect body of yours. You know exactly how to sit.

To walk. To breathe." Hedge's gaze locked to hers again, as if he didn't dare look at her body again. "And the dress. When you wear the dress, you leave a man defenseless. He can't even lie to you."

She couldn't take anymore. She jumped to her feet and paced around the bench. Hedge reached out to catch her hand, but she pulled away. "This is a fantastic pep talk."

Hedge dropped his hand in his lap. His voice sounded more somber. "It's not a pep talk. Just an explanation. The only one I've got." He paused, and after another second, Evan sat back down to listen. "You awe me. I see you work. I watch as every man —every man—begs for the breadcrumbs you might throw his way."

Evan drew another deep breath. She didn't want to hear this, and she certainly didn't want to acknowledge it. "Every man but you."

Hedge laughed. "Including me. You have no idea how much I want you."

What? She almost smiled in relief.

"But you scare me," he whispered. "You don't even mean to manipulate me. At least I hope not."

She shook her head. "I would never."

"You don't intend to do it. For you, it's second nature. Maybe first nature. I never really understood that expression." Hedge laughed again.

Evan didn't know if he had amused himself or if he was deflecting. Maybe he thought a little joke would ease the pain of the arrow he'd sent through her. She could laugh, too. She could turn on her pout or tears or a hundred other little tricks she'd learned along the way. But that would prove his point. Nope. He was laying it out for her, and she'd show the same courtesy to him. She would let him know she heard him. Loud and clear.

"So my life will be filled with getting whatever I want from men, as long as it's for the job and not for myself?"

Hedge shook his head. "That's not what I'm saying."

"But you said that I can't help myself. It's who I am." She held out her hands in surrender.

Hedge didn't respond. She could tell that he had expected a sarcastic comeback. She wouldn't oblige this time.

She stood up again. "And you can't trust me not to be that way with you?" Still no answer. "Can we go back now?"

Hedge got to his feet slowly. Evan could see the pain in his face. She didn't know if it was from his injury or from the one he gave her.

"Listen," he said. "I don't want you to change. We need you, just as you are, for this mission."

Evan froze and glared. "This mission?"

Hedge nodded. "We need your lashes, your legs, and your gorgeous pouty lips."

"*We* need?" She felt as though her head was going to explode. She wanted to run all the way back to the room.

"I need. Is that what you want me to say?" His face flushed red, too. He took another step toward her.

Evan glanced around the park. People were starting their day around them, and she had no intention of being the morning's topic for them. She lowered her tone and stood toe-to-toe with Hedge. "Yes, Hedge. What exactly do you need?"

He didn't flinch. "What I need is for you to go to Mr. Cooper and be your perfectly manipulative self. You do your thing. Work your magic. Be whatever he wants. Do whatever is necessary to get him talking."

Evan blinked to clear some of the fury from her eyes. "And how far do you want me to go?"

"As far as necessary." Hedge turned and left her standing on the sidewalk.

Now she had no response. She just shook her head and in a few quick steps was caught up to him.

He stared straight ahead as he walked. "Sometimes it's part of the job."

Evan didn't even turn to look at him. She couldn't. "Yessir."

They remained silent until they reached the hotel steps again. Hedge opened the door for her. "We're clear now, about everything?"

Evan flashed her hottest glare. "As you like to say, *crystal*."

CHAPTER TWENTY-THREE

After a short but blistering shower, Evan suited up for the day. She had decided that if Hedge wanted her to be charming and manipulative, she would. He would regret every word he'd said that morning. At least, that's how Evan had concluded after several more imaginary arguments in the shower. Now she was ready to turn it on.

Dressing in a black strapless cocktail dress at nine thirty in the morning seemed crazy, but once she layered a red floral silk scarf around her neck and slipped into a lightweight gray cashmere cardigan, she felt more presentable to the world. She adjusted the side ruching on the skirt until the hem sat even with her knees.

She knotted her hair into a loose bun at the nape of her neck and applied a natural-looking makeup. She coated her lashes with dramatic black mascara, but the rest of her face looked fresh and innocent, just as she preferred.

Evan examined her right earlobe in the mirror. It was healing nicely. *A few days make a big difference.* She secured her new earrings in place, and when she heard a digital click, she whispered, "Red, can you hear me?"

"I've got you," Kirk replied.

Evan suddenly felt as though things were back to normal between them. She liked having his voice in her ear. It was like a security blanket, and for a moment, she was afraid she had lost it.

She sat on the edge of her bed and strapped her thigh holster to her leg. Once it was secure, she checked her Springfield to make sure she had a round chambered, and then put the weapon into place. She stood to inspect her ensemble in the mirror. Something was off. Evan shifted her holster to minimize the visibility of her pistol.

"What am I missing?" she muttered to herself.

"Your shoes," Kirk answered.

Evan laughed. "You're right." She grabbed her red shoes and joined her team in the sitting room.

Teo wore a black tee shirt and jeans, which meant he would be on his own, probably tracking down names of anyone who might have been seen coming or going from the Tambar estate in the last week.

Kirk wore his typical white button shirt and khakis. He'd be staying in and keeping the team linked in constant communication.

Evan pulled her shoes on and waited for Hedge. She checked through her clutch purse. Lipstick, ID, credit card, cash—she was ready.

Hedge walked out of his bedroom, and Evan's jaw dropped.

Hedge Parker wore his charcoal slacks and a crisp ecru dress shirt with a steel blue and gold striped necktie knotted in a perfect half-Windsor. What surprised Evan was that he was clean-shaven.

"Your face is nekkid!" she gasped.

Teo looked up and nodded. "Yeah, that's what's different. You shaved your goatee."

Kirk glanced up and shrugged. "You had a goatee?"

Evan lunged across the room and placed her hands on either side of his jaw. "I can't help myself."

Hedge took hold of her hands and gently removed them from his face. "Uhn-uh," he said and clicked his tongue. "Kiss of death, remember?"

It was as though he was using the same playbook she was. Evan sighed. "I'm gonna miss it."

"It'll grow back," Hedge assured her. "I needed to change my look." He put on his suit jacket and pulled a small black pouch from the inside breast pocket. "These are phase two of the transformation." He unfolded a pair of glasses and put them on. The silver wire frames enhanced the tiny gray hairs at his temples.

Evan smiled. "That'll do," she said. She didn't know why, but the glasses certainly worked for her. She wanted ice to flow through her veins, but every time she looked at Hedge, she melted. *This may be harder than I thought.*

"Do I look like a nerd?" he asked.

"Yes," said Teo.

"Yes," said Kirk.

"Not even a little bit," Evan said. "I think they make you look very distinguished."

"Nerd," Kirk and Ramos replied simultaneously.

"Let's get out of here." Hedge offered his elbow to Evan, and she slipped her hand into the comfortable bend in his arm. They made their way back to the street, and this time Hedge gestured south.

"What's the plan?" she asked. *Keep it professional.*

"We are going back to Tambar's office. Kirk hacked in and set up an appointment for us in half an hour. There should be sufficient confusion in the office so that nobody will notice one way or another." Hedge hailed a cab. "I expect that they'll tell us that he's not available, but we can insist that they allow us to speak to someone."

Evan waited as Hedge opened the car door for her. She noticed him glance at her legs as she slid into the back seat. *Good.* "How long do you expect they'll make us wait?"

"I'm figuring an hour or two. Long enough for most people to give up and leave."

Hedge gave the driver the address and leaned back in the seat, looking back over his shoulder to check that no one followed.

"I hate to be there all day, Sweetheart," Evan said, slipping into her cover identity. She lowered her voice and added a raspy whisper. "I wanted to visit the spa later."

Hedge smiled. "Don't worry too much about it. Think about how good that massage is going to feel when we're all done with our meeting."

The cab driver peered at them in the back seat as he drove.

Hedge stretched his arm across the back of the seat and drew her closer to him. "It'll be just like a second honeymoon," he said, just loud enough for the man to hear.

Evan snuggled under his arm. "Where are we going for dinner?"

Hedge spoke up. "Sir, what would you suggest for a nice restaurant nearby?"

"No English," the driver said automatically.

Hedge nodded. Now for the test. He and Evan faced forward and smiled placidly. She was to go first.

"Honey, what did you think of my new dress?"

"I didn't like it." Hedge noticed the driver's eyebrows rise.

"Awh, why not, babe?" Evan whined. "I got it jus' for our trip."

Evan and Hedge were careful to use their voices only and keep their gestures to a minimum.

"Does it make me look fat?" Evan said, sounding slightly upset.

"Nothing like that," Hedge said. He paid close attention to the driver's expression. "But I prefer you without any clothes at all."

The man started laughing immediately.

Evan nodded as they pulled up to the curb. Hedge helped her out of the car and then turned back, acting as though he was getting out his money to pay. Instead, he snapped a photo of the driver with his phone, and the man immediately sped away without waiting for his fare.

"Hmm," Evan said. "I guess someone knows we're here."

"Kirk," Hedge said.

"I've got him," Kirk hummed efficiently in Evan's ear. "What should I do with him?"

"Trace where he goes, tap his radio and snag his calls for the rest of the day," she answered. "We need to know who he reports to."

"On it," Kirk replied.

Hedge and Evan checked the sidewalk either way over each other's shoulders. "Let's go," said Hedge.

He led the way into the office he'd visited the day before. The room was empty except for the receptionist at the desk. Her eyes were red, her cheeks tear-stained.

Hedge approached her. "Mr. and Mrs. Brandon Hedger to see Señor Tambar. We have an appointment."

The young woman looked up. She blinked several times but seemed unable to place him. "I am very sorry, but Señor Tambar is not available today."

Hedge feigned resentment. "We have an appointment. We flew all the way over here from the United States to see him. What? Is he out playing golf or watching a football game or whatever it is you do over here?"

The woman burst into a fit of tears. Evan's cue.

"Honey, why don't you have a seat over there," she said to Hedge, gesturing to the leather armchairs near the garden windows. "Let me talk to her."

The secretary dabbed at her eyes with a well-worn tissue. Evan took the opportunity to retrieve a few fresh tissues from the small table at Hedge's elbow. She offered them to the woman. "Here you go." Evan circled the desk enough to pat the woman on the shoulder and to see the list of names on her computer screen.

"Gracias," she said.

"I'm sorry about that. My husband can be so insensitive sometimes. He gets a thought into his head and then can't get it out."

The receptionist looked confused.

Evan continued. "I can see that you're having a bad day. Is there something that I can do for you?"

"No, but thank you," she responded.

"Well, can you tell me if Señor Tambar is sick? Is he expected to come in later today? This meeting is real important to my husband's business. It's been a real bad year for us, you know." Evan let her Texas drawl spill out.

The woman sobbed. "Señor Tambar won't be in again. Not today." She shivered as she spoke.

Evan walked to the water cooler and poured a drink for her.

"Red, are you catching the stuff on her computer and her desk?" she whispered under her breath.

"Already got it," he assured her.

She offered the drink to the woman who gulped it down quickly.

"Gracias."

Evan waited for her to regain her calm. "Jus' take a deep breath." Evan demonstrated. Hedge snickered. The woman inhaled and exhaled. Her face lost its blotchiness.

Evan tilted her head in her most kind and charming manner. "It's obvious that something very bad has happened, and I'm so sorry about that. Maybe there is someone else that we could speak with? Other than Señor Tambar?"

The woman chewed on her lip for a second. "Un momento," she said.

Evan seized the opportunity. "I'm sorry, but I don't understand Spanish. I no hab-lo ess-pan-yol," she pieced together in her most incompetent way.

The woman looked at her and smiled. "Please wait here."

"Oh, certainly."

The woman motioned to a man in the next office, who strode promptly to her side.

"Tienen una cita con el Señor Tambar. ¿Que les debo decirle?" she asked the man.

"Puede reprogramar?" he responded.

Kirk whispered. "She asked what to do with you, and he wants to know if you can be rescheduled."

"I know," she huffed under her breath. "Spanish I understand."

The woman shook her head. "No, son los estadounidenses. ¿Que puede cumplir con ellos?"

The man looked at his watch and then back down the hall behind him. "Llevarlos al Señor Vasquez. El sera el nuevo Secretario pronto."

"Gracias," she said, and the man disappeared.

"Vasquez," Kirk murmured. "Got it."

The woman returned. "If you can wait just a few minutes," she said, speaking slowly. "Señor Vasquez will see you."

Hedge sighed as though this whole thing was a huge inconvenience, and Evan patted his shoulder to console and calm him.

Evan sat down at his side, and he reached out for her hand. "Honey, don't you worry. He's gonna see us, and we'll get all straightened out," she said. "Do you have one of your business cards?"

"Right here in my pocket." He patted his jacket. He motioned to the windows. "I want to show you something."

They walked to the windows and peered out to the gardens. "Two men in the doorway trying to figure out if they recognize me."

Evan put her arm around his waist. "Should we go?"

He stepped closer to her and cupped her face in his hand. "If we run, they'll chase us. Right now it looks like they aren't sure."

Evan leaned up, moving her lips to within inches of his. "So we need to make them look away?" she whispered.

"Do you want me to pick my nose or kiss you?" he asked.

Evan pressed her eyes closed, trying not to laugh or hit him. "I know which one I'd prefer," she said.

Hedge lowered his lips to cover hers, but just as they touched, her phone began to ring. She sighed and took a step back. Looking at her phone, she saw the name.

"Crap, it's Cooper. What should I do?"

"Take it, of course," Hedge said. He gestured to the receptionist who had returned to the side of her desk. The other men had disappeared.

"Señor Valdez is ready for you."

Hedge patted her elbow. "Take the call, and then join me when you're done."

Evan nodded. "This is Eve," she chirped as she answered the call.

CHAPTER TWENTY-FOUR

"I need you," Cooper said. His voice sounded strained.

"That's very sweet, Michael," she started to say.

"It's not sweet," he interrupted. "I'm in trouble. I'm not crying wolf this time. I'm in trouble."

Evan sighed. "What happened?" she asked. She looked out the window to the garden, trying to maintain a calm façade.

"I received a call this morning. The man's voice sounded like it might have been distorted. He said he needed a favor, but didn't say what he wanted."

Evan kept her voice even. "Did he say that he would contact you again?"

"Yes."

"But he hasn't?"

"He sent me a photo." Cooper's voice was losing strength. "It was Tambar—in his car. He looked as though he was dead."

"Was there a message?" she asked.

"He said that this was my future if I contacted the authorities or refused his requests."

Evan cleared her throat. "I can meet with you in an hour. Back at the Cathedral?"

"Thank you, Eve."

"I'll see you soon," she replied and clicked off.

Evan dropped her phone back into her purse and turned to face the woman at the desk. She smiled as she approached. "Where might I find my husband?"

"I'll take you to him."

Once Evan sat at Hedge's side, she struggled to concentrate on the conversation. Hedge and Vasquez talked about Spain's plans to expand opportunities for foreign investment in energy resources. In her mind, this meeting was like something of a form letter. No real substance, just a fishing trip, but without the excitement of standing silently for hours.

"Do you have any questions, honey?" Hedge asked her.

She felt like she was floating in a haze of confusion and anxiety. Hedge tapped her knee.

"Honey?" he repeated. "Any questions you may have?"

She pressed her finger to her temple. "No, dear. You brought up all my questions. Thank you, Señor Vasquez."

Hedge knit his brows. "Are you all right?"

She forced a smile. "It's just a little headache," she said. "I'm fine."

Hedge stood and shook hands with Vasquez. "Thank you for seeing us. We'll be in touch."

Hedge led her out to the street before asking, "What is it? What's wrong?"

"Cooper was contacted."

"You're certain this isn't just a second date?" Hedge asked.

"They sent him a photo of Tambar, dead in his car." Evan clutched at his arm. "It was murder, Hedge."

"Cooper wants to meet with you?"

"Drop me back at the Cathedral. I'm dressed. I'll let you know if I need you." Evan paced in a circle while Hedge found a taxi. "I won't take any crazy chances."

Hedge and Evan climbed into the cab. "I'll get out a block before the Cathedral and walk the rest of the way. I don't want Cooper to see me with anyone else," she said.

As they pulled to the curb, Hedge opened the door and helped her out. "Do you think I should stay?"

Evan looked up at the clear blue sky and then shook her head and patted his shoulder. "No, Hedge. I'm sure we won't stay here long. If he sees anyone following, he may clam up."

Hedge nodded. "Keep Kirk in the loop," he said.

"I will," she assured him. She watched him drive away and then walked the short block to the chapel. She saw Cooper standing at the front steps, his arms crossed over his chest.

As she approached, Cooper's shoulders relaxed. He reached

out to greet her.

Evan took his hands and kissed his cheek. "Has he contacted you again?"

"No," he said, handing his phone to Evan. "Look at the message he sent before."

Evan looked at the picture and read the message. Her stomach turned at the sight of Tambar sitting slumped next to his wife. She gave the phone back. "I can help."

"Before, I thought this guy might be looking for some kind of payoff," he said, walking to a nearby bench. "You mentioned blackmail."

Evan nodded. "This man is completely sadistic. His methods are ruthless." She stood next to him at the bench. "We need to get somewhere that we can talk in private."

"So you know who this man is?" he asked. "You've been tracking him. You knew he would come to me."

Evan licked her lips and reached for Cooper's hand. "We need to talk."

CHAPTER TWENTY-FIVE

Evan sat on the red leather couch in Cooper's penthouse suite. The ultra-modern living room smelled of lavender and mint. She took a deep breath as Cooper instructed his assistant in the foyer.

"I'm leaving Barcelona this afternoon. I'm going to London a day early. I can't stay here, knowing that the man who killed my friend is here." Cooper smoothed his palms over the front of his jacket and sat down next to her.

"If he knows your itinerary, which we must assume he does, he may already be in London." Evan took his hands in hers. They felt cool and damp like Tambar's had before. "What did he sound like?"

"As I mentioned, his voice sounded very low and distorted. It was a bit gravelly, like from drinking too much whiskey." Cooper closed his eyes slowly and opened them again. He appeared to be looking through Evan more than at her.

"Did he have an accent, or sound like he was from any particular place?" she asked.

"No, not really."

"Maybe a little bit?"

Cooper paused for a second. "The way he said a particular word—I can't remember what exactly—but I thought perhaps he was Russian or Ukrainian, maybe Czech."

"That's good," she replied. She patted his hand. "But he didn't give you any instructions? He didn't tell you what he expected from you?"

"Only that I shouldn't go to the police," he answered.

"Did he say 'police' specifically? Did he use that word?" Evan watched Cooper's expression. He appeared flustered.

"I don't remember now," he stammered. "No authorities, but I think he did say the word *police*." He shook his head. "Perhaps he didn't. I'm sorry, but I'm not used to being in this position. I'm usually in control."

"I understand," Evan said. "Michael, I'll be honest with you. I don't know who he is, but I've dealt with people like him on several occasions."

Cooper ran his fingers through his light brown hair and laced them together at the back of his neck. He rocked his head back and stared at the ceiling for several seconds. "I've been attacked in the media, and I've had people try to take me down financially before. I've never had anyone who wanted to kill me. What does he want?"

Evan shrugged. "He appears irrational, but when you look at everything he's done in the last year, he has a plan. We have to pull at one good thread for it to unravel."

"You've been after him for a year?"

"Yes."

"All this time and no authorities have been called in?" Cooper asked.

Evan swallowed and nodded. "Who does one call? He's connected with situations in Greece, Italy, France, Spain, Egypt, and the United Kingdom. Probably more, but I can't be sure."

"If you haven't stopped him in a year, how can you be sure you can stop him before he kills me?"

Evan took a deep breath. "He hasn't made this much contact with anyone so far—not that they've admitted to me."

"Tell me the truth, Eve," Cooper said, holding his breath in short bursts. "Did I get my friend killed? Did he murder Tambar to get to me?" His voice sounded icy and scared.

Evan shook her head. "No, Michael. The same way I found you, I found Tambar. He was on this man's blackmail list as well."

Cooper coughed and cleared his throat. "He killed Elena, too."

"I know, but it wasn't your fault."

"What could Tambar have done to deserve this?" Cooper stared at the phone in his hands.

"Nobody deserves this," she said. "But don't worry. This is going to stop soon."

"How?" he asked.

"I have my methods."

CHAPTER TWENTY-SIX

Sunlight poured through the window wall of Cooper's suite, amplifying the heat of the early afternoon. As they ate lunch, Cooper explained where he was and what he was doing when the mystery man called. He gave the phone number to Evan, which was unnecessary since Kirk already had snagged it from Cooper's phone. Evan had to pretend that it was procedure, of course, and Cooper was glad to offer the information.

They talked for another hour, with Kirk listening in on everything, and processing at the speed of light. The call had come from a disposable phone, which was probably at the bottom of a river by now. The picture of Tambar and his wife was authentic. It had been taken only minutes before Hedge and Teo arrived at the garage.

"I'll do everything I can to protect you," Evan assured Cooper. "Both your life and your business."

"Thank you, Eve," he said. He exhaled slowly, and an even color returned to his cheeks.

Evan smiled and nodded. She finally felt as though she was gaining ground on this job.

He checked his watch. "I suppose we should get going now," Cooper said, standing. He reached out for Evan's hand.

She took it and stood at his side. "I'll get my people working on all of this right away. I've already messaged them the basic information, and after I give my staff a run-down on the rest, we should be able to get a step ahead."

Cooper put his arm around her waist. "It's such a comfort to have you with me."

She smiled. "I'm good at my job." She didn't want to dwell on her failures of the last week. She tried not to imagine what would happen to Cooper if she failed him.

"I know you are," Cooper agreed. He led her to the door of his suite and down to the lobby.

As they reached the street, the valet brought Cooper's silver coupe to a stop in front of them. Cooper helped her inside his Morgan sportscar. As he circled the car to the driver's seat, she did her best to inhale the luxury of the vehicle. She'd seen Morgans before, but this was the first time she'd ever been inside one. The steely black leather interior smelled rich and felt like calf-skin to the touch.

"Do you like it?" Cooper asked as he secured his safety belt.

"It's very nice," she answered. *Understatement.*

"I keep it here, so I don't have to rent," he explained.

"And what kind of car do you have in London?" she asked, teasing.

"I keep two in London," he replied. "I have an Aston Martin for the city and a Range Rover for trips to the country. You can't pack much into a sports coupe."

Evan nodded. Anything more than her clutch purse would have caused crowding in this car.

As they drove toward the Cathedral, Evan released a deep sigh. "You can drop me up here, and I'll have my assistant pick me up."

Cooper chortled. "I don't think I'll let you go so soon."

The car passed the Cathedral.

"Oh," she said. "Have you thought of something else?"

"I have," he said, driving on.

"What is it? I'll phone my staff right away. Maybe we can get a jump on this man before you get to London."

Cooper squinted as he drove. He shot a quick grin to Evan, and then shifted his focus back to the road.

Evan paused, hoping he would answer. He didn't.

"Michael, if you'll tell me before you leave, I can do more with your information."

He nodded. "Before we leave."

She shook her head, noticing that they were at the turnoff for a private airport. "Yes, well, before you and your team leave

Barcelona, I mean."

"What I thought of," he said, "is that I don't know that much about you or your business."

Evan frowned. "What do you mean?"

"What I mean is that I should be cautious, right?"

"Of course."

He nodded, turning the bullet-car toward the small hangar at the end of the road. "I like you very much, Eve. I do. That's not in question at all."

"I like you, too, Michael," she said. She started to wonder where this was going.

"My problem," he continued, "is that I don't know enough about you to be sure that you really can help me. You say that you can, but you weren't able to help Tambar."

"I know," she conceded. She looked around at the small landing strip. A private jet sat on the side of the runway. Two men were loading it with luggage and boxes.

Cooper glanced her direction. "Don't worry; I don't doubt you. I simply want to see some evidence of your ability."

Evan lightened her expression. "What can I do to prove myself?" she asked. She was confident that whatever he requested, Kirk would hear and make it happen.

He pulled the car to a stop. "I want you to come with me to London."

"I'll be in London tomorrow," she said. "I guarantee it." She sighed with relief.

Cooper got out and walked around the car to open her door.

"I'm here for you, Evan," Kirk whispered.

"Thanks," she said, under her breath as the door opened.

"Come and see my plane," Cooper requested.

Evan's mind raced through a dozen scenarios. What if the mystery man simply wanted Cooper out of the way? What if he made contact with him only to scare him into going to London earlier than planned? What if he planted a bomb on Cooper's jet?

"I'd love to see your plane," Evan said. She took Cooper's arm and walked to the tarmac to examine the small jet.

KIM BLACK

"I'm assuming you want me to scan it?" Kirk asked.

"Oh my, yes," Evan said, as she walked under the wing.

"You have such a charming way of speaking," Cooper said.

Evan tilted her chin and smiled. "How do the wheels go up?" she asked.

"Come here, and I'll show you."

Cooper led her to the landing gear and showed her the compartment into which it would retract.

"Everything looks good there," Kirk said. "Wheels, wings, all good so far."

"May I see inside?" she asked.

"Absolutely."

Cooper walked her up the flip-down steps into the main cabin. The jet contained every luxury she could imagine. A large television screen spanned the back wall, with a wet bar underneath. She inspected all of the leather upholstered captain's chairs and the side tables as well.

"Nothing out of the ordinary—so to speak," Kirk said. "It's a beautiful jet."

Cooper smiled at her broad grin. "You are impressed?"

"Yes, I am," she admitted. She fixed a coy expression on her face. "May I see the cockpit?"

Cooper shrugged. "Do you know anything about airplanes?"

Evan shook her head. "Not really, but I like things with lots of buttons and gadgets."

Cooper walked to the door of the cockpit. "My pilot isn't in there yet, but I suppose it's all right for you to peek inside."

Evan took a step into the tiny room. She placed her hands on the backs of both of the pilots' seats, allowing the multitude of mini cameras on her dress to see every last inch of the compartment.

"I don't see anything out of place," Kirk said. "But of course, if there were something placed within the control panels, we wouldn't be able to see it."

"This all looks amazing," Evan said. "What else can I see?"

Cooper gestured back to the cabin. "You didn't ask to see the

142

back."

Evan looped her arm around Cooper's. "May I please see the back of the plane?"

He led her past to the back wall, through a narrow hall. "The lavatory is on this side," he said, gesturing to a door. "And this is the kitchen." He pointed to the cabinet behind him. "Back here." He opened another door. "This is my bedroom."

Evan gasped before she could stop herself. The tiny room was almost all bed, but still rivaled the most expensive hotel suites she'd ever visited. The bronze-colored duvet had golden silk piping around the edge and fat tassels on the corners. The multitude of pillows covered at least one-third of the king-sized mattress.

"Lovely," she said.

"A bomb could be anywhere in this place," Kirk said. "Inside a pillow, under the mattress. I'm not picking up any unusual signals or heat signatures, though."

"Go ahead," Cooper suggested. "You can lie down."

Evan shook her head. "Oh, I don't think so," she said. She looked back over her shoulder. "May I powder my nose, though?"

Cooper smiled and took a step backward. He opened the lavatory door for her. "Please, be my guest."

Once securely inside, Evan turned on the faucet for noise. She held her hands under the cool water for a second to calm herself. "Wow," she said to Kirk.

"That's what I was thinking," he answered. "I haven't seen any sign of foul play or tampering. And there are no hidden cameras. It looks like Cooper is safe for his trip to London. Come on back, and we'll get on the move, too."

"I'm on my way," she said. Suddenly the engines roared to life on either side of her. She turned the water off. "He's ready to leave," she whispered.

She opened the door and joined Cooper in the cabin. The outside door was closed and sealed.

"I think you forgot something," she said.

Cooper looked around. "I don't believe so." He took her hand

and gestured to a seat. "Please sit down."

She took a deep breath. "How long before you take off?"

Cooper laughed. "My dear Eve, you're coming with me."

"Crap," Kirk muttered. "I was afraid of this."

"Oh, Michael, I can't come with you right now," she said.

The plane began to taxi, and the sudden movement sent Evan off her feet and into Cooper's arms.

"You must."

"But I can't. My passport is back at my hotel," she explained.

The plane continued its taxi.

"This is where I test you and your staff," Cooper said, helping her to her seat, and buckling her lap belt. "You may make one call, right now, to your assistant. Tell him you'll be landing at this airfield in 90 minutes, give or take." He handed her a card for another private airfield located north of London. "You may have him meet you there with all of your necessities."

Evan started to laugh but quickly realized that he wasn't joking in the slightest. "An hour and a half?"

"Is plenty of time for a fairy godmother like you," Cooper finished.

Evan shot him a fierce glance and began punching in Teo's number on her phone, though it wasn't needed. Kirk already had a plan in motion.

"Yes, this is Eve," she said casually. "I'm on my way to London as we speak. I'm here with Michael Cooper in his private jet." She paused to listen to Teo swear for a second. "I know it's impulsive, but this is our chance to prove to him just how capable we are." She listened to Hedge's scolding for another second. "I'm sending you the address for the airfield so that you can get the directions online. I'll be there in ninety minutes. Thank you, goodbye."

She hung up in the middle of the tirade that both Teo and Hedge had launched. The wheels of the jet left the tarmac and retracted into place. Evan prayed that, whoever the madman might be, he hadn't had the chance to hide a bomb on this plane.

CHAPTER TWENTY-SEVEN

As the plane punched through the low clouds and approached the little strip in England, Evan breathed a sigh of relief. The private jet hadn't exploded on take-off or in mid-air. All that was left was to land safely. Kirk had assured her that he would take care of everything she needed before her ear-piece went out of range of his transmitter over the English Channel.

Cooper seemed to sense that Evan was afraid of something—not just because of the surprise trip. He had spoken very little as they flew.

"We're almost there," he said. Another ten minutes and we'll be on the ground."

"And then what?" she asked. "Do you plan to keep me locked up? I have to be able to get around to do my job. It's you who should stay holed up."

Cooper grinned as if she were joking. "I'd stay holed up all week if you promised not to leave my side."

Evan clicked her tongue. "Michael Cooper, don't tempt me. You know I could spend a month just listening to your voice. The problem is that in another month you wouldn't be any safer than you are now. My job is making you safe."

"That's another thing that concerns me." He turned his seat to face her. "You haven't brought up your fee. Everyone who works for me always wants me to know what they charge."

"And you're worried that since you have almost unlimited resources, I'm going to take advantage of you?"

Cooper shrugged. "I would be happy for you to take advantage of me," he said with a gleam. "But the reason I have almost unlimited resources, as you say, is because I'm careful with my money."

"I understand," Evan said. "I can have an associate bring a

contract for you to look over, but most of my clients like to minimize any paper trails. Discretion is my hallmark. I'm certain that we can come to an agreement about fees, and about not pressing kidnapping charges against you."

Cooper chuckled. "You're quite right, of course. I should be ashamed. I suppose if I wasn't a target, I might be."

Evan shook her head. "I doubt that. You don't seem the type that wears shame well."

"Hmm, I like that." He tapped his index finger to his lips. "Yes, I like that idea very much."

Cooper gestured to Evan to lock her seat into place, and he did the same. The plane began its descent to the green rolling hills of England. A light rain came down evenly, and the small jet took its time landing.

Evan's stomach was in knots as she waited anxiously to see if her team had been able to beat them to London. As the plane taxied up to the small hangar, she looked for any other planes on the runway or tarmac. Nothing in sight.

Cooper stood and helped her to her feet. "We've arrived," he said. "Let's see how efficient your assistant is."

Cooper stepped out onto the small stairway first and opened a wide black umbrella. He waited for her to step into its shelter before heading down to the asphalt. As Evan reached the last step, she looked up to see a woman in a navy-blue pantsuit and a leopard-print scarf walking toward them in the shadow of a bright red umbrella. Instantly Evan felt complete relief. *Eleanor.*

"Mr. Cooper, I'd like you to meet one of my most trusted assistants," she said as Agent McKinnon-Grey approached.

Eleanor handed the envelope in her right hand to Evan and then shook Cooper's hand. "I'm Ms. Fleming. It's a pleasure to meet you, Mr. Cooper." She turned to Evan and nodded. "Ms. Taylor."

"Thank you, Ms. Fleming."

Cooper smiled proudly and walked both women back to the tiny terminal. "A blonde and a redhead on either side of me," he chirped. "All I need is a brunette, and my collection will be complete."

Eleanor and Evan exchanged glances. "Mr. Cooper," Evan said. "I'd like to get you to a safe place before you start getting too familiar."

"Of course," he replied. "I apologize. It's just that you're both so lovely. I thought all your assistants might be like the one in the nightclub."

Eleanor gestured to the envelope. "Ms. Taylor, besides your passport, I took the liberty to include a client contract for Mr. Cooper to peruse. I know you didn't request one, but I thought it might save time."

Evan smiled. "Thank you. That's perfect."

They all went through the quick check in customs and took a seat at a table.

Cooper addressed Eleanor. "I'm assuming that you're in charge of the financial end of your business?"

"Yes, sir."

He looked over the paperwork and then pushed it back across the table. "And so you understand that, even though the terms are agreeable, I won't be signing any documentation?"

She nodded and smiled, taking a small device from her bag. It looked like a cell phone. "We have a perfectly legal means around paperwork. If you'll place your right thumb in the center of this pad." She flipped a switch on the side of the device, and the digital face lit up with a green square in the middle.

"That's clever," he said, placing his thumb on the pad. "If I'm still alive when this is all over, will you share with me where you get one of those. I must have one."

Evan smiled. "I'll see what I can do."

Eleanor stood up. "It's time to go, now. Ms. Taylor, I was able to bump your reservation up one night without too much inconvenience. All of your things are waiting for you there. I'll drive you in."

Cooper protested. "Please allow me to escort you both."

Evan took a step closer. "Mr. Cooper, you've already altered your plans too much."

KIM BLACK

"It's no trouble," he said.

"That's not what I mean." She took a firm grip of his arm just above his elbow. "You've shown your hand to this man. By changing your itinerary, he can see that he's gotten to you. It's important to keep as close to your original plans as possible."

Cooper sighed. "I see your point."

"I don't want him to think that you've contacted anyone about your situation. You need to go to your hotel alone. And don't change your reservations to another site or suite or anything. Do you understand?"

Cooper lowered his chin. "I understand."

"Good. Now go into the city. I'll wait for twenty minutes or so before I leave here. I'll contact you tonight and we can meet. At that point, I can update you on everything I know."

Evan looked at Cooper and then to the exit doors of the airport, telling him that it was time to go.

Cooper glanced at Eleanor and grinned politely. "Excuse us for just one moment, if you will, Ms. Fleming." He gently took Evan's arm and led her half a dozen steps away.

"What is it, Michael?" Evan asked.

"Eve, you promise to see me tonight?"

"I promise."

He looked over Evan's shoulder at Eleanor and then back into Evan's blue-green eyes. "Have dinner with me?"

"I suppose that would appear the most innocent."

He bent down and kissed her. "I'll see you tonight."

Evan regained her breath and watched him walk out to a dark green Range Rover at the door. *Oh, he was pretty.* She joined Eleanor and watched him drive away.

"He's a real charmer, isn't he?" Eleanor said, motioning to the table.

Evan grabbed two cups of coffee from the small credenza in the corner of the room and sat down across from her superior officer.

"I can't tell you how glad I am to see you here," Evan said.

Eleanor sighed. "You did well to keep your calm and your

148

cover. Do you know how difficult it is to get a passport put together in half an hour? I was still in the air when Kirk called me, and it takes forty-five minutes to drive out here from town."

Evan grimaced. "Is there any chance he knows we're InDIGO?"

Eleanor shrugged. "There's always a chance. But since we've had him under our watch, he's done nothing to indicate that."

"He scares me," Evan said, half under her breath. She looked up to see Eleanor's serious expression. "He seems to ask all the right questions and then demand the impossible."

Eleanor glanced over her shoulder at the doors. "He looks like an Adonis, and he's obviously infatuated with you."

"Another reason he scares me."

CHAPTER TWENTY-EIGHT

Eleanor pulled up to the curb in front of Le Méridien Piccadilly hotel with an abrupt stop. "The others should be here within the hour. "You're on the third floor, as always."

"Won't you come up?" Evan asked.

Eleanor tapped on the envelope again. "Everything you need is in here. If I were you, I'd go up and have a nice hot bath while you can. Once the boys arrive, its full speed ahead."

"I suppose Hedge and the others are pretty angry?"

"You made a call. I'd have done the same thing. So, yes, they're angry." Eleanor smiled. "I know you've had a tough time this week."

Evan shrugged. "I'm not used to losing two so close together. I don't want to make it three."

"See that you don't," Eleanor replied. "We are getting closer."

"Is there anything concrete?"

Eleanor waved toward the elegant cut-stone façade. "Go on in. Kirk will give you everything we have."

Evan nodded and stepped out to the still-damp sidewalk. She leaned down to tell Eleanor goodbye. "Thank you," she added.

"I'll see you again, Evan."

Evan waited for her to disappear into bustling afternoon traffic. She suddenly felt exhausted. Walking through the heavy wood doors, Evan could smell the energizing aroma of citrus and vanilla. The foyer was elegant but spacious. She checked in at the front desk and rode the elevator up to the suite.

Evan dropped her clutch purse on the gray tweed couch and smiled when she realized that the throw pillow at each end was the same red as her handbag. "This room seems to be the perfect accessory," she quipped to herself.

"You're there," Kirk's voice hummed in her ear once again.

"So are you," she answered. "I'm in our room, where are y'all?"

"We just touched down at Heathrow. We'll be in soon."

"Good," she said with a long sigh. "You guys get here soon, and I'll make sure the tub works."

"Evan, Hedge says you need to be ready to go when we get there. MI6 has requested a meeting with us."

"For what?" she asked. "How do they know we're here?"

"That's a very good question."

CHAPTER TWENTY-NINE

Evan sat in the oak-paneled waiting area of the Secret Service offices with her team as British officials scurried from one door to the next, shuffling folders from desk to desk. Everyone appeared to be in an efficient hurry, creating a symphony of keyboards tapping, footsteps clicking, file drawers sliding, and people whispering.

Evan uncrossed and re-crossed her legs in the other direction. Hedge buttoned and unbuttoned his jacket several times. Ramos stared at his hands while bouncing his right knee. Kirk sat back in his chair with his eyes closed. Evan wondered if he hadn't fallen asleep.

After nearly a half hour of waiting, the heavy-looking raised panel door in the corner opened slowly.

Eleanor walked out, escorted by a stout man in a gray flannel suit who had apparently said something funny because Eleanor was still laughing. She smiled at the team and gave Evan a nod.

Evan finally relaxed. She hadn't realized that she'd been holding her breath. She stood when Eleanor held out her hand to her.

"Colonel Fitzhume, this is Agent Tyler," Eleanor said, placing a hand on Evan's shoulder.

"Agent Tyler," Fitzhume said, taking Evan's right hand and shaking it vigorously. "I'm delighted that you would agree to meet with me. You're just what I envisioned."

Evan suddenly felt disadvantaged. To make matters worse, Fitzhume was leading her by the arm through the heavy door and away from the others. He closed the door and offered her a seat in a red velvet, wingback chair. As he sat in a matching chair to her right, she realized that all of the sounds that flooded her in the waiting room were gone. The only thing she could hear was her heart beating in her ears.

This much smaller room held only the two chairs flanking a small hearth, a leather-topped desk, a credenza stocked with liquor bottles, and a narrow bookcase behind the door. The wall opposite them was made entirely of bare windows. Natural light poured into the room and bounced around the white-washed walls, raising the temperature at least five degrees over the waiting room.

Evan waited for Fitzhume to speak. He seemed to be evaluating her. His brown-black eyes bore through her defenses. His pursed lips tightened as though he'd tasted something tart. He didn't blink; he stared.

And then without warning, he began to chuckle.

Evan jumped in surprise.

"Very good, my dear," Fitzhume cackled. "Cool as a cucumber, what?"

Evan raised her brows and took a deep breath before she spoke. "Thank you for inviting me here. Your office is lovely."

Another burst of laughter. "Aren't you wonderful?" He regarded the chamber with a wave of his hand. "This isn't my office. No, this is where I meet delightful people such as yourself." He patted his knee. "If I was to take you to my office, well—that's top secret, you know. It would be the end of both our careers." He made a teasing gesture of a knife across his throat.

Evan blinked, unsure of exactly what she should say or do.

Fitzhume quickly became serious, lacing his fingers together and letting them settle on his chest. "I wanted to meet you in person, Agent Tyler. I wanted to thank you in person."

Evan swallowed hard. He was thanking her. She shuffled through all of the things that she might have done for the British government recently. Nothing sprang to mind. She hurried to show her best manners.

"Colonel Fitzhume, how kind, but," she began.

"But you don't quite know of what I speak, do you?"

She shook her head. "No, sir."

"You met a friend of mine in Paris a few weeks ago. His name was Robert Charles."

Evan smiled instantly. Robert Charles had, at the time, called himself Adam Dooley. He was working for MI6 and had kidnapped her before he knew that she was InDIGO. They were both trying to infiltrate Anton Hrevic's operation, from different angles. He was handsome and charming and had died at the hands of her own team member, Jarrett Brawn.

"Yes, I knew him," she said.

"My dear Agent Tyler, I saw the little video that you made with him. You more than 'knew' him." Fitzhume tilted his double chin forward and poked his elbow toward her in a nudge-nudge sort of way.

"Well, that was duty," she confessed.

"If I knew Charles, he enjoyed every minute of it." Fitzhume straightened himself in his chair.

"I'm sorry that he was lost," Evan said in a softer tone. "He was your friend."

"He knew what he faced every time he left this building," Fitzhume explained. "Just as you do, I'm sure. People like you have a higher calling. You offer your bodies as sacrifices, both in life and death, so that the ideals of your country might prevail against the evils without."

Evan's heart swelled. Though Fitzhume spoke in a tailored British voice, his words reminded her of her father back home. Her eyes glazed in a pool of tears.

"Thank you, Colonel," was all she could manage.

"Allow me to thank you, Agent Tyler. I understand that you were the one who killed Charles' murderer. You are my avenging angel." Fitzhume offered his right hand again.

Evan took hold again, but this time Fitzhume didn't pump it. He merely held it in a firm grip.

With her left hand, Evan brushed away an escaping tear. "Pardon me, sir."

"You Americans can get away with showing emotions. We Brits have to keep that stiff upper lip. Rubbish, you know. When I heard Charles was dead, I cried like a babe."

"He was a good man," Evan said. "I was fortunate to know him."

"He liked you, right off," Fitzhume explained. "Called me the first night he met you and said he found the Eve to his Adam. Of course, Charles didn't have any family. He rarely spoke of women at all. He said that you were something special. He was right."

Evan smiled through the blush that reddened her cheeks. "You're too kind."

"Not at all," he answered. He reached into his breast pocket as he stood.

Evan rose to her feet as he handed her a calling card with the initials G. F. and a telephone number.

"If you need anything from me, don't hesitate to call."

Evan memorized the number in a matter of seconds and handed the card back to Fitzhume. "Thank you, Colonel. You're a kind man."

He grinned broadly. "Would you mind starting that rumor in this office?" He laughed. "Kindness is certainly not the attribute for which I am best known."

He opened the door and waited for her to join her team before following her out. He shook hands with all of the men and then kissed Eleanor on the cheek. "It's good to see you again, Elle," he said, and then added, "Don't break my city while you're here."

Fitzhume began laughing again as he strolled away through another hall.

Eleanor gestured to the others and led them to the exit.

"That was it?" Hedge asked. "What was this all about? He brings us all down here, chats with the women, and then dismisses us with a joke?"

Evan grinned at Hedge. "He probably just likes to speak with the ones in charge," she teased. Eleanor laughed.

Ramos waved his hands and shrugged. "Don't bother me if I don't have to go to the Principal's office. I think it's cool that we got to see this place in person. We might have been talking to James Bond, you know?"

Hedge laughed. "He didn't look like Bond to me."

Eleanor tilted her head. "Looks can be deceiving."

As they all got into the black Porsche SUV, Eleanor cleared her throat. She barely waited for Kirk's foot to leave the pavement before hitting the accelerator and lunging the vehicle into traffic.

"Status report?"

Hedge began. "We are still working on the information pulled from Cooper's phone, but so far we're hitting multiple dead ends. This guy is smart. He knows his technology."

Eleanor blinked and changed lanes. "You have Kirk. He eats, drinks, and sleeps technology."

Kirk nodded. "Yes, but it's like he knows me. He's anticipating my strategies."

"Then work out some new ones." Eleanor didn't accept excuses.

"Yes, ma'am." Kirk rarely called her ma'am.

Hedge gestured for Evan to report.

"I'll be on Cooper tonight," she said, and then realized how her words sounded. "I mean, I'll be with him. I'll meet him this evening for dinner."

Hedge and Teo both grimaced at her.

"I'll do my best to get everything I can from him—all the information." Evan huffed. "He's our best lead."

Eleanor grinned. She understood completely. "The rest of you, can you handle a little more?"

Hedge nodded. "What do you need?"

"The US ambassador to the UK is here in London, and as you know, his name came up on one of Hrevic's lists. He says that no one has contacted him, but I have my doubts. He couldn't wait to end our phone conversation, and that's not like him." Eleanor glanced at Hedge in the rearview mirror.

"We planned to make contact with him right away, but this thing with Cooper came up first," he explained.

"Well, I'm concerned because his wife and children are in town this week for a sight-seeing tour. They'll be spending a great deal of time with the Prime Minister's wife," she said.

Hedge nodded. "And if our man is targeting the Ambassador, what better time to strike?"

Eleanor blinked a 'yes.'

Kirk, sitting beside her, turned back to face the others in the back seat. "What better leverage could he find?"

Teo shook his head. "We have to stop this guy soon. We can't let him hurt anyone else."

Eleanor pulled up to the curb of the hotel and gave the keys to the valet. She took Hedge's arm and pulled him and Evan aside while the others went in. "We need to make sure that we stop him from disrupting the trade summit. We need him gone. And we need to be certain that he's the top man on the totem pole. Is that clear?"

"Crystal," Hedge said.

"Yes, ma'am," Evan answered. She felt recharged after her meeting with Fitzhume, and the bath didn't hurt, either. "We will get him."

Eleanor looked up at Hedge. "I'll message you all the information I have about the Ambassador's family shortly. I want you guys to protect them. So far our madman has focused on Europe, but Hrevic's lists included plenty of American politicians. This might be his way into US affairs. We don't want to give him that foothold."

"Crystal clear," Hedge repeated.

Eleanor faced Evan. "You get dressed and get to Cooper's side. I want every scrap of intel you can pry from him. Do whatever it takes."

"Yes, ma'am." *Whatever it takes.*

Eleanor patted her shoulder. "And have fun on your date."

CHAPTER THIRTY

Evan slipped into her freshly charged secret weapon and stared at herself in the full-length mirror. Not a hair out of place. Perfect lipstick. Perfect everything. *At least on the outside.*

She'd spent the last hour silently chanting the same mantra over and over. *This is the job. This is the job. This is the job.* Why did Eleanor have to call it a date?

It was bad enough that Michael Cooper was beautiful, charming and a billionaire—worse was the fact that he kissed her in a way that left an electric sizzle on her lips. *This is the job.*

She wrapped the sheer black sash around her waist and then crossed it over the bodice, creating a halter effect at the neckline. The look was very different than any way she'd worn the dress before, and she liked it. The hem sat just above her knees, her favorite length. She put all of her bare necessities into the tiny black sequined wristlet purse.

She put on her holster and completed the ensemble with the Springfield her father gave her as well as an extra magazine.

A rap at the door gave her a start.

"It's Hedge," he said.

"Come in."

He looked at her with a surprised expression. His deep blue eyes fixed upon her shoulders and then studied every detail. Evan was confident that if anything were amiss, Hedge would see it.

He reached out with his right index finger and picked up a curl from the back of her neck. "Nice touch," he said.

"What do you think about the sash?" she asked.

"It's good. It covers more skin, but in a hard-to-get way. Cooper's imagination will drive him crazy." Hedge nodded. "And you've become extremely efficient in positioning your weapon to keep it from showing."

"How do you know I have it on already?" she asked. She placed her left fingertip on her bottom lip, in a tease. *After all, he asked for it.*

"Save that for him," he replied, pointing to her mouth. "I know you're wearing it because I saw you bring it in with you, and I don't see it now."

Evan grinned. "Are we ready?"

Hedge took a step closer and slid his hand under her jaw and behind her right ear. "How is your earlobe?"

Her heart pounded until she was certain he could hear it. She licked her lips. "It's healing."

He lowered his face to within an inch of her neck. His lips skimmed her left ear. "What perfume are you wearing?" he whispered.

"Orchid," she answered, trying to maintain even breaths.

"I like it."

Her knees felt warm and weak. She reached out and stopped his right hand from traveling any further up her skirt. "Don't touch my pistol," she whispered firmly.

He took a step back and grinned. "You're ready."

Evan took her turn. She dropped her hands to her hips and gave him a once over. "Aren't you going to put on a tie?"

"Nope," he chirped. "I don't have to, because I'm not going out." He led her to the living room and made a sweeping gesture to Teo. "Cooper has seen him already, so he will be walking you over to the Brown's Hotel."

Teo looked dapper in his dark brown suit with a golden yellow dress shirt and mango-colored tie. The warm tones complemented his bourbon skin and thick black hair. Evan reached out for his arm.

"Shall we?"

"I'm ready when you are," Teo said.

Hedge went to the door. "Don't let her get out of range," he said to Teo.

"They won't see me, but I'll be there," he said with a salute.

Hedge turned to face Evan. "And don't drop your guard. Get him to talk, but don't give him any advantage. Anything he can give you—no matter how insignificant—may lead us to our terrorist."

"Got it," she said. "Don't wait up, Dad."

Hedge twisted his bottom lip. "I'd prefer you come back tonight. We'll be able to strategize more efficiently if we're all in one place. But do whatever is necessary." He held open the door for Evan and Teo to leave.

As they walked to the elevator, Teo choked out a nervous laugh. "He was kidding, right? He doesn't want you to spend the night with Cooper."

Evan raised her eyebrow as they entered the lift. She didn't say a word.

"Naw," Teo said. "Because I don't think I can stay out all night. I need my rest. It's better if you end this dinner date before midnight, don't you think?"

Evan laughed as they walked to the street. "Teo, are you jealous of Mr. Cooper?"

Teo shook his head. "Evan, this is tough. I know Hedge doesn't like fraternization. I get that. It can cause problems. But he can't just send you out here and expect that this stranger can meet your needs."

Evan stopped mid-step and turned to face him. "My needs?" She laughed. "What is this about?"

Teo shrugged. "The other day, I guess. We had some fun, you know. The henna. Okay," he said. "Maybe it's not your needs; maybe it's mine. Maybe it's all of us."

Evan smiled and began walking again, pulling him along by the elbow. She did find Teo attractive. She couldn't help it. But she felt for him as she did for Michael Cooper. There was a handsome face, a healthy body, and charm, but the connection was more of a feeling of responsibility than anything else. There was friendship, of course, but she didn't dare risk anything deeper than that.

She considered Kirk. With Kirk, there was a bond that comes

with time and the knowledge that without him, she wouldn't be alive today. She had saved his life before as well. The fact that he'd kissed her just a few nights ago didn't even feel awkward anymore. It was just something that happened. It would never happen again. She smiled.

Hedge was another story altogether. She tried not to feel anything for him, but he just seemed to know exactly what buttons to push for her. "He's just aggravating," she muttered as she walked.

"Hmm? I don't suppose you're talking about me," Teo said, sounding disappointed. "I don't want to be aggravating, but it would be nice to have a place up there right now." He pointed to the side of her head.

"I'm sorry, Teo," she said. "I'm just trying to get my mind straight before I see him."

"Cooper is the aggravating one?" he asked. The look of relief on his face raised a pang of guilt in Evan's heart.

"Yeah," she lied. "I jus' wish this whole thing was simpler."

As they approached the entrance to the Brown's hotel, Evan turned and faced him. She took hold of his tie and straightened it, more as a friendly gesture than anything else. "I'll try to end the evening before midnight. I wouldn't want you to turn into a pumpkin."

"I'm sure he'll drive you back to our place—if he's a gentleman, anyway." Teo looked around. "I wish I could kiss you, but he could be watching. You look beautiful, though."

"Thanks, Teo," she replied. "Stay close. You're my paladin tonight."

"My pleasure."

Evan left him at the street and went inside. The ebony wood of the long reception counter contrasted with the white walls and barrel-vaulted ceiling above. The middle-aged woman at the desk smiled and nodded as she made her way through the foyer.

Michael Cooper waited at the doors to the Albemarle Bar. He wore a midnight blue suit tailored to fit his every angle. His silver tie was dotted with tiny blue starbursts in a pseudorandom pattern. The stark difference between the colors of the suit and the tie played a game with his eye color. Evan couldn't keep from staring.

"Lovely," he said as a greeting. He put his arm around her and kissed her cheek, moving toward a small table in the corner of the bar in the process.

"Has he contacted you today?" she asked, trying to remember her mantra.

"No." Cooper motioned to a waiter who responded with a nod. "I suppose my change of plans sent him a pretty clear message of who is in control."

Evan scoffed. "I'm sure. By changing your plans and racing to London a day early, you've broadcast the message that you're scared and that he's controlling you."

Cooper winced. "What have you found?"

"My staff is still digging. There are several things that we suspect about him, but without proof, it's only speculation." She took a deep breath and relaxed her shoulders.

"Tell me," he insisted. "Maybe your ideas will trigger something for me."

"That's not how it works," she explained. "If I share my suspicions, they will certainly color your perspective."

Cooper released an exasperated sigh. "But wouldn't that work the other way, too?" He paused as the waiter brought two champagne flutes to their table.

Evan shook her head. "What are we celebrating?" she asked.

"I always drink champagne with my friends," he answered. "It would be unusual if I didn't. I suppose it's the first thing I've done to resume my routine."

Evan picked up her crystal and held it toward Cooper. "Then let's toast to the evening."

Cooper tapped his flute to hers and smiled. "To us."

CHAPTER THIRTY-ONE

After drinks, Cooper drove Evan to Les Trois Garcons in Whitechapel. The dark interior of the restaurant enhanced the sparkle of the crystal chandeliers and gilt candlesticks that seemed to be everywhere.

The host at the door took them directly to an alcove where they could dine privately. Evan wondered if Ramos would have any difficulty getting in, but since Kirk had remained silent, she wasn't worried.

"I considered skipping the auction tomorrow, but I can't bear the thought of giving up my prize," Cooper said. "The egg in question was originally owned by the Tsarina of Russia, Alexandra Romanov."

"How interesting." After Xandra's delusional tirade about taking over Russia as a natural successor to the Imperial family, Evan was less than interested in hearing anything more about the Romanovs. "Do you have a collection of Russian art?"

Cooper shrugged as the wait staff assembled a full meal at their tiny table in a matter of seconds. When they finished, he continued. "I have a gallery at my home in Dublin that contains antiquities from every major royal or dynastic family in the world. I have a ring that once belonged to William the Conqueror's brother. Legend has it that William sliced it from his finger and kept it on his person until the day he died."

Evan cringed as she looked down at her plate. "Hmmm, do you have any other less gruesome treasures?"

Cooper grinned and swallowed his bite of truffles. "Right, I should keep to lighter fare while we eat."

Evan dipped a spoonful of soup. "If you don't mind."

"I have several tapestries that are from Norwegian Things," he said, watching her face for a reaction."

"What kind of things?"

He laughed. "Nobody ever knows what a Thing is. I kind of love that." His face became animated as he explained. "In the days of Vikings and such, the villages had great meeting halls where the elders would sort of hold court and make decisions and discuss ideas. The buildings were called Things. Eventually, the meetings or ideas were called things. That's where the word comes from."

"You're kidding," she said with a giggle. There was no ticking in her ear from her lie detector. "I guess you're not."

"You're funny, Eve."

"Why am I funny?" she asked.

"The way you act like you don't trust me one minute, and then you do the next."

Evan let her lashes bounce for a few seconds while Cooper watched. "I suppose that goes with my job. In some ways, it's hard to know so many secrets about people."

"Everybody has secrets," he said, taking a bite of seasoned lamb.

"Yes," she replied with a sigh. "It's nicer to think of people like they are in photographs and portraits. They wear their finest clothes and paste a perfect smile on their face. At that moment their life is fairy-tale perfect."

"You and I were clearly raised with different fairy tales. Or perhaps mine were more real. Mine had the Baba Yagas and the armless princesses."

Evan cringed again. "Nothing gruesome, remember?"

"Sorry about that," he repeated. He raised his index finger, and a waiter suddenly appeared. "Dessert."

The young man nodded with the entire upper half of his body and ducked behind a draped wall.

"What is dessert?" Evan asked.

"It's a surprise. You do like chocolate, I assume?"

"It's my favorite. The darker, the better."

Cooper's lip curled in a teasing grin. "To be safe, I ordered a torte with a layer in every shade of chocolate."

"Perfect," she said. She sat back in her chair and surveyed the remains of the feast that once dominated the small table. She sighed. "What exactly is your topic for the meeting you're planning during the summit?"

"I'm going to facilitate a discussion about generating new business opportunities in the energy industry throughout Europe. There will be speakers from American companies, the Middle East and Asia, too." Cooper seemed as if this meeting was a common occurrence for him. "It should be interesting."

Evan nodded. "Do you think the man who called you could be one of the attendees at the meeting?"

He considered only for a second. "It's possible, perhaps. But what difference would that make? It's a routine interaction among leaders in the industry. There will be no major decisions made. No earth-shaking revelations to announce."

"What is your overall opinion of the Summit?" Evan asked. "A few big names will attend."

Cooper cocked his head to one side. "A few, yes. But no heads of state. They'll be signing little treaties and agreements that will be obsolete in a few months."

"What do you mean? Why will they be obsolete?" Evan pulled the pressed linen napkin from her lap and placed it in a heap on the table. She leaned forward eagerly to listen to his explanation.

Cooper held up his hands as if he was surrendering. "I'm not suggesting that anything is going to happen. It's always the case that men sign their names to documents in grand gestures at big meetings. A few months later they leave office and along comes another man who signs the next paper to reverse the previous one. It's always the way."

The waiter returned with a silver platter with two slices of cake and two cups of coffee. He cleared the dinner dishes and arranged the dessert meticulously in front of the guests.

"Thank you," Cooper said with a nod.

Evan stared for several seconds at the scrumptious layers of brown and black and white silk cake and frostings. The coffee aroma mixed with the bittersweet smell of the cocoa powder and Evan beamed.

"You do like chocolate," he said. "I'm glad I guessed correctly."

"Me, too."

They finished their desserts and started back to the Brown's Hotel. As they approached Le Méridien, Evan turned to Cooper. "This is where I'm staying."

He started to drive past, but Evan gave him a sigh. He made the next block and turned back. "I was hoping you would come back with me."

Evan worried that by circling the block, Cooper might notice that Teo was following their car. She placed her hand over Cooper's on the gear shift. "I still have a great deal to do before tomorrow."

He puffed out a breath and then smiled. "Once around Piccadilly Circus and then I'll take you home. Is that a deal?"

Evan smiled. "I think I can live with that."

As he drove, he spoke quickly, trying to push as much business into the conversation as he could manage. "Tomorrow afternoon is the auction at Sotheby's. The next afternoon is the meeting before the summit. Wednesday is the major summit. I won't attend, but several of my colleagues have asked me to keep myself available for questions and concerns that I might be able to address."

"And then for Thursday?" she asked.

"If I'm able, I'll be on my way to Zurich. I have a meeting scheduled there with a banker." Cooper navigated around the circular parkway. "Friday I'll be in a cozy spa resort for the night, and Saturday I'll be back in Paris for a week."

"So busy," she murmured. "And you have no idea what kind of demands this man might make of you?"

Cooper shook his head. "If he makes any demands at all, it should be limited to money. Otherwise, I doubt I could deliver. I don't think I have much influence."

"Money buys influence," Evan suggested.

"This is true," he agreed. "But not as much as you'd think. There is always someone with more than you."

Evan laughed. "I think you're right about that. But in your case, there are far fewer than in mine."

He laughed. "But you have the real influence because whatever sway you can attain with money, you can buy two or three times that much with the right information. As a keeper of secrets, you must understand that."

Evan looked around at the lights on the street. "I do understand. You know, the easiest way to stop a blackmailer is to hold a press conference and tell the world whatever it might be that they plan to use against you. Confession of the sin takes the power away."

"The power of the sin or the power of the blackmailer?"

"Yes, both."

Cooper drove back to her hotel. "Are you suggesting that whatever the blackmailer says he'll expose against me, I should confess to the world?"

"I can't make you do anything you don't wish to do, but I will say that I've seen that work before." Evan sighed. "I suppose it depends a great deal upon what sins you've committed, and against whom."

Cooper got out and circled the car to open her door. "What if I'm accused of something I didn't do?"

"You can always attempt to refute him." Evan turned to the valet. "He'll be right back down," she said.

"I will?" he asked.

"Yes, you will." She smiled at him as she took his arm. "You need to rest tonight. Remember that if you're going to fight him, you'll need energy for a battle."

Cooper wrapped his arm around her waist as he walked her through the lobby. "And what do I do if he doesn't accuse me of anything? What if he only threatens to kill me if I don't do what he says?"

Evan didn't want to think about that. He verbalized the fear that had been scratching at the back of her brain.

"That's a possibility," she said. "And that's why we need to identify him. If we know him, we can find something on him.

That's where we have leverage."

Cooper stopped in front of the elevator and pressed the button. "I understand. I need to concentrate on something to identify him."

The elevator doors opened, and Teo stepped out. "I'll take her from here, sir," he said to Cooper.

Cooper blinked at his efficiency. He squeezed Evan's hand. "May I have a second to say goodnight?"

Evan held up a finger to Teo. "I'll be right there." She led Cooper a few steps away. "Don't worry too much, Michael. I'm working on your problem."

Cooper placed his hands on her shoulders, making circles with his thumbs over her collarbones. "When this is over, I should like to spend more time with you. Perhaps I could find a place for you in business."

Evan tilted her face toward his. "We'll see. You may find that you don't like my tactics."

"I doubt there's anything about you that I wouldn't like," he said. He raised her face to his and kissed her.

She took a step back. "May I come with you to the auction tomorrow?"

"I would be very upset if you didn't."

CHAPTER THIRTY-TWO

Evan and Cooper sat in the fourth row on the aisle of Sotheby's. The cream-white walls were bathed in natural light from the overhead windows, and the black-draped section of wall to the right of the podium appeared infinitely deep. This created the illusion that the paintings displayed there were levitating in space. The audience gathered and whispered about several of the items listed in the catalog. The dozens of workers in blue ties and black aprons shifted items around behind the curtains to the side of the stage.

"Is this your first auction?" Cooper asked.

"No, but it is my first at Sotheby's," she said. Evan wore her gray suit jacket over the black dress. She tied her hair into a neat, low bun and wore black button earrings. The whole ensemble screamed executive, which made her feel quite comfortable in the formal surroundings.

The gallery was composed mostly of men and women in their fifties and sixties, with a few that were much older. Evan felt like a token twenty-something, while Cooper was among a handful of people in their early thirties. The auctioneer was a distinguished-looking gentleman with silver hair and a long narrow nose. He carried around a gavel like a retired barrister with a prized possession.

Evan flipped through the catalog for the hundredth time, using it as a prop as she scouted the room and everyone present. All day she had felt a distinct sensation of being watched.

Cooper pointed to a man with an umbrella at his side. "Didn't look like rain to me. What do you think?" he asked her.

"It's London. You should know that it rains here if a kitchen mouse so much as sneezes hard," Evan said.

Cooper laughed until others around them began to stare.

"Where do you come up with such ideas?"

Evan shrugged. "I'm from Texas. We don't get rain nearly enough there, so we tend to notice how often others do."

He smiled. "Just a few minutes and the sale will begin."

"Once you have what you want, are you going to leave then, or stay for the whole thing?"

Cooper raised his brow. "I like to stay for everything. I never know when there might be a piece that catches my fancy."

Evan nodded. "What's your favorite auction find so far?"

He placed his finger to his bottom lip, appearing deep in thought. From behind them, an older man with a marked limp approached and slapped Cooper on the shoulder.

"Coop, you bandit! I haven't seen you in a year," the man cried out in a brash Aussie tenor. "What do you plan to make off with today?"

Cooper stood and matched his friend's slap. "Gavin Stafford, good to see you." Cooper made a face and tilted back at the waist to look at the man. "That is the name you're still going by, right?"

The man burst into a roar and held his sides. "Who's this beaut, Cooper? She's not some Sheila you just picked up here, is she?" He turned to Evan and pretended to whisper to her. "He's no good, you know. Never worked an honest day in 'is life."

Evan smiled, stood, and took the man's hand. "Mr. Stafford, it's a pleasure to meet you. I was beginning to suspect as much of Mr. Cooper. I'm Eve Taylor."

"Aww no, mate. She's too good for you." Stafford pushed his way into the row of chairs with Cooper and Evan, bumping her slightly and causing her to stumble. Stafford caught her elbows, and once she was settled, he planted himself in the next seat.

"I know that's for sure," Cooper agreed. He glanced back at the rest of the room. "Where's Helen?"

Stafford dropped his chin and crossed himself. "Helen passed last August. Bad pneumonia after that brutal winter."

Evan placed her hand on his shoulder. "I'm sorry for your loss, Mr. Stafford."

Cooper nodded with a solemn look. "Yes, rest her soul."

Stafford shrugged and casually dropped his hand on Evan's knee. "The good news is that I'm back on the market, dear."

Evan laughed, and Cooper brushed Stafford's hand away. "The frozen food is back there," he said, pitching his thumb over his shoulder.

A woman two rows back gasped, taking his remark personally. Both men giggled like school children, and the auctioneer glared at them both as he stepped up to the podium.

The auction began right away and progressed rapidly through the catalog. The gallery behaved in an orderly fashion, offering the appropriate oohs and ahhs at the objects d 'arts. A sixteenth-century vase with a country meadow painted on the side went for several thousand Euros, and Cooper suggested, in hushed tones, that the buyer paid too much. A Persian rug that appeared to be on its last thread sold for nearly a quarter of a million dollars and Cooper whispered that it was a steal. Evan couldn't wrap her head around the quantities of cash changing hands.

After nearly an hour, the Faberge egg appeared on the table, awaiting presentation. Evan noticed a light turn on in Cooper's eyes. She glanced to her left to see a similar expression on Stafford's face.

As soon as the auctioneer began his description, Stafford's bidding paddle shot into the air. Cooper straightened his shoulders and raised the bid. A few other bidders joined the challenge, and Evan's stomach began to tingle. Her nerves got the best of her, and her right knee bounced with excitement.

Stafford's bids came more quickly, and Cooper answered with his own. The woman who had been raising the bid in every turn soon dropped out. Stafford, Cooper, and another man, sitting in the row behind and to their right, took turns bidding. The crowd all seemed to notice, as a low hum filled the room. The paddles rose higher each round, never settling back down.

Cooper's arm stayed extended, and at his turn, he simply fanned his paddle forward. Stafford began waving at the auctioneer, and the other man was nearly on his feet. The auctioneer started to perspire. He had difficulty keeping up with the current price. Twice he had to call the room to quiet.

Evan stared, bewildered at the men on either side of her. Their arms jerked with each bid, and she found herself dodging their elbows. A couple at the back of the room, who hadn't bid on the egg at all, broke into an argument.

They were getting shushed by several others around them. Evan couldn't believe her eyes and ears. In the hour leading up to this masterpiece of gilding and enamel, the room had been nearly silent. Now it was all the auctioneer could do to keep from bursting into tears.

"They're like animals," Evan whispered to herself. The bids continued to rise without signs of stopping.

Kirk chuckled in her ear. "You know why, don't you?"

"No," she replied. She barely lowered her voice, because it was unnecessary amidst all the chaos.

"You turned on the agitator about ten minutes ago. I thought you meant to do it," Kirk explained.

"Oh no," she said. She tapped again at her heel, and within another minute, the room had calmed back down.

The auctioneer waved his arms over his head and begged for a pause, which the gallery was suddenly willing to oblige.

"Now," he announced with a dramatic sigh. "We are standing at nine million Euros, ladies, and gentlemen." The gallery drew a collective gasp. "This will set a new record for an egg by Carl Faberge. We have nine million. Do I have nine million and five?"

Stafford held the bid with nine million. His paddle shook in his hand, and the other gentleman quickly dropped his paddle. The room stared at Cooper.

"Last call for nine million and five," the auctioneer said with a breath of utter amazement. "If I have no other bids?"

Cooper raised his paddle once more. "I say nine million and five."

Evan blinked, trying to decide if this was real or a dream.

The gavel came down, and Cooper was the proud owner of a very expensive jeweled egg.

Stafford slumped into his chair in obvious relief. "What was I doing?" he muttered.

Cooper leaned forward and gave his friend a wink. "You were giving me a good run. I had half a mind to let you pay it."

Evan chewed at her lip. "I'm glad that's over."

Cooper handed the paddle to her. "You can keep this as a souvenir if you like." He nodded. "I don't think I'll be bidding on anything else this afternoon."

Evan laughed. "I suppose one record is plenty."

Stafford shook Cooper's hand. "Let me buy you both a drink."

Cooper chuckled. "Let me buy you one. I got the egg, and I've got the girl. It's the least I can do."

Stafford cackled. "You don't have any money left. And you ought to be careful about how you talk about women, lad. If you keep referring to them like property, you won't have them at your side very long. Am I right?"

"You are," Evan agreed.

Cooper went back to the desk to close his transaction, and Stafford chatted with Evan as they walked to the exit door.

"How long have you known Mr. Cooper?" she asked.

"Most of his life, I'd say," he answered. "I knew his mother. She was a lovely redhead like yourself. And then I knew his father. He was a tough old badger. Came home from Afghanistan a changed man. It was difficult for Bridget and Mick. It was hard for all of us to see him so angry."

"Bridget was Michael's mother?" she asked.

"Yes, such a sweet girl." Stafford seemed to recall a fond memory.

"What happened to his parents?"

Stafford shook his head. "Not much good comes from war if anything at all. No happily-ever-afters there."

Evan frowned. "That's a shame. Mr. Cooper seems to have pulled himself up by his bootstraps, though."

Stafford chuckled as Cooper returned.

"What's she said that has you laughing like an idiot?" Cooper asked.

"She calls you *Mister Cooper* and *Michael*, Mick. How long have you been seeing each other?" he asked. "Do you insist that she also say *yes, sir*?"

Cooper scoffed. "Don't be stupid, Gav. First, she's from the part of America where they still teach their children manners, so it's natural for her. Secondly, Ms. Taylor is a business associate of mine."

"Oh, I'm sorry," Stafford said, but his words dripped with sarcasm. "So you won't be chasing her around your desk until after the deal is sealed?"

Cooper scowled. "Gav, you're acting like you've already had too much to drink. Perhaps it would be best if we got together another time."

Stafford stepped back with a wobbly limp. "Maybe you're right. I'm not feeling too well, Mick."

Evan shrugged and squeezed Cooper's arm. "Can we give him a ride back to his place? If he's ill, I don't want to leave him."

Cooper smiled weakly. "You scold me for the way I speak about women, and then you say such awful things, and she still wants to take care of you. I'm telling you, she's an angel."

Stafford nodded. "She's that, alright." He took Evan's hand, and the threesome walked out to the curb and waited for a cab. "Let me see the egg, Mick."

Cooper shook his head. "Sorry, Stafford," he apologized. "I had it shipped. I don't have it with me. After all, it was a pretty penny. I'm not going to let it fall out of a pocket."

Stafford shrugged. "It wasss almosss mine," he said. Evan noticed the sudden slur in his speech.

She shot a concerned glance at Cooper. "What's wrong, Mr. Stafford? Are you ill?"

Gavin Stafford coughed for several seconds. He pounded his fist sideways against his chest. "Don't worry, love. I may be old, but I'm strong."

Cooper turned to face Evan. His expression was serious. "Would you be angry if I took Stafford home without you? I want to run him by a doctor, and I hate to make you wait."

"I don't mind waiting with you both." She forced a smile as

she nodded toward Stafford.

"No, no. I couldn't ask you to do it. I'll call you when I get back to my room." Cooper's voice sounded low and somber. "Stafford has had health problems for years. It's probably nothing, but I don't want to leave him."

Evan nodded. "You go on, then. You're a good friend."

Cooper helped his friend into the cab. He took a quick step to her and kissed her cheek before climbing in after the older man. "I'll call you soon," he said as he closed the door and the taxi drove away.

Within seconds, a black SUV pulled to the curb in front of her, and the door opened wide.

"Get in," Hedge demanded. "You got played."

"I did not. The man was sick," she explained.

"Uh-huh," he said with a laugh. "They ditched you. Now we have to see if they are going out for a night on the town, or if they have a business meeting lined up."

Evan protested. "No ticking in my ear means no deception. Not from either of them."

Kirk joined the conversation. "Sorry, girl. Maybe they just know how to lie."

"Seriously?" she spat out. "How do you know they were acting?"

Kirk continued. "They acted like their meeting was by chance?"

"Yeah."

"We've been monitoring Cooper's calls since Barcelona. The Aussie texted him first thing this morning that he would be there at the auction," Kirk explained.

"That doesn't mean anything," she said.

Hedge smirked. "The actual message went something like, 'I'll pretend to get sick so you can lose your friend. We need to talk.'"

"Why, those little jerks." Evan said.

Hedge laughed. "Yeah, so I'm gonna say they deceived you. Neither you nor the dress picked up on their game."

Evan shook her head. "Why didn't you say something? I could

have put a micro transmitter on them both."

Hedge shook his head. "We can't just pin one on every man you meet. You especially can't use them just to see if your sweetheart is out with his wingman picking up women."

Evan waved her hands in protest. "I don't care if they're on their way to a disco. What if Stafford is Cooper's blackmailer?"

Hedge and Kirk answered at the same time.

"That would make him our terrorist."

CHAPTER THIRTY-THREE

Hedge and Evan made their way back to the hotel suite to track Cooper's meeting with Stafford. According to the GPS coordinates, Cooper's phone was back at the Brown's hotel. He never took Stafford anywhere else.

"That arrogant fool!" Evan said. "If he didn't want me around, he could have just said so. I'm not his wife. He doesn't have to lie about a sick friend."

Kirk took a deep breath. "What concerns me is that he did lie —and neither of us recognized it."

"That jus' chaps my hide." Evan crossed her arms and plopped down in the center of the couch.

Teo sat at the table, sketching on a piece of paper. Hedge paced, and Kirk worked at his notebook.

"The way I see it," Evan began. She decided to enjoy her internal dialog aloud, mostly because she was ticked off and nobody else was talking. "We have limited options. If Stafford is our man, we either have to wait for Cooper to tell us what's transpiring, or we confront Cooper and hope that he'll be honest with us. With both options, we have to hope and pray that Stafford doesn't decide to kill him before we have the evidence we need to stop him."

No response from any of the men. Evan glared, stood, and began pacing with an aggressive stomp.

"Maybe I should go to Cooper's hotel room," she said.

Hedge snarled. "You can't. If you show up and everything is innocent, he'll think you're spying on him."

"I am spying on him."

"I know that. All of us are, remember? I don't want you to scare him off," Hedge explained.

"I'm so overbearing that I'll scare him away?" Her voice

jumped an octave. She wanted to punch him.

"I didn't mean that," Hedge answered with a huff.

"That's what you said." Evan planted her hands on her hips.

Hedge marched to face her. "May I have a word with you in private?" he growled.

"That would be fine with me."

Evan stomped to her bedroom door and held it open for Hedge. "After you," she barked.

"Evan?" Kirk said, looking up with a grimace on his face.

Hedge held his hand up to Kirk. "You can talk to her later."

"Yessir," Kirk muttered.

Evan slammed the door once Hedge was inside. "I don't know why you have to treat me like a child," she griped. "Anything you need to say to me you can say in front of the others."

Hedge deliberately stepped into her personal space and stared at her with cold blue eyes. Evan noticed a twitch in his right cheek. He pressed his lips into a straight line.

Evan tried to calm down. She didn't understand how Hedge could push her buttons and raise her fury the way he did. She didn't know why he was angry. Maybe she should have just kept her thoughts to herself.

By this time the silence was coming to a full boil. Hedge's chin was tense, and he was clenching his fists.

Evan inched back a half step. "Are you going to hit me?" she asked, unable to bear the silent steam any longer.

Hedge shook his head, and creases broke across his forehead. "I would never hit you. Why would you ever think that?"

Evan trembled. "You look angry." She punctuated her statement with another stomp.

Hedge rolled his eyes and looked up at the ceiling for a split second. "You're making me crazy, not angry." He took another step toward her and wrapped his arms around her waist. He pulled her to his body and held her tightly as he covered her lips with a strong kiss.

She smoothed her hands up his arms and around his shoulders. She clutched at his neck and jaw, holding his face to hers. She wanted this. This wasn't a kiss for cover or for spite. This was delicious and electric and stirring. His lips were full and soft. His hands covered her back and sides. Her knees felt hot and weak, and she stumbled back against the door. His body followed and sandwiched her between his hands and his lips.

They both gasped for air and then dove right back into their passionate exchange. Hedge moved his lips to her neck and shoulders, and Evan shuddered in his grasp.

"Oh my," she whispered.

"Mmm, hmm," Hedge mumbled.

"But we weren't going to do this."

"Hunh-uh."

They ignored the first knock at the door. A second, louder rap caused them to freeze in place, their lips still firmly pressed together. A third knock sent them apart and into the center of the room.

"What is it?" Evan asked, trying to sound casual and failing.

"Give me your shoe, Evan." Kirk opened the door and scowled at them both. He held out his hands. "Give it to me."

"Why?" she asked.

Hedge knit his brow, but it was difficult for him to be taken seriously with Evan's lipstick smeared over his lips and jaw. "Is something wrong?"

Kirk glared and pointed an accusing finger at Evan. "She doesn't know how to control her heels. Every time I turn the agitator off, she stomps and turns it back on. I'm taking the thing out until you learn some self-discipline."

Evan slipped out of her red shoes and handed them to Kirk. "I'm sorry." *But not really.*

Kirk disappeared with the red pumps, and Evan closed the door after him. She looked at Hedge and sighed. It was plain to her that the heat had left him. She handed him a tissue, and he dabbed at his face until the traces of lipstick were gone.

"What was that about with Kirk?" he asked.

"He was trying out something with my shoes." She shrugged.

"It didn't work?" Hedge asked. He took a series of deep

breaths. Evan assumed that he was working his way back to normal.

"Oh, I think it worked," she explained. "But not the way he expected."

Hedge and Evan stared for several seconds in awkward silence. Hedge gestured to the door. "I suppose we should get back out with the others."

"Yeah," she replied. Neither moved.

Hedge planted his hands at his waist, and then let them fall to his sides. "What we did just now," he started and then paused.

"It was my fault." she stammered.

"Don't." He shook his head.

"Okay."

They went back into the sitting room and looked around. Teo was picking up a dozen papers strewn across the room while Kirk was sopping up a spilled can of soda from the floor.

"What happened in here?" Hedge asked.

Teo glared at Kirk. "Ask him."

Evan could plainly see that Kirk and Teo had scuffled with each other, or at least *at* each other.

Kirk sighed. "It was just a big mistake."

Teo nodded. "Probably a lot like what was going on in there with you two."

"No!" Kirk, Hedge, and Evan all said simultaneously.

Evan's phone began to ring from within her purse. She grabbed it and answered. "This is Eve."

She paused for a moment to listen.

"Eve, this is Cooper. I need you right now. It's urgent."

She looked at the other three men and nodded.

"I'll be right over."

"Hurry," he said and clicked off.

Evan grabbed her shoes and waved them at Kirk. "Did you do what you needed to do?"

"Done."

Hedge opened his gear bag and handed her a small black velvet pouch. "I want you to take some micro-dot trackers and put one on Cooper and one on Stafford if he's still there. I'm giving you a few extra just in case you meet anyone else along the way."

"Thanks," she said, dropping the pouch into her clutch. She tugged on her shoes and pulled a comb through her hair. She smoothed her palms over her gray jacket and applied another coat of lipstick. "I think I'm ready to go."

Hedge gestured to Teo. "Drive her over and stay close. I want you to be within sixty seconds of her at all times."

"Yes, sir." Ramos nodded and tucked his Glock into his waistband. He pulled his shirttail over the weapon and headed for the door.

Hedge caught Evan's arm and pulled her aside. "If you need anything, call him. And if you need us, just say the word, and we'll be there."

Evan nodded and smiled. "I appreciate that, but you know I can take care of myself." As soon as the words were out of her mouth, she regretted saying them. Hedge's face darkened, and he nodded with a detached expression. "I know."

She walked out the door on Teo's arm, wishing she had the time to go back and speak to Hedge. For once she was sorry.

CHAPTER THIRTY-FOUR

"You okay?" Teo asked as he maneuvered through the narrow London streets.

"I'm fine."

"Did you get a full-fledged 'come-to-Jesus' back there?" Teo glanced sideways at her. "Hedge was acting a little stressed out."

Evan sucked all the lipstick off her bottom lip. "No. I mean, yes, he's stressed. But no, I'm not in trouble or anything."

"It got quiet when you two left the room, at least until Kirk started tossing my notes around. I don't know what he's got against paper. Did Hedge give you another dressing down?" Evan didn't want to talk at all, but she especially didn't want to talk about Hedge with Teo. "Is your earbud working?" she asked, hoping to turn the subject to the business at hand.

Teo put his hand to his ear and directed his face away from Evan. "Say again."

Evan lowered her voice to something just above a whisper. "Can you hear me all right?"

"Copy," Teo said. He reached out and rubbed Evan's right shoulder. "Don't worry about a thing. You got this."

She nodded and drew a deep breath. "I'm not worried. I just can't figure out how I didn't get any signal that Stafford was lying to me."

As they got closer to Cooper's hotel, Teo shrugged. "What usually happens when your lie-detector thingy goes off?"

"The dress measures people's vocal patterns and rhythm. When there is a difference, an anomaly in their meter and tone, I get a ticking in my ear." Evan reapplied her lipstick in the mirror. "It didn't pick up on anything."

"But Kirk said that if people worked at it, they could trick the dress, just like beating a regular lie-detector, right?" Teo drove past the front of the hotel and parked half a block down the street.

"Yeah," Evan said. "But that doesn't give me a lot of comfort. That could mean that this guy is a pro."

Teo squeezed her hand as she started to get out of the car. "Or maybe he believes his own lies. We men are known to do that, Evan."

She smiled and gave him a nod. "Not sure that's any better, Teo."

Before she could close the door, he said, "Evan, be careful. I want to talk to you later. When we can be alone." He wiggled his eyebrows at her and grinned.

"I'm always careful," she said. As she closed the car door, she blew him a kiss through the window. Maybe she shouldn't. But he smiled, and that made her feel better.

She listened to the tires squeal as he pulled away from the curb behind her. She started the short walk down the block to the entrance of the Brown. *Breathe in, breathe out.*

The doorman nodded as he pulled the door open and bowed as she stepped inside. Cooper was coming out of the elevator as her eyes adjusted to the dark interior.

"Thank you for coming so quickly," he said. He reached out for her hands and kissed her cheek. "I didn't know who else to call."

"What did the doctor say about Stafford?" she asked, anxious to hear his explanation.

Cooper shook his head. "Stafford? He's fine. He came to see me be-because," he stammered. "Eve, this is bad. Whoever is trying to hurt me is using my friends to get to me."

"What do you mean?" she asked.

"I suppose you figured out that Stafford was putting on about being sick."

Evan raised her eyebrows and sighed. "I suspected as much."

Cooper followed her into the tiny lift and punched the close *door button.* "I knew you knew." He slipped his hand under her jaw and rested his thumb on her bottom lip.

Evan barely acknowledged the touch. "So why did y'all ditch

me?" she asked.

"What? What is that?" he asked with a knitted brow. "Are you angry?"

"You know, you could have told me that you needed some privacy to talk business. You didn't have to come up with a near-stroke." She shifted her clutch purse from one side to the other, placing it conspicuously between their bodies. "If you want me to take care of your secrets, you have to trust me with them."

Cooper nodded. As the elevator stopped at his floor, he held the door open and let her exit before leading the way to his room. Once the door was closed securely behind them, Cooper turned to face her, holding up a USB flash drive.

Evan took it from his hand and examined it as thoroughly as possible with the human eye. She could see that it was identical to the ones she and Hedge found at Hrevic's estate. "Where did you get this?" she asked.

"That's what I'm talking about," Cooper said. He took it back from her and crossed the room to his computer. "Stafford gave it to me. He said that a man gave it to him to deliver to me. He said that if he didn't give it to me today, both he and I would be dead by morning."

Evan wrinkled her nose. "What's on it?" She crossed her arms and twisted her lips from side to side.

Cooper shrugged. "I haven't looked. I didn't want to open it without you being here."

"Stafford didn't stay to see?"

"As soon as he put it in my hand, he bolted. I asked him who the man was and what he looked like. He just said that he didn't know him." Cooper plugged the flash drive into the computer port.

Evan watched as a pop-up announced that it recognized the device and wanted permission to open the files in the directory.

"I suppose we should open the one marked *Watch First*?" he suggested.

"Probably," Evan said.

As Cooper clicked on the icon, Evan sat down on the chair

next to the small desk. "It's a video?" She hoped Kirk had gleaned the information from the drive already.

Cooper pulled a larger chair from the other side of the desk around to her side and waited for the media file to open.

A small animated hour-glass began to flip in the center of the screen until the download was complete and the video window opened.

Instantly Evan recognized the woman in the foreground. It was Nastya, sitting in a chair. Her face looked pale with a dark bruise under her left eye.

Cooper's face grew tense, and Evan could hear his breath shorten. "That's Nastya," he said. "Where is she?"

Evan scanned the background of the room in the video, but it was dark. All she could manage to see was a figure in black, with a ski mask hiding his face. He paced from one side of the screen to the other, keeping a few yards behind the frightened-looking blonde.

Nastya stared at someone behind or beside the camera. She nodded at them and then began. "Michael, he has me. He says that you will know who he is. He says that you have to do what he asks."

She coughed for a second, interrupting her Russian accent. "Michael, please, do this for me. I do not want to die."

Cooper reached out for Evan's hand. "What can I do?"

Evan shook her head. "We will find her, don't worry, Michael."

Kirk's voice whispered. "Working on it."

They studied the video for any hints as to where it was taken. Evan held Michael's hand, knowing there was nothing that she could do until Kirk could analyze the drive.

"Michael," Nastya started again. "This man is powerful. He can hurt you. He can hurt anyone at any time. He is unpredictable."

A sharp pop sounded on the video, and Nastya slumped forward in the chair.

"What happened?!" Cooper cried out.

Evan knew. Her stomach turned and twisted. She clutched at

Michael's arm, trying to maintain a sense of calm.

"No," she gasped. Her heart slammed against her spine and in her ears. She saw the man in the background step forward and grab Nastya's hair. He raised her head to face the camera, and the hole in her forehead distorted her once-beautiful appearance.

"NOOO!" Michael cried. Glassy tears poured over his cheeks as he slid from his seat and sank to his knees.

The video ended and the picture froze on Nastya's dead face. Cooper buried his face in Evan's lap and wept for several seconds.

Evan reached forward and closed the video window, bringing the flash drive menu back to the center of the screen.

"You okay, Evan?" Kirk whispered in her ear.

Evan took a deep breath and held Cooper until his sobs faded.

"Okay," she said, both to Kirk and to Michael. "I'm here. We're okay."

Cooper sat back and shook his head. "What kind of monster does that? She didn't do anything. He killed her because she knew me. That's all."

Evan took his face in her hands. "Michael, we will get him." As she wiped the damp streaks from his cheeks, she realized that her hands were trembling as badly as Cooper's body. "Do you think you can stand to see what else is on the flash drive?"

Cooper climbed back into his chair and nodded. "I don't have a choice, I suppose."

Evan clicked the other icon, labeled *Next*, and a text document filled the screen.

Michael Cooper,

Now you see what I can do to you and anyone close to you. You know that I will not hesitate to act if you don't obey me. Do not think you can play games. Do not think that you can beat me. I have already taken away one that you love. I will not stop at her. Others will die. Only you decide who.

You will pick up a package tomorrow on your way to the summit. I will send word in the morning where you will find it. It will have your instructions attached. If you fail to pick it up, I will kill your new friend. If you fail to obey, I will kill your friend. If you call for help or alert authorities, I will kill her. If you fail to meet my demands in any way, I will kill both you and her.

Cooper finished reading and sat back in his chair. For the first time since they met, Evan thought that he looked like a defeated child.

"What can I do?" he asked again. He looked at Evan and reached a weak hand up to touch her face. "Your only sin is that you know me. I don't want you to die, too."

Evan shook her head. "I'm not going to die." She hadn't decided if she was speaking to him or herself. "We are going to get this beast."

Cooper's hand dropped to the chair arm, and he chuffed through a heavy breath. "How? We don't know who he is?"

"Nastya said that you would know. *He* thinks you do know."

Cooper raked his fingers through his hair. "But I don't. If I knew, I would tell you."

Evan nodded. Her stomach was almost settled enough for her to stand. Just another minute or two.

Cooper chewed his lip and pressed the heels of his palms over his eyes. "I cannot believe she's dead. Nastya. I can't believe it."

Evan sat forward. "If you let me take the flash drive with me, I think I have a friend who can figure out where the video was taken. Maybe even who took it."

Cooper shrugged. "What difference will that make? By the time your friend knows anything, I will have already done whatever terrible deed he wants me to accomplish."

Evan stood and walked to the side of the computer, within inches of the USB drive. She hoped she was close enough. "Maybe you're right about how long it would take to analyze the information, but don't you think it's worth a chance?" Evan continued. "Just because he threatens you doesn't mean you have to do what he tells you."

"He will kill you," he said, letting his body go limp.

Evan shook her head and propped her hands on her hips. "I have dozens of people threaten me every day," she said. "Anyone who knows the secrets I know can say the same thing. I take measures to make sure I'm safe."

"He'll kill me."

"I will protect you."

He flipped his hand toward his computer. "He killed Nastya." Cooper's tone was flat and indifferent. His tears had dried and, apparently, so had his emotions.

"Starting to pull meta now," Kirk hummed.

"Nastya wasn't with me," Evan said. She crossed to stand in front of Cooper. "I won't let anyone hurt you."

Cooper took her hands and pulled her into his lap. "Will you stay here and protect me?"

Evan sighed. She wanted to get back to the others, but she knew that she couldn't let Cooper out of her sight. "I'll stay."

"I would like that." He leaned against her shoulder and snugged his arms around her waist. "I don't think I can be alone after that."

Evan kissed his forehead. "I don't think you should get back out again tonight. Don't make any calls or even leave the room."

"As long as you're with me, Eve," he said, holding her tighter. "I don't need to leave the room again."

Evan nodded. She got up from his lap and checked out the window. The sky was turning a dark shade of lavender, and the street lights began to flicker to life. She saw the black SUV flash its lights. Teo would watch over her tonight.

She turned back to Cooper. "I won't leave you." As she moved back to his side, he stood and took her into his arms. She could still feel a tremor in his muscles. "We'll be safe for the night."

Cooper kissed her. "I feel better knowing you're with me."

She patted his cheek. "And maybe we can figure out who this man is."

"I don't want to talk about him right now, please."

Evan reached up and kissed his lips. "Then maybe we can talk later."

CHAPTER THIRTY-FIVE

"This guy is sick," Kirk said as his diagnostic programs began analyzing the video of Nastya's execution frame by frame.

Hedge paced their room with a frown. "How soon will we be able to track down an IP or something?"

Kirk sighed. "He's good. Without an active connection, I have to trace signatures embedded in the drive itself. That takes a lot more time. It's like a fingerprint, but the problem is that when a flash drive gets used over and over, it's like layers of prints, one on top of the other."

"So he's covered his tracks?"

"Nobody is invincible," Kirk said. "But it will take some time to sort."

"Evan may not have time," Hedge barked.

Kirk didn't respond beyond focusing back on the monitor of his notebook.

Satisfied with that, Hedge gave up his pacing and parked himself in a chair at the small table in the corner. "What do we know about this man?" he muttered to himself.

"That he's watching Cooper closely enough to know that Evan is with him," Ramos replied through his com connection.

Hedge didn't expect an answer, and when Ramos spoke, Hedge almost jumped. "Yeah," he said, trying to minimize the reaction. "And we know that he's been watching Cooper long enough to know about his relationship to Nastya. He's probably been following him for longer than we have."

"Yeah, but I haven't seen any sign of a tail," Ramos said. "And I haven't let the two of them out of my sight."

Hedge turned back to Kirk. "Is there any way we can find out if someone besides Ramos has been following them?" he asked. "You know, use the micro-cameras on the dress?"

Kirk nodded. "I thought about that. The dress cams are always on and always processing. I can adjust the settings to broader variables and send the last three days of interaction with Cooper back through the FRS analysis."

Hedge chewed on his bottom lip and let his eyebrow twitch for a second. "If you do that, won't it mess with the real-time processing with the dress?"

Kirk nodded. "It will take it down to a minimum, but frankly," he said, wishing he didn't have to vocalize his thoughts. "I don't think Evan's using the dress for that right now."

Hedge hopped back to his feet and resumed his pacing. "This is making me crazy."

"Me, too," Ramos said.

Kirk tapped at his keyboard. "I've adjusted the settings. It may take an hour, but I think we'll have at least that much time before she'll need to be working at full capacity."

Hedge growled. "What can we do right now?"

"At least we know, for now anyway, she seems to be safe," Kirk said. A beep on his notebook alerted him. "I have the first hit."

Hedge crossed the room in two steps, anxious to get a look. "Who is it?"

Kirk frowned. "It's the doorman at the Brown's Hotel. Probably nothing, but I'll send him through local law and Interpol. Could be a great cover."

"Do it," Hedge ordered.

"I've got another," Kirk said as a second face popped up. "Okay, it's another hotel employee."

"Send them through, too. I don't care if you get a hundred hits," Hedge said. "Send everyone through until we get something we can work with."

"You got it," Kirk said. "I can run it in the background, and it will signal me if I get anything more than a parking ticket."

Hedge sighed. "I guess that will be good enough. Although, if the parking tickets are in any of our recent cities, I want to know that, too."

Kirk tapped away again. "I can do that."

"If you get something," Ramos said, sounding angrier each time his voice came over the com. "I want to know."

Hedge snorted. "We'll get him, Ramos."

CHAPTER THIRTY-SIX

Evan woke up and looked around the still-dark room. She found herself alone on the floor, covered with the faux fur blanket from the foot of the bed. She scanned the room for Cooper.

She saw a light coming from the narrow gap under the bathroom door and silently got to her feet, adjusting her dress back into place on the way up. She removed her Springfield from her purse and held it out of sight as she tiptoed to the side of the door. She could hear water running.

She peeked into the bedroom, where everything looked untouched from last night. The digital clock on the nightstand glowed a neon blue 5:30.

"Anybody awake?" she whispered in her lowest tone.

"Romeo here," Teo answered with his call sign. His voice sounded tired.

"Kilo here," Kirk whispered groggily.

"We're all up," Hedge said. His voice carried no hint of fatigue at all. "Report."

Evan cleared her throat as quietly as possible. "I think Cooper is in the shower. I don't see anything out of place." She scanned the room for whatever else might have roused her. A glint of something shiny at the main door caught her eye. "Wait," she whispered. "I see something."

She moved across the room like a cat on a cloud. She peered out the peephole but saw nothing out of place. She holstered her weapon to her thigh and reached down to pick up the jump drive on the floor.

"Another flash drive," she said, holding it against the dress for a second so that Kirk's program could scan whatever was on it. "You got it, Red?"

"Got it."

"Good, now I need to get back to work."

Evan could hear Kirk tapping at his notebook. "I'm scanning contents and fingerprints. I'll check hotel security footage to see if I can catch whoever dropped it."

"Out," she responded.

"What's out?" Cooper asked, stepping out of the bathroom wearing only a towel cinched at his waist. The vanity lights cast a glow around his dark silhouette, and a few drops of water sparkled on his carved shoulders. As Evan's eyes adjusted to the sudden influx of light, she became aware that she was staring at his near-perfect figure.

Evan straightened her back and held up the flash drive. "You are, now," she replied. "This was on the floor next to your door." She let her eyes wander for the appropriate few seconds and continued. "It may be the instructions. We should see what's on here."

Cooper rolled his eyes. "I was hoping we could wait the business until later."

Evan swallowed hard, grateful that the dim lighting was camouflaging the blush she felt in her cheeks. Cooper approached, and she decided to close the gap with a few steps of her own. Before he could say anything else, she reached her arms around his neck and kissed him.

Her heart slammed in her chest. It was a dangerous play, but she had to make it before he took control of the situation.

His hands surrounded her and began a desperate search for the zipper on her dress. *It's working.* She started a trail of kisses leading down his neck, as his hands continued their hunt over her back.

"Where is your zipper?" he asked.

She pushed him back a few inches. "Oh, Michael, I can't do this." She made sure he could hear the longing in her breathless voice. He didn't need to know that the longing wasn't for him.

He pulled her body back against his. "Yes, you can," he said. "But you're going to have to show me where your bloody zipper is."

Evan eased back out of his arms. "I can't. You're upset about Nastya." She placed her hands on his bare chest, pressing the flash drive against his skin. "I am, too. And the only way we can stop this beast from hurting anyone else is if we can catch him."

Cooper took hold of her wrists and held them against his body until she could feel his heartbeat. "I need you," he insisted.

Evan let a slight curve form in the corners of her lips. "Be reasonable, Michael."

"I don't want to be reasonable."

She took a deep breath and inched back a little more. "Then I have to be reasonable for both of us. Your blackmailer, or whatever we're calling him today, is already a step ahead of us. We need to see what's on this drive right away."

"It's five-thirty in the morning. He cannot possibly expect me to be up at this hour." His hands slid up to her shoulders, and he started to pull her closer.

She resisted. She didn't expect him to be quite so demanding, but she was determined. "Darling," she said, tilting her head for effect. "When this mess is over, we will have plenty of time for pleasure."

He dropped his chin and let his eyes beg.

"You can't use those big puppy-dog eyes on me," she said. "We have to keep a professional relationship until I have rescued you from the big bad wolf. I have a reputation to maintain."

Cooper seemed sincerely disappointed. "If we both survive this, I'm going to hire you to work as my *very* personal assistant. Then we'll see what kind of reputation you have."

"Go get dressed. I'll put myself together and see if I can wake my contact at the British government." She reached up and kissed his cheek. "Hurry," she said, giving his backside a firm slap.

"Watch out," he said over his shoulder. "Or your reputation is going to include a charge of sexual harassment." As he retreated to the bedroom, he let his towel slip enough to flash a bit of cheek her direction.

"What was that?" Kirk asked Evan. "And I don't mean his butt."

She laughed under her breath. "He has to trust me, Red," she whispered. She made a loop around the room, turning on all the lights as she finger-brushed her hair. "If I didn't make it look good, he would suspect something. I had to behave like any other woman in my position."

"Do your best to stay in the *upright* position," he said.

"What do you have for me?"

Kirk tapped at his keyboard. "I got into the hotel security feed with no trouble, but I couldn't find anything suspicious. I have two hotel workers down his hall between midnight and five, but I couldn't see anything that would indicate either of them slipped the drive under his door. I'm running both individuals through FRS as we speak."

"What about the drive?" she asked.

"It doesn't contain any video this time. Only some instructions on where to retrieve a package. Looks like you're going to the park."

Evan sighed. "Easy enough. Is that it?"

Kirk clicked his tongue. "Not exactly. The blackmailer says he intends to dump Nastya's body in a manner and place that will suggest Cooper had a hand in her murder."

"More threats?" she asked.

"Looks like."

"Okay, let me know if anything pops," she whispered.

"You too," he replied.

Evan dropped the jump drive beside the computer on the desk, grabbed her purse and skipped into the bathroom and relieved her very insistent bladder. That task completed, she pulled her comb through her hair and then twisted it back into a bun, securing it with the half-dozen bobby pins from the bottom of her clutch. She used a tissue to dab around her eyes for a clean, subtle look, and then she dragged her tube of nude lipstick across her mouth. A spritz of tangerine and gardenia at her ankles and wrists made her feel as though she could deal with the rest of the morning. *Good enough; now to work.*

She went back into the parlor and pulled her gray jacket on and slipped back into her red heels. Cooper joined her a few seconds later, fully dressed in a light cocoa-colored sports suit with a pale blue shirt. The exact color of his eyes, she noticed. He wore a lemon-yellow tie with blue and beige diagonal stripes. His pocket square was solid yellow, and his cufflinks and tie bar were platinum.

Wow, was all that she could manage. She suddenly realized that she had no idea whether she said that aloud or just thought it.

By his reaction, she probably shouted it. *Oh well, there goes cool and calculated.* "You look nice," she said, hoping to downplay the situation.

Cooper shot her a serious glance. "Let's get to business. I want to get this taken care of and get you out of that dull dress."

Evan raised her brow. "You liked it last night," she said, trying to extend the tease just a little longer.

Cooper all but ignored her. "Let's see what this one says." He plugged the drive into the port and clicked on the pop-up.

Mr. Cooper,

Take Ms. Taylor with you when you leave this morning and proceed directly to Jubilee Gardens. Be there by 9:00 AM. Go to the carousel booth and ask for two tickets. Take a ride, sitting in the blue swan bench seat. Beneath it, you will find a small tote bag with a package inside. When the ride stops, carry the bag and package with you and get into line at the London Eye. Check the bag at the ticket counter and leave it there when you board your capsule. When you pick it up after your ride in the Eye, you will find orders for its final placement.

Follow these instructions to the letter. Do not miss a step. Do not take any side-trips or detours. Do not allow Ms. Taylor out of your sight.

If you follow my direction, I will contact you again with the location of Nastya Alenko's body. If you take any liberties with my orders, you will find yourself arrested for her murder.

Cooper stared at the note with cold eyes.

"Are you all right?" Evan asked, reading the note twice.

He pressed his lips into a tight line. "No, I would have to say that I am definitely not all right."

Evan placed her hands on his shoulders. "Let me call my friend. He has contacts at the police."

"No, Eve." Cooper used his foot to push out the chair beside him. "Sit down."

Evan took a seat and held his right hand in both of hers. "My friends," she started.

Cooper shook his head. "They couldn't do anything. We can't risk it. I can't risk it. He's already murdered Nastya. He fully intends to murder you, too."

"I can take care of myself," she said.

"No. Nastya died simply for knowing me," he started.

Evan interrupted. "That's not true, Michael. Perhaps you don't know what she was involved in, but I do."

Cooper pulled his hand from hers. "What do you mean?"

"Nastya was working for a man, actually a woman, but that's not important. She was collecting information about powerful people for someone. That's how I came to find you."

"Nastya would never tell secrets about me to anyone. We've been friends since we were children."

"I know that," Evan responded. "But she was selling secrets about other men. Very powerful men who worked in very powerful places. I tried to help your friend Benito."

"Yes, and they killed him. They know who you are. They will use you to manipulate me." Cooper rested his hand against her cheek. "I can't let him touch you."

Evan turned her head so that her lips were in his palm. She kissed his hand softly, letting her lips part and linger over his fingertips. "Please let me help you," she whispered. "I don't want anyone to hurt you simply because you left me behind. I want to be at your side, no matter what happens."

He pulled her face to his and kissed her again. "You are brave, Eve Taylor. I give you that."

"I will want more from you than a compliment," she said, raising her eyes to meet his in the most beguiling expression she could manufacture. "When this is over, I will want so much more than that."

Cooper finally smiled. "What do we do, then?"

She looked around the room. "We have a little while before we have to go. Order breakfast for us, and I'll make a quick phone call. Don't worry, either. I won't say anything that could be overheard or misconstrued. My friend is quite discreet."

She rose to her feet slowly, allowing his gaze to follow her curves. She bent at the waist to kiss his forehead. "Order whatever you like for breakfast."

"I already tried that, and you said, 'no.'"

She shot him a scolding look as she walked to her purse. "Behave."

"What do you want for breakfast?" he asked, sighing as he picked up the hotel phone.

"I don't suppose y'all have biscuits and gravy here?" she asked.

He knit his brows and shook his head. "That sounds horrible."

"Oh yeah, I forget you call cookies *biscuits*. That does sound disgusting. I guess that would depend on what kind of gravy it is, though. My Aunt Deirdre makes chocolate gravy, and I think that would be okay on cookies."

Cooper looked at her as if she'd lost her mind. "And they say Scottish food is dreadful."

"Jus' get me a pastry or something like that. And coffee. The real stuff—black."

Cooper laughed at her casual demeanor as she picked up her phone and began punching buttons.

"Hi, this is Eve Taylor. May I please speak with Barbara?" she said when Hedge picked up the line.

"We have half of MI6 on the way to Jubilee Gardens now. We have teams checking all the piers and bridges in the area, as well as traffic cams, too," he said, not bothering with pleasantries.

"Hi, Barb, this is Evie. It's so great to talk to you, are you busy?" she said in a sing-song drawl.

"Listen," Hedge continued. "Follow the directions to the letter. Try not to call any attention to yourself."

"I know," she interrupted. "I wish I wasn't always so busy when I come to London. I'm actually with a client. His name is Michael Cooper."

"We will have the situation handled by the time you get there."

"Oh, you've heard of him," she said. She shot a broad grin to Cooper as he was ordering their breakfast. "Yes, he is handsome."

Hedge's voice took a sharp tone. "Listen to me. Do your best to keep out of the open spaces as much as you can. We don't know what to expect, and there's only so much we can do."

"I know, Barb. I think he's going to take me to the London Eye this morning, and later he has a meeting with that energy summit thingy." She nodded to Cooper. "Who all is going to be at that meeting? Do you know?"

Hedge continued, getting frustrated with her exaggerated accent. "Try to get close enough to the package for Kirk to scan it. We should be able to tell if it's an IED or what. Also, if you can get us a look at the next set of instructions, that would be good, too."

"Oh sure, Barb. I just figured they wouldn't let me in the meeting, so maybe you and I could go get some tea and biscuits or something?" Evan pushed out a giggle. "Maybe you have a better idea."

Hedge chuffed. "If it is an explosive, we can always deactivate it with a Sonic EMP from the dress. You were able to figure out that little trick. I'm a little worried you might knock out the power on the Eye. I don't want our target to get spooked and start improvising."

"I know; me too," she said.

Hedge paused. "Was that for Barb or me?" he asked, sounding a little confused.

"You are so funny," she answered. "We have just got to make this work so we can get together later," she said. She wished she could say more. She ached to tell Hedge everything she was feeling right now.

"I know," he replied. "Be safe. I mean it."

"It was good to talk to you, too," she said. "I hope I see you later." She clicked the phone off and turned to Cooper. "All done."

"I thought you were going to talk to your friend at Scotland Yard or something." He pinched the bridge of his nose as if he had a headache.

"I did. Barb works for Scotland Yard. Didn't you hear me talking to her?" Evan dropped her phone into her purse. She slinked across the room to sit next to him, letting her knees bump his.

"Yes, I heard. It sounds like you two will have a lovely afternoon together." He patted her knee and gave her a distinct look of pity.

Evan smoothed her palms over her jacket and skirt. "Would you like to know what Barbara said?"

"Why not?"

Evan reached out and pretended to straighten Cooper's perfect yellow tie. "She said that she'd send out extra officers to the garden, and they will make sure, starting now, that all cameras are in good working order and that they will be recording every square inch of the park."

"She did not," he said, one eyebrow raised into a sharp arch.

"And she said that you should do as you're told, but don't do anything you wouldn't typically do."

"Like what?"

She watched his eyes as they studied her face and neck. As his gaze drifted downward, she took a deep breath and then used her index finger to raise his face back to hers. "Like, if you were going to take me for a spin in the London Eye, how would you do it?"

"Certainly not first thing in the morning," he replied. "I would take you at night so that you could appreciate the city lights."

"That sounds lovely," she said. "Very romantic."

"It would be. And I would reserve a private capsule," he said. "With champagne."

"Mmm," she said, easing closer to him. "Do they only do that at night?"

Cooper laughed. "No," he said and paused. "Have you never been up in the Eye?"

"Nope."

He laughed. "Then champagne it is. For another fifty Euros, we'll ride alone."

"I definitely think we should have a private capsule, or whatever it's called." She bit her lower lip, and Cooper seemed to notice.

"Even the private rides come with an obligatory host, but I could even get a more private capsule than that," he said. "Money is influence."

"Hmm, maybe we should keep the host, for now. I wouldn't want this guy to think we were pulling something." She shifted her shoulders back and forth and slid her ankle over his leg. "But when this is over, maybe a *completely* private capsule."

He was about to reach for her hand, but a knock at the door stopped him.

"Room service."

Evan shifted to the other chair, and Cooper answered the door. The waiter rolled in the tray of fruit, pastries, and thin-sliced ham. He positioned the cart between the couple and poured out two cups of steaming black coffee.

"Sugar? Milk?" the young man asked.

"No, thank you," Evan answered.

The man walked around the table and picked up the napkin from Evan's antique white plate. "May I?" he asked, bowing his head as he flicked the folded linen open.

"Yes, please," Evan said as she inched back in her chair, allowing the waiter to slide the napkin across her lap. He positioned the napkin to cover the extra magazine of ammunition he dropped into her left hand.

"Ma'am," he said, backing away with a bow.

"Thank you," she said. "I jus' love London," she added with a sigh. As soon as she had the magazine tucked into the holster on her thigh, she reached across the tray for Cooper's hand. "Thank you for sharing this with me."

The waiter bowed again and excused himself from the room.

"You do have a way, don't you?" Cooper asked.

Evan sipped her coffee. "My daddy used to say that I could charm the scales off a rattler," she said. She let her lashes rise and fall.

"I have no idea what that means." Cooper laughed. "I like it, though."

He drank his coffee and trudged through his breakfast, getting slower the later it got. Evan ate a wedge of melon wrapped in the prosciutto, and then devoured a croissant with butter. She gulped at her cooling coffee and then poured another cup.

"What's wrong, Michael? Don't you like it?" she asked.

"It's delicious," he said. He picked up his napkin and threw it onto his plate. "But I'm starting to get the feeling this is my last meal."

Evan shook her head and made her way to his side. She dropped to her knees and rested her head on his arm. "Don't say things like that."

He took a deep breath and held it for several seconds before letting it out. "I know you said that Nastya was involved with some bad things. I don't know what to think about that."

"It's true, Michael."

"Maybe it is, but I can't help but think that if I hadn't been seeing her, she would still be alive."

Evan shook her head. "You can't blame yourself. She made choices, too. It wasn't her fault that she was killed, either. I'm not saying that. It's this shadow we're chasing. He's the one to blame."

Cooper looked at her and swallowed hard. He stared directly into her eyes for several seconds without speaking. He moved his thumb to rest on her bottom lip. Evan wished Hedge were here. She wished for a whisper from Kirk. Anything.

Cooper seemed to sense that her thoughts were clouding. "We all make choices. You're correct in that. We all have feelings for people. Sometimes they see them, and sometimes they don't.

Sometimes they return those feelings, and sometimes they don't."

"Michael, for now, let's focus on your situation."

"Like you and your assistant," Cooper said. He snapped his fingers. "Not Ms. Fleming, the gentleman, the one in Barcelona."

"What about Heathcliff?" she asked. She was surprised that Cooper even remembered Teo, and almost startled that he brought him up at all.

"He's certainly got feelings for you, Eve."

She scoffed. "No matter what you might think, my darling Michael, not every man walking the planet has feelings for me."

He shook his head. "As far as I can see, all the ones that have met you do."

"Don't be silly," she chided.

"I'm not, not with Heathcliff." He raised his eyebrows. "His name is Heathcliff? Really?"

"And don't make fun of his name, just because you have the most handsome name there is." She tilted her face away for a second. "Heathcliff is a very nice man."

Cooper laughed. "He's a very nice man who would like to rub your bare back with coconut oil on a secluded beach somewhere."

"You shouldn't say things like that." It was true, but she didn't want him to say it.

"I saw the way he looked at you. I know that look." He pointed to his face. "It's the same look I'm giving you now."

Evan realized that was exactly how Michael was looking at her. "Don't."

"I feel bad for the man," Cooper added. "He's going to be hurt because of it."

Evan leaned back a few inches and studied Cooper's expression. One moment it was filled with lust and want, the next with sadness. As it waxed from one look to the other, his eyes seemed to flash with something else.

"What do you mean?" she asked, trying to keep her innocent air.

"I mean," he said with a laugh. "That if anyone is going to be massaging oil into your bare skin, it's going to be me."

He pulled her into his lap and covered her lips with his. After only a few seconds, though, his eyes flashed on his gold watch face. He stopped mid-kiss and eased back in his chair.

"What is it?" she asked.

"It's time. We have to go."

Evan felt his hand squeeze her hip as she picked herself up from his lap. "Hey, now," she warned. "My daddy always told me not to go out with men whose hands wandered."

"I have a feeling your father wouldn't care for me very much." Cooper stood in front of the hall mirror for a second and adjusted his tie.

Evan followed him to the door and put her purse on the small console table under the mirror. She positioned herself behind Cooper and slid her arms under his and around his chest, hugging tightly. "My daddy likes whoever I like," she said. She leaned her head against his shoulder. "Don't worry. I'm right behind you."

Cooper smiled at her reflection in the mirror and checked his watch again. "Are you sure you are ready for this?"

"You don't think I can take care of myself?"

Cooper turned around, still in her arms, and faced her. He held her tight and kissed her again. "I think you probably can when it comes to your business. It's obvious you are very good at what you do." He kissed her again. "I know you want this to stay a professional relationship. You don't want anyone to get hurt. I understand that."

"Michael, all we have to do is figure out who he is. When we have that information, we can stop him." She stared into his icy blue eyes. "I'm good at getting information."

Cooper opened the door to the hall and peered out in both directions.

Evan nudged his arm. "Don't look conspicuous," she said.

Cooper raised his eyebrows. "You're the one wearing the same dress as last night."

Evan glared at him as she passed him through the doorway. She waited as he pulled the latch closed.

"Evan," Kirk whispered. His voice gave her a start. "We are making a little progress on the video. We should have the location where it was shot soon."

"Hmm," Evan hummed her acknowledgment.

"Ramos will be right with you. Hedge and I are on our way to the gardens."

"Okay," she said, taking Cooper's arm. "Let's go."

Cooper gestured to the elevator. "I'll call over to the Eye and make our reservation."

"Hang on a sec," she said. "Before you start your call, make sure we're alone in the lift."

"Good advice," Cooper said.

Evan could hear Kirk tapping his keys. "I don't read any signals in the car," he said.

Evan nodded to Cooper as the doors slid closed. "You're good to go," she said.

He pulled out his phone, looked at it, and then dropped it back into his breast pocket. "I'll call from the car," he said. He pulled her into his arms and kissed her again. "While I'm doing that, you can fix your lipstick."

CHAPTER THIRTY-SEVEN

Cooper made arrangements for their private ride at the London Eye as Evan texted her "assistant" about her plans for the day.

Kirk informed her that they had a general location for where Nastya had been murdered and that MI6 was on the way there to confirm the data.

Evan wondered aloud if any of the attendees of the energy summit had plans to be in Jubilee Gardens for the day.

Cooper, still on the phone with the London Eye people, shrugged and whispered, "I don't know about that. Shall I look into that?"

She shook her head. "I'll see what I can find out."

"I don't see anyone from the summit," Kirk murmured. "Let me run through the agendas for government—this could be something."

Evan hummed as though she was waiting for a reply text.

Kirk continued. "I have the US ambassador's wife and kids scheduled to be sight-seeing today. They have stops at the Garden and the Eye on their itinerary."

"What's our time frame?" she asked both Kirk and Cooper.

Cooper shot a glance down at this watch. "We're good." He smiled as he finished his reservation.

"It looks to me as though the ambassador's wife is en route as we speak," Kirk said. "I'll alert our friends to keep her in sight at all times. Hedge says he's going to call the ambassador and see if he still denies being contacted."

A knot formed in Evan's stomach and tightened the closer they got to the park. This whole set-up was giving her fits. Something wasn't right, but she couldn't put her finger on what specifically bothered her.

As they crossed the bridge north of the Eye, she began to tumble the last few weeks in her brain. Someone was gathering dirt on as many influential world leaders as possible, but for what reason? Blackmail for money is always the easy answer, but this person, or persons, had a great deal of cash and jewels at their disposal already.

What kind of person has millions and still wants more? She sighed and almost laughed. Every millionaire she'd ever met pretty much fell into that category. She stared at Cooper as he now worked on his tablet. *He has billions, and here he sits working in his car between traffic signals.*

She looked out the window at the age-old city. London was a mix of old and new. As they parked the car, she could see between the spokes of the Eye across the Thames to Big Ben. It was like looking through a modern frame at an antique postcard. And someone in this town was determined to cause hurt and destroy lives.

Cooper took her hand and led her away from his sports car toward the carousel. "This way," he said.

Evan noticed a look of anxiety and distraction in his eyes. He stared at everyone they passed on the walkway.

"What's wrong?" Evan asked. "Do you recognize someone?"

"No," he replied. "But don't you feel as though someone is watching us?" He wrapped his arm around her waist and cinched her to his hip.

"Don't worry," she answered. "There is always security in the park; maybe Barb was able to get it beefed up a bit."

"I suppose."

"But if you do see someone you recognize, don't point them out, Jus' tell me where they are and what they are wearing." Evan looked up into his eyes and smiled. "I am very good at being nonchalant."

Cooper grinned, but the expression wasn't convincing. "I feel like a pawn in someone's twisted game."

"That's what you are for now," she said. "I'm doing my best to get you out from under this guy's thumb."

"Hmmph," he snorted. "I don't want him using me to hurt other people."

"I know."

They reached the carousel just as the manager opened the ride. "Welcome," the chubby dark-haired man said, spreading his arms out wide. "What a beautiful morning it is."

Evan smiled. She wondered if the man was the regular manager or an agency asset. "It's a lovely day."

Cooper held up two fingers. "I'd like to take my lady fair on a trip around your beautiful carousel."

"Of course, of course," the man replied and handed Cooper a receipt for two fares. "Enjoy."

Cooper gave him some money and nodded. "Keep the change."

The man looked at the cash and raised his brows as high as his round forehead would allow. "Too much. You gave me too much."

"No mistake, friend. I'd like you to start the ride with only the two of us. I want to purchase every place on the ride."

"Oh, I see. Very romantic," he winked at Evan. "This happens sometimes—always the man has something important to say."

Evan grinned and dipped her chin. "Thank you."

Cooper gave him a salute and walked Evan up the steps to the carousel platform. They walked between the large painted horses, around to the far side, where they found the blue swan bench seat.

"Are you ready?" the manager called out.

"Yes, whenever you are," Cooper responded.

As they sat down, Evan couldn't help but stare into Cooper's eyes. "Are you ready?" she asked as the ride began to turn.

"I don't have a choice, do I?" he answered.

"Did you see if the package was under the seat?"

"No. I didn't look. I want to take one turn without thinking about what's under us." His lips became tight, and his breathing quickened.

Evan nodded and put her head on his shoulder. "It will be okay, Michael."

"It must."

"You trust me, don't you?" she asked.

"I trust you," he slid his fingers under her chin and raised her face to his. "But whoever is doing this—didn't even make any demands on me until after he murdered Nastya. I don't trust him to keep his word."

Evan nodded. "I won't let it come to that." She leaned up slightly and kissed him.

As his lips left hers, she thought about what he had said. There were no demands on Cooper until *after* Nastya was dead. She wasn't ransomed. She was a message. That was what had been bothering her.

Evan inhaled a deep breath and waited for the carousel to take them out of view of the ticket man. "Do you want to look, or shall I?" she asked.

"I'll look," he said.

Cooper held his breath as though he were diving under water. He bent over; and in another second, he pulled out the small black nylon tote bag and set it between them on the seat.

In silence, they made another pass by the ticket booth. A line of children and parents was forming at the counter. All Evan could think about was what damage a bomb could do in this park. Her heart pounded in her ears.

"Did you say something?" she asked Cooper, trying to focus on what was actually happening and not her imagination.

"I didn't say anything," he answered.

"I did," Kirk buzzed in her ear. "You okay?"

"Mmm," she responded quietly.

"We just got the call from MI6. Looks like they found the warehouse and Nastya's body. They'll collect the evidence and keep us in the loop."

Evan sighed. "When shall we look inside and see what we're sitting next to?" she asked Cooper.

He draped his arm over the back of the seat and rested his hand on her shoulder. "We shouldn't wait too long. Our ride will be over soon."

Evan carefully pulled back the side of the bag. Inside was a small package, about the size of a toaster, wrapped in brown shipping paper. It was completely encased in clear plastic packing tape. She hoped that somehow Kirk was getting some kind of reading from it.

"It looks ominous," Cooper said. "What do you think is inside?"

"I have no idea. Do you see any markings or anything?"

Cooper looked all the way around the package, carefully replacing it in the bag before they passed the ticket booth again. "I can't find anything on it. I don't think I should shake it."

"No, don't shake it," she said. "That's a hundred bad ideas in one."

He laughed at her expression. "You say the funniest things."

As they passed the booth again, Evan noticed the line of people now intently watched them go by. "That's not awkward at all," she said, sarcasm dripping from every word.

"They're expecting me to propose to you, I think." He gestured to the package. "Maybe I put this here to surprise you. Don't you think that's what they're waiting for?"

Evan shrugged. The idea never occurred to her that the people in the line were waiting for anything more than a turn on the carousel.

"I think we should do it," he said. As they rounded to the side of the line, Cooper got out of his seat and knelt before her on the platform. He pulled off the small diamond ring from his pinky finger and held it out to her.

"What are you doing?" she asked, genuinely admiring his intuition.

Cooper waited until they were right in front of the line before he said, "Evelyn Dianne Taylor, will you do me the honor of becoming my wife?"

Evan wiped an invisible tear from her eye and nodded. "Yes, I will," she said, and then pulled him to her in a long kiss.

Applause and cheers from the crowd in the ticket line followed, and the carousel slowed to a stop.

As Evan and Cooper exited the ride, a makeshift reception line formed. Evan slipped the tote bag over her arm, and the couple was greeted with cheers and congratulations from everyone in the line. An older woman even kissed Cooper on his cheek.

"That's for good luck and many children," she said with a wink.

At the end of the line stood the manager. "Very good, my friend. She said *yes*, I see."

Cooper shook his hand. "Yes, thank you very much."

As they cleared the crowd with the package, Evan slipped the diamond off her finger to return it to Cooper. "That's the first time anyone's ever proposed to me. You did a lovely job."

Cooper shook his head. "Put it back on," he said. "Tonight, when this is all over, then you can decide whether to give it back to me."

Evan slid it back into place on her finger. "What do you mean?"

"Maybe you'll decide I wasn't play acting."

She bit her bottom lip. Maybe her plan to win his complete trust was working—maybe too well.

"You shouldn't toy like that with a woman's heart," she said.

"We'll see," he said. "Let's survive the day, shall we?"

"Let's."

"Evan, stop where you are," Kirk said loudly in her ear. "Stop now."

Evan froze in place.

"What's wrong?" Cooper asked. "Are you all right?"

"The package you're carrying contains a bomb. It's small, but it just armed. Do you read me?" Kirk said plainly.

"Yes," she answered both of them. "I'm fine." She looked at Cooper. "I'm a little dizzy all of a sudden. Maybe from the carousel, and then walking in sight of the river. Can we rest for a second?"

Cooper knit his brow. He leaned down to whisper in her ear. "Only for a second, I don't want anyone to get suspicious. I don't want anyone to think we're not following directions."

"I know, Michael. Jus' give me a second. I'll be okay." She placed the back of her hand against her forehead. "I need to let my eyes adjust."

Cooper nodded and rubbed her back. "Breathe, love. Breathe."

Kirk began again. "The signal just popped up, and I don't have time to do much analysis. I hate to do this, but can you stand a little hiccup?"

Evan knew what that meant. Setting off the Sonic Electromagnetic Pulse in her dress caused a tight squeeze around her middle and felt somewhat like a giant hiccup. The pulse would also zap any electronic devices within a few yards of her.

"Yeah," she said, inhaling deeply. "I think I need to catch my breath. I hate to feel so disconnected." Evan hoped Kirk got her message.

"We won't lose contact. The shoes should reboot you right away. You'll be fine." Kirk's voice reassured her.

"Yes, just a second more," Evan said drawing another deep breath.

Cooper nodded and held her hand. "I'm here, Eve."

"I don't mean to rush you, but the ambassador's wife is just a few meters behind you. You need to activate the SEMP now," Kirk said.

"Now!" she heard Hedge's voice yell over Kirk's.

She raised her hand to her chest and discreetly pinched at the notch in the corset between her breasts. As the contacts touched, she felt the whole dress compress around her. Though she wasn't dizzy before, she certainly was now.

Cooper blinked and scanned the area around them. "Did you feel that?" he asked.

"What?" Evan stood up straight to catch her breath.

"I don't know," Cooper said and shrugged. "It almost felt like a tremor. Just a slight one. You didn't feel it?"

"I'm still dizzy from the carousel," she said, laughing.

Evan heard a crackle in her ear. The SEMP had worked. She didn't have to wonder if it deactivated the electronics nearby, because suddenly everyone around them had lost the use of their cell phones. Wherever they turned, they could hear people cursing at their phones.

"Feeling better?" he asked her.

"It's deactivated," Kirk whispered. "Good job."

"I think so," she said. "Let's walk in the shade of the trees for as long as we can, though, okay?" Though the SEMP knocked out the bomb and the other devices around her, it would do nothing to a pistol or sniper rifle, and she didn't want either of them to be anyone's easy target.

She casually turned to look around them and saw two men approach the ambassador's wife and children. She had never seen the woman before, but with her training, she found the operatives' actions obvious. They directed the woman and children into a black government sedan and drove them safely away.

Over Cooper's shoulder, she could see Teo leaning against a car in the parking lot. He gave her a boy-scout salute and blew her a kiss.

She turned to face Cooper and fixed a smile on her pink lips. "Let's get this show on the road."

Cooper squeezed her hand. "The things you say."

Evan leaned against his arm, wrapped around the now-benign explosives. "I guess my mind gets a little bit silly when I'm scared. My daddy says it's my defense mechanism."

Cooper leaned down and kissed her forehead. "It seems I'll be meeting your father soon, that is if you decide to keep the ring."

Evan wrinkled her nose with a coy smile. "He's tough, but I have him wrapped around my little finger," she said.

The idea of her father brightened her thoughts. She was relieved that the bomb was diffused. After a half-hour long trip around the Eye, Kirk would have a few more clues about who was behind this plot. And if she needed help, she could rely on Teo to back her up.

They reached the London Eye ticket pavilion without incident, and Cooper stepped up to the counter marked *Priority*

Guests.

"Michael Cooper, I have a reservation," he announced.

"Yes, Mr. Cooper," the young woman behind the counter said. "Our computers went down a few minutes ago, but I had already reviewed your information."

Cooper frowned. "Your computers are down? How do you operate the Eye?"

"Don't worry, Mr. Cooper," she said politely. "Only the ticketing computer went down, and it's back now. Everything else was fine. It appears it suffered a mild power surge. I assure you, we wouldn't run the Eye if it weren't completely safe."

Evan nodded. "It's fine, Michael."

The woman gestured to a man in a gray tweed vest and navy bow tie. "August will be your host this morning. I hope you will find everything to your satisfaction, Mr. Cooper."

August took a step toward the couple. "If you will follow me," he said.

Evan tugged on Cooper's jacket. "Honey, why don't we leave the bag down here. I'd hate for your mother's gift to get broken."

The young woman nodded. "Of course, I can check your bag, and you can retrieve it when your ride is complete."

Cooper handed the tote bag to the woman, who immediately placed it behind the counter. She noticed that he was studying where she put it.

"It will be perfectly safe with me," she said.

"Thank you," he replied.

They followed August into the big glass capsule and took a seat on a bench on the far end. August secured the door and stepped to the small bar area on one side. "Would you prefer your champagne right away, or would you like to wait until you reach the top?" he asked.

Cooper shrugged. "How about a glass for now and another when we reach the top? This is a celebration, August. This beautiful creature has just agreed to marry me."

"Congratulations, sir," he said. "And best wishes to you both."

"Thank you," Evan said.

Cooper took her hand and stared out at the river as the gondola began to rise.

Evan patted his knee as August delivered their champagne flutes.

"Michael, your champagne," she whispered when he didn't turn right away.

"Oh, thank you, August," he said. His tone sounded polite but detached.

Evan took her glass and thanked the host.

"I'll leave you to your privacy," August said. "I'll be at hand if you need me."

"Thank you," Evan said. She watched him return to his station and turned back to see Cooper already sipping at his glass.

"Okay," she said softly. "I thought you might have wanted to make a toast or something."

Cooper shook off his distraction and turned toward her with a smile. "Sorry about that. How rude of me." He lifted his glass an inch. "I've had too much time alone. Here's to no longer being alone."

They let their flutes chime together and then sipped simultaneously as the car rose closer to its apex. Evan watched Michael's eyes study her face. She hated the idea of lying to him this way. Though deception was almost always a part of gaining an asset, the fact that he had actually proposed made her a little woozy.

Seeing a handsome billionaire on his knees in front of her with a diamond ring was nothing she ever expected from her life. *Even if it wasn't real, he was just so dang good. This would not end well.*

"This is it, isn't it?" Cooper asked in a whisper. "He has us, doesn't he?"

Evan recognized the desperation in his eyes. She set her glass down on the small side table and took his from him, placing it beside hers. She leaned close to his face. "Don't give in now," she said. "We can beat him."

"How?" he asked. "We haven't done a single thing to thwart his plan so far. We're just running around, carrying out his every order."

"Don't be so sure about that, Michael." She placed her hand against his cheek. "I have my methods. My staff is working on this situation. Just because we don't see anything, doesn't mean nothing is happening."

"You're so trusting," he said. He pulled her face to his and smothered her with a heated kiss that sizzled all the way down her spine.

As he pulled away, he stared into her eyes and grinned. "I wish we had left August down on the pier," he whispered.

"You're a very bad man," she said.

He moved his lips to her ear and began to kiss her neck. "You have no idea, love," he said.

Her thoughts scattered a million different directions as she felt his hands around her waist. Suddenly her brain snapped back to the job at hand. She realized that several minutes had passed, and she was eager to hear from Kirk.

"Simmer down," she said, shifting just out of reach of his lips. "We don't want to embarrass our host."

She reached for her purse. "I need to message my assistant again and see if he's made progress." When she pulled out her phone, it was dead. The SEMP had knocked it out. "Great. My phone is dead. I must have forgotten to charge it."

Cooper pulled out his phone and punched the button on the side. The face lit up. "Use mine. It's fully charged."

Evan looked at it and shook her head. *He must have a surge protector built into his phone or the case. Billionaires.* She shook her head and handed it back. "I suppose it can wait until we get down." She smiled and dropped the phone back into his hand.

"We have the ambassador's family in a safe house," she heard Kirk's voice in her ear. *Thank heavens.*

"Michael, let's finish our champagne and get ready for our view from the top," she said.

"Good idea," he replied.

Kirk said. "Ramos is going through their car as we speak. Hedge and I are on our way to the warehouse where they found Nastya."

"Very good," she said. She looped her arm around Cooper's and looked out over the river. "The city is gorgeous from up here." She gazed across the river at the House of Parliament. The carved stone pediments and spires seemed to go on forever.

"Let's save Big Ben for the climax," Cooper said. He gestured to the carousel. "Just a few minutes ago we were spinning in circles down there."

She looked down at the brightly colored roof over the carousel. "What now?" she asked, hoping each of her men would answer.

Kirk responded first. "It looks like our man planned to set up Cooper for Nastya's murder. They found a dozen perfect fingerprints on site that are a match to your fiancé."

Evan laughed nervously. That feeling was back.

"Eve, look over here at how quickly the car park has filled up." Cooper pointed down to the parking lot. Evan stepped closer to the glass to see if she could find Teo among the cars. It took her only a second to spot her friend half inside the long silver sedan.

"Oh my, well this is a beautiful view."

She'd barely finished her thought when a ball of orange and yellow fire exploded before her eyes and reflected on the glass, and split second later, a loud *boom* shook the capsule. She dropped her champagne flute and pressed herself against the glass.

"NOOO!" she shouted. Black smoke obscured her view, but she knew it was the silver car. Teo was gone.

"Tango, do you copy?" Kirk screamed in her ear. "Evan, answer me, are you all right."

Cooper and August rushed to the glass beside her, trying to see what had happened below.

"Teo?" she whispered, knowing that Kirk was the only person listening to her.

Kirk's voice was frantic. "Evan, there was an explosion. A

second bomb. I can't reach Ramos."

Tears flooded over her cheeks. "I saw the car explode," she sobbed. "Gone. He's gone."

"Who is gone?" Cooper asked. He reached down to the floor of the cabin where Evan had sunk in her despair. "Did you see it?" he asked.

She tried to collect her emotions, but they shattered in ragged pieces, along with her heart. She nodded and cried.

August ran back to his station and grabbed a radio. "Capsule one, we are safe for now. Is there any disruption in operation?"

A voice crackled through the static. "Waiting official direction. Keep passengers calm. Will report momentarily."

Evan continued to cry as she listened for Kirk's voice. "Evan, I have confirmation. Ramos is gone. We had a cell net over the whole area, though. If it was detonated by phone, we should have a location soon."

"How? Why?" she poured into a sob.

"Hedge and I are heading to you right now. You're not alone up there. August is ours. And we may be there by the time you get back down. Sit tight."

Cooper held her in his arms as she wept and shivered. She struggled to remain professional, but crying was an acceptable part of her cover. She didn't care, anyway. *An explosion shouldn't get to me like this. But it's Teo.* She could still see him blowing that last kiss.

"You're in shock," Cooper said. "That's normal when you witness something like this." He took off his jacket and wrapped it around her shoulders. "This will help."

She nodded and sat down again. The capsule continued its journey. They had passed the halfway apex and begun their descent.

Cooper picked up the champagne flute from the floor and hailed August. "Maybe this seems out of place, considering the situation, but I think it might help Eve to have another glass of champagne."

"Yes, Mr. Cooper," he answered and went back to pour another flute. "Why don't I just bring you the bottle?"

Cooper nodded. "That would be appreciated." He handed Evan a fresh glass. "Drink. Go ahead. You'll feel better."

Evan gulped too much at first, and the dense bubbles filled her throat and choked her. She shook her head and handed the glass back to Cooper. She pulled his jacket close around her.

Cooper stared out over the chaos on the ground. Thick black smoke still billowed as first responders worked to snuff the flames and keep bystanders safe at the same time.

"People get hurt all around us," Cooper muttered. "We are helpless to stop it." He tipped his glass back and emptied it quickly. He spun back around and held the flute toward their host. "August, do you mind refilling me?"

Kirk's controlled voice. "Evan, the car bomb was detonated by phone, and we have a location for the signal. The phone is still on. Do you copy?"

"Mmmhmm," she said, finished with her tears for now. She knew they would return, but there was too much to do to linger in them.

"Are you okay?" Cooper asked her again.

"Yes, just shaken," she replied.

"It was like a movie, wasn't it?"

Evan shook her head. "No, not really."

Cooper twisted his lip to one side. "Really felt it, didn't you?" he asked.

Kirk hummed in her ear again. "Evan, I'm tracking the signal right now, and it's coming from you."

August filled Cooper's glass and handed it back to him. Evan tugged Cooper's sports jacket tighter around her arms. Her heart pounded hard again as she slipped her fingers into the inside breast pocket and his cell phone.

It hadn't been fried by the SEM pulse. He'd used it against them. She'd been blinded by his charm. The Faberge Egg had been just another payoff, and she had sat there and watched it all happen. He'd lied, cheated, he'd even murdered Nastya. She'd been played. Again.

"Oh, Michael," she said. She held out his phone to him. "It's you. You did this."

August turned toward Evan, ready to follow her lead.

Before she could say another word, Cooper grabbed the pistol tucked under August's vest and shot him through the back. The man blinked once and fell face down on the floor of the capsule.

"NOOO!" she screamed. She started to reach for her weapon, but Cooper was too fast. He leveled the pistol even with her heart.

"I told you that your friend was going to get hurt," Cooper said. "You didn't listen to me then, so you had better listen now."

Evan stood slowly and let his jacket fall from her shoulders. She dropped the phones and held out her hands, palms up and shrugged. "I'm listening to you, Michael. Tell me what you want."

He shook his head and gestured to August, lying dead between them. "I didn't want this. I had no intention of this happening."

"I know, Michael. I understand. This was my fault."

He nodded and shook the firearm from side to side in front of her. "You should sit down."

"I will," she said, taking a steady step away from the bench seat.

"Nastya—that wasn't what I wanted either." His collected façade seemed to be crumbling before her eyes. She could see that he was not used to facing consequences.

"I know," she said. "I know that you loved her. I know that she loved you."

"But people get hurt, see?" he said. "You need to sit down, Eve." Calm was beginning to return to his voice. Evan knew he was much more dangerous when he was in control, and she needed to wrench that control back.

"I will," she said again. "I just need to see if I can help August. I know you didn't mean to kill him. If he's still alive, you'll want me to help."

He interrupted her by firing three more rounds into August's back.

She froze in place.

"You see," he said, now matter-of-factly. "I did mean to kill him. Now sit down!"

Evan backed up to the seat again. "What can I do for you?" she asked.

Kirk was there. "Hang in there, Evan. We're almost to you."

Evan tried to remember all the functions in her dress. Cameras, microphones, body armor, SEMP. Not much use at the moment, beyond recording a confession. Her lie detector never seemed to work with him. He was just that good.

Cooper remained calm and cold. In another five minutes, the ride would be over, one way or another. "There is only one thing left for you to do," he said.

"What is that, Michael?" She kept her palms up to him.

"You're going to be my hostage. When we get back down, there will be police. We're going to walk away from all this, and I may need you to be my shield." His tone revealed no emotion.

Evan thought that she had been seducing him, all the while being suckered. He had turned her own game on her. *It had felt real. Maybe a little, anyway. Might as well play it all the way through.*

"Michael, you don't need the gun," she said. "I'll go with you wherever you want. You know how I feel about you."

Cooper hissed. "Let's see how you feel about me when I'm taking your other friends apart, piece by piece. I'll let you watch."

Evan felt a stone forming in her gut. She couldn't take it any longer. She stood again and pulled off her gray jacket, dropping it to the bench. She licked her lips and took a small step toward him. "You need me alive, Michael. If I'm dead, then so are you and I find it highly unlikely that being dead is part of your plan."

"You know nothing about my plan."

She shrugged her bare shoulders and tried sultry one more time. "You're right about that. I have no idea why a man like you—a man with everything under the sun—would want to hurt other people with bombs and blackmail. For what? Money? Power? Fame? You already have all that."

Cooper's gaze roamed her body as she slipped closer to him. She watched his eyes move up and down and let her muscles tighten and twitch accordingly, as though his stare was physically touching her. This held his attention long enough for her to get within arm's reach of him.

"Michael," she whispered, drawing his attention to her mouth.

His arm dropped an inch, and Evan knew that was her only opportunity to take him down.

She struck out like lightning, jabbing the heel of her palm into his throat and slicing the pistol from his grip with her other wrist. It fired again when it hit the floor and slid under the seat.

He stumbled back a step, but grabbed her arm and pulled her with him as he crashed into the glass shell of the capsule.

She spun around and shot her elbow up under his chin, smashing the back of his head into the glass again.

He pushed off the wall and propelled them both into the center of the capsule floor, just a few feet from August's body. He landed heavily on top of her and closed his hands around her neck.

She raised her knee to meet his groin, but he was sitting on her waist—too high for any contact. She pushed down with her legs to arch her back and flip him over her, but he was too heavy, and she couldn't get enough leverage.

"Hang on, Evan," Kirk cheered her.

She wanted to answer, but she couldn't move any air through her windpipe. She scratched at his eyes and kicked with her legs. She heard fabric rip as the stiletto heel from one of her shoes went through his pant leg. She repeated the motion and caught skin this time.

"Aaughhh!" Cooper yelled. He jumped back and grabbed his leg.

Evan tried to reach for her Springfield, but Cooper caught her hand and yanked hard, dislocating her shoulder.

Pain shot through her whole body and blinded her for several seconds. When she finally focused on Cooper, he was holding his bloody shin and grinning.

Her right arm hung limp and twisted as she pushed herself back to standing with her left.

"What are you going to do, Eve? You need me alive just as much as I need you," he said. He clamored back to his feet.

Evan weighed her options. Her right arm was useless, and her left wasn't in the right position to draw her weapon. She was afraid to get too close to Cooper now, worried that he would take her pistol and use it against her.

Cooper lunged at her. "Come over here," he said. "We're almost down."

Evan's arm burned from the marrow out. She took a deep breath and squelched out the screams in her mind. Her brain was spent. The dress had nothing left for her. Her body ached from every pore. All she had left was her shoes.

Evan worked up her fiercest growl and took two swift steps toward him. On the third step, she spun in place, turning her head quickly to spot her target. Evan plunged the heel of her right shoe into his thigh. He howled like a wild dog and clutched at his wound. A fountain of thick crimson pumped out from the hole, and he exchanged his moaning with a steady flow of curses.

"Shut up and let me help you," she said. She quickly unfastened and removed his belt, and cinched his leg as tightly as she could with only one hand. "I hit your artery. If you don't sit still, you're going to bleed out and die." She gestured to his hands. "You'd better keep pressure on that with both hands, too, if you know what's good for you."

The capsule came to a stop at the bottom of the Eye, and Hedge was the first man through the door, with his sidearm trained on Cooper's head.

"Do not tempt me, Cooper," he warned. "You have no idea how badly I want to squeeze this trigger."

"Just get me to a hospital," he moaned. His voice was

weakening.

Evan nodded. "You'd better hurry. He's already lost a lot of blood."

Two other officers grabbed Cooper and began working on his leg. A third came in to see after August.

"Dead," Hedge said. He looked up at Evan. "What about you?"

"Dislocated shoulder," she answered. "Other than that I'm fine."

Hedge sat her down on the bench and took her arm in his hands. He inched his fingers up the inside of her arm until his hand was in her armpit. "This is going to hurt."

"It's okay. Do it. I'm not going to the hospital again." She took a deep breath and focused on the men carrying Cooper out of the capsule. "I'm ready."

Hedge held tightly and pushed back on her shoulder as he cupped her shoulder blade with his other hand. Evan tried not to scream, but a sharp shriek escaped anyway. After a few seconds, her whole arm began to tingle, and she knew she would be okay. She leaned into Hedge's shoulder, aching from every cell of her body.

"It was Cooper all along," she said. "He played me—I thought I had him, but he had me."

"Shut up," Hedge barked. "He played all of us. He's going to suffer for what he did to Teo."

Hedge helped Evan back to her feet, and they walked out to where four men were securing Cooper to a stretcher.

"Cooper, it was a mistake not to tell us your plan before. You are not going to like what we do to you now," Hedge said.

"You can't do anything to me," Cooper said. "You know nothing." Without warning a bullet pierced his brain.

CHAPTER THIRTY-EIGHT

Evan climbed into the car with Hedge and Kirk. No one spoke a word as they drove back to Le Méridien and shuffled into their room.

Eleanor stood in the middle of the suite, directing two men who were packing up Teo Ramos' belongings into boxes. "Come in and sit," she said. Her tone was flat and short. She looked exhausted.

Evan's first impulse was to offer a preemptive apology, but she swallowed it before it would escape her lips. Teo would have hated an apology.

Hedge and Kirk took their positions at opposite ends of the sofa and waited for Evan to sit between them. She sunk into the center cushion and let her feet rest side by side in front of her. She didn't have the energy to even cross her legs.

"What do we know about Michael Cooper? Whom did he work for? Who took him out?" Eleanor asked.

She might as well have asked the name of Michael Cooper's favorite boy band from the nineties. Evan had no clue. She drew a breath to speak, but Hedge stopped her.

"Agent McKinnon-Grey, we are field operatives. We work from intelligence provided to us by others. This assignment has us chasing shadows and digging for our own intel. You gave us a lead, and since then we have been wading through lies and half-truths. You had half a dozen women in custody, and you're telling me that your interrogators couldn't get anything?"

Eleanor blinked. Hedge had turned the table so quickly she couldn't seem to manage a response.

Hedge continued as Evan and Kirk listened with brows raised, surprised at his audacity. "Agent Tyler has spent the last week in the hands of this nut-job. We know now that he is the one who actually murdered Nastya Alenko. He's the one who pulled the trigger and ended the woman with whom he'd had a decades-long relationship."

Eleanor held up her hand to interrupt him, but he continued. "Evan is lucky to be alive. I lost one team member. I could have easily lost two."

Eleanor huffed and took a step toward Hedge. Evan thought that it almost looked like Eleanor was stamping her feet.

"We all lost Ramos," Eleanor said. "We will all miss him. We all needed him. But he knew what kind of assignment this was. And he wasn't afraid to die."

Hedge growled. "None of us are afraid to die in the line of duty, ma'am. You know that."

Hedge called Eleanor 'ma'am.' Evan stood up, eager to cut through the tension. "I never suspected that he was our blackmailer. I certainly didn't think he could be working for someone else. None of us did. Why would a billionaire place himself in that position? We all assumed that he was a victim, not a perp."

Eleanor halted in place and took a deep breath. "That's true."

Kirk looked lost without his notebook in his lap. "If I had the chance to do a little more digging, maybe I could come up with something."

Evan nodded. "Give me tonight to go through a few things in my mind. Maybe I missed a clue."

Hedge glared at Eleanor. "Our team has suffered a blow. We're down, but we're not out. The three of us are strong. We can sift through this mess if you give us a little time."

"How much time do you need?" Eleanor asked.

"I think that depends on what your intelligence sources can provide for us."

Eleanor glanced down at Kirk. "What do you need?"

"I need to run through all of Evan's conversations with Cooper. The dress should have the audio and video in storage. I can flag a few things to look for, and then send them all through my data scanner." Kirk sounded excited. "I should be able to glean anything useful by morning."

Eleanor looked at Evan and nodded. "What do you need?"

Evan wanted to shrug, but her shoulder still ached. "I'll work through the data files with Kirk."

Eleanor nodded and turned toward Hedge. "And you?"

"I need a little latitude. The sniper could have just as easily taken out Evan or myself. They knew they had one shot, and we have to assume they used it to their greatest advantage." He paused and glanced at Evan. "That means Cooper had become more of a liability than an asset."

Eleanor nodded. "I expect Evan had a big role in that. Maybe he was charmed by her more than we thought. Whoever had him killed may have been worried."

Evan furrowed her brow and shook her head. "He had already made a mistake. He had already given me too much information."

"What do you mean? What information?" Eleanor asked,

"I don't know yet. But something." Evan had a feeling that there was probably more to their conversations than she first thought. Hindsight would give a better perspective.

Kirk nodded. "We'll find it."

Eleanor nodded. "Fischer is screaming for you all to come in. But I can buy you another day or two."

Hedge took a step between Eleanor and the team. "You'll need to buy us more time than that."

"Give me something for leverage; I need it fast." Elle gave everyone a quick nod. "Get after it now. We can all grieve later."

Evan turned to Kirk. "What do we do to start?"

Kirk punched a few keys to reconfigure the program for review. "How much privacy would you like?"

Evan appreciated his consideration but shook her head. "I want zero privacy. The more eyes and ears on this, the better."

Hedge pulled a chair over to join their conversation, but Elle tapped his shoulder before he could sit. "One minute before I leave?" The two of them moved a whispered conversation to the balcony.

A high-speed video montage filled the left half of the monitor as transcribed audio filled the right. A few signal bars and line graphs underlined the whole program, with a couple of pulsing icons in the corners of the screen indicating other programs running simultaneously.

"I'm not sure what we're looking for, Kirk." Evan blinked at all the information the dress could gather at one time.

"The dress is always set to flag pertinent names and places mentioned. I've just dialed it up a notch for this review. I also have FRS scanning faces for anyone in our databases." Kirk looked pleased with his design.

Evan nodded. "There was something weird that Cooper talked about. I meant to ask, but with everything that happened, I forgot. It was about a fairy tale or something."

"Baba Yaga?" Kirk asked.

"Yes!" Evan's jaw dropped as the name popped up, highlighted in orange onscreen. "Who or what is a Baba Yaga?"

"She's a cross between Santa and a witch-type character in Russian folklore. Parents scare their children into good behavior with stories of her. She sneaks into homes and snatches the bad children. It's a little difficult to explain to Americans who enjoy nothing but good cheer at Christmas." Kirk shrugged. "So why would a good Irish Catholic woman like Bridget Cooper tell her son bedtime stories of Baba Yaga?"

Evan nodded. "Maybe for the same reason her son had a Russian roommate in college?" She took a deep breath. "Stafford mentioned Cooper's father had spent time in Afghanistan. I didn't think much of it at the time, but what if Cooper's father was Russian? Can we find that information?"

Kirk raised a brow and smirked. "You ask like you don't already know the answer."

"I ask because you didn't get this information before I met the man." Evan leaned against her dear friend and drenched her words with sarcasm. "You're slacking, Red."

Hedge and Elle returned to the room, and instead of Hedge joining them, he gestured to Evan. "We need to talk."

CHAPTER THIRTY-NINE

Evan followed Hedge into the suite's bedroom, inhaling his musk as she walked past him. He closed the door.

"I talked to Elle. We're going to finish our assignment, without backup team members." Hedge's voice was low. His eyes looked dark.

Evan wanted to reach out for his hand. She wanted to touch his face and ease the worry lines from his forehead. She knew she couldn't. That wasn't their relationship now. She couldn't be that close. She couldn't apologize. All she could do was assure him that she was on his side.

"I was played. I was duped."

Hedge shook his hand. "Don't tell me you're sorry."

"I'm not. Please, jus' listen to me." She sat on the side of the bed and waited for his expression to clear. He took a seat at her side. "I was charmed by his pretty face." The words were bitter on her tongue. "I was manipulated. I know how that feels now. It hurts."

Hedge shifted his gaze away from her and back to the door. He said nothing.

"I know it might be hard to believe, but you can trust me. I will take care with you. I will do everything I can not to manipulate you." Evan took a deep breath. "You're the boss. I'll follow your lead."

Hedge swallowed hard—loudly enough that Evan heard it. She saw the twitch in the corner of his eye and wondered if it was pain or something else. He turned to face her.

"First off, you did nothing wrong." His hands gripped his thighs just above his knees. "We didn't back you up the way we should have. None of us. Eleanor just gave me an earful about it, and she's right."

Evan felt her chin quiver as she tried to stay calm. "We can all do better."

Hedge flexed his jaw. "We can, and we will." He nodded. He started to say something else and then stopped short. He stared into Evan's eyes with a frustrated expression, then looked away. Whatever it was he wanted to tell her, she guessed he'd changed his mind.

Evan dropped her gaze to the floor. *Too much and not enough.* She took a deep breath and stood. "Anything else?"

Hedge shook his head. "Not from me. You need to talk to Kirk." He stood and walked back to the door.

That was the last thing she expected him to say. Kirk? She closed her eyes for a long second, and when she opened them again, she saw that Hedge was gone and Kirk was coming into the room.

"I guess we need a little privacy after all," he said. His upper lip looked heavy and frozen. Evan knew from experience that meant he had bad news.

"What's wrong?" she asked, sitting again.

Kirk sat in the chair at the side of the bed. "You and Hedge are going to be all right." It was a statement more than a question. "You are going to get this guy."

Evan nodded. "Yeah. The three of us make a good team." She ached to say three instead of four.

Kirk dropped his head. "We did. Even when it was just the two of us, but not anymore."

Evan shook her head. "No. Don't say anything else. You're my partner. You're the voice in my ear. I can't do this without you." Tears threatened again. This couldn't be happening.

"You call me Red for a reason. I'm your Red Shirt. I'm the sacrifice when everything goes south. Right now we're about as far south as it gets. This is my choice. I worked it out with Elle. If I go back with her to DC, it will buy you and Hedge more time. It's my choice." Kirk's face remained stolid.

Evan pinched her lips into a thin line and squeezed her eyes closed. "Let me talk to Elle."

"No. It's settled."

"It's not."

"It is." His voice rattled this time.

Evan clenched her fists. "But why?"

Kirk looked at her, and his expression crumbled. "The other day, when I kissed you." His voice faltered.

"That will never happen again. It was a fluke. An accident." Her protests seemed to injure him more.

"No, it isn't that." Kirk rubbed the back of his neck and slumped his shoulders. "It reminded me of all the choices I've made. Right and wrong. When I was recruited, I didn't think I had a choice. I joined and left everything else behind." He looked into her eyes, and Evan saw something she'd never seen before. His emotions were bare to her.

"I don't—"

He interrupted her. "That kiss. That moment. You gave me a glimpse of what I abandoned before. I want that back. I can go back to a desk. I can still be there for you and Hedge, but I can be there for me, too. Not in your ear, but Hedge can do that. I'll be there in a keystroke."

"My heart is breaking, Red. Rowan." Evan leaned forward to take his hands. Everything ached.

"Let Hedge put it back together." Kirk pushed her hair from her eyes. "You two have more than you know."

Evan shook her head. "What will we do without you?"

"You won't be without me. You just won't have to drag me along behind you. You'll be able to move more discreetly as a couple. You'll draw less attention. You'll be unstoppable."

"Stop being reasonable." She forced a smile. "Are you gonna run off and find your old girlfriend?

Kirk laughed. "I already found her again. I put in a friend request this morning. Fingers crossed."

Evan rolled her eyes. "Is she prettier than me?" she asked facetiously.

"Nobody's prettier than you." He leaned forward and kissed her forehead. He leaned back and hesitated, glancing down at her lips.

"Once more for old-times?" She offered a perfect pink pucker.

"Better not."

She laughed. "Well, you know what you're missing." She sniffed. Her thoughts wandered back to Hedge. He was losing another team member, too. *What next?*

A strange beeping signaled from the other room, and Kirk's expression changed. "We have a hit."

"Get in here." Hedge's voice sounded more strained than before.

Kirk and Evan hurried to where Elle and Hedge stood over Kirk's computer.

Hedge's gaze never shifted away from the screen. "Facial recognition found a match from our files."

Evan studied the man's face. Pale complexion, light hair, grey eyes, a long nose, and a straight mouth. Average. She hadn't seen him before. He had been just another face in the gallery at the Sotheby's auction. Cooper hadn't spoken to him, or even noticed him, as far as she could tell. "Who is he?"

Kirk answered. "FRS says he's Costa Alenko. He's Nastya's brother."

Elle took a deep breath. "Nastya's *dead* brother?"

"The same." Hedge shook his head. "I guess we know why Cooper's dead now."

Evan's heart slammed in her chest. "So, Nastya and Cooper weren't grieving Costa's death. They were planning. The three of them, planning together."

"Planning what?" Elle asked.

"Something terrible." Kirk picked up the notebook. "I'll make some calls."

Evan took Hedge's arm without thinking. She nodded toward Kirk. "Your poker buddies?"

"Uh-huh." He was already sending messages.

Evan shot a look to Elle and then to Hedge, but both were focused solely on Kirk. She swallowed hard and nodded, more to herself than to the others. She knew Kirk was in his element.

This was his show, and right now he needed a dark room and a bigger computer. She could do this. She could let him go.

"Okay, so this should be plenty to give us more time. Elle, you and Kirk get home and get to work. Hedge and I will track him and take him down." Evan planted her hands on her hips. "We don't have time to waste. He's been two steps ahead of us all along."

Hedge raised his brows as he finally made eye-contact. "And who's the boss here?"

She smiled, and he smiled back. She pointed to Elle. "Technically, she is."

Elle tipped her chin toward Evan. "And the boss says to do what she says." She nudged Kirk's shoulder. "Can you be ready to go home in an hour?"

"We can be wheels up in half an hour." He closed his notebook and met Evan's gaze. "Are you good, Evan?"

"You go change into that red shirt and get out of here." *Fake it 'til you make it, girl.* Evan turned to face Hedge. "Are we good, sir?"

Hedge's expression filled with determination and he nodded back to her. "Better than good." His gaze rose from her red heels up over the black dress and stopped at her eyes. "You're a better partner than I deserve, and I trust you with my life."

Evan smiled, feeling his gaze and his words embrace her. She had everything she needed in him. "Then let's go get him."

THE END

ABOUT THE AUTHOR

Kim Black is an award-winning writer and designer. She is a member of the Texas High Plains Writers and has served as President of that organization.
Kim writes novels and keeps a blog from her home in the Texas Panhandle. She enjoys spending time with her husband, Riley, and kids, Sam, Whitney, and Sean.
She writes Historical Christian Fiction and Children's books under the name Kimberly Black.

For more information and links to other books by Kim Black, visit

www.kimblackink.com

www.ingramcontent.com/pod-product-compliance
Lightning Source LLC
Chambersburg PA
CBHW071305210626
46818CB00015B/2992